Andrew Sarkady

ever-life

Time Trust

SOUL FIRE
PRESS

www.christophermatthewspub.com
Bozeman, Montana

What readers have said about *Ever-Life*

Ever-Life: Time Trust

Editor: Jeremy Soldevilla
Cover design: Armen Kojoyian
Interior illustrations: Andrew Sarkady
Typeface: Georgia

Paperback ISBN 9781938985652
ebook ISBN 9781938985669

Published by
Soul Fire Press

An imprint of
CHRISTOPHER MATTHEWS PUBLISHING
http://christophermatthewspub.com
Bozeman, Montana

Printed in the United States of America

For my family.

Acknowledgements

There are those without whose encouragement, I never would have finished this labor of love. It is with the utmost sincerity and affection that I thank my close loved ones and family for supporting me.

To all my children and grandchildren, thank you for giving my life meaning and hope, and, in the end, for a reason to write. And hi, Mom and Dad—thank you! I know you are watching.

Finally, thank you, Karen and Jeremy, for your undying patience and support during rewrites and the final edits.

Table of Contents

PREFACE

My story is quite an exciting one, really. I am simply an ordinary man having no scientific or medical background; but I am the world's first real time-traveler. The purpose of my recounting all that happened was to get it out of my head, and it did haunt me until I finished. I know, you're thinking, here we go; what kind of idiot would believe that statement? I don't blame you if you walk away and forget about it. I wrote this to relieve my mind and for my family and those loved ones who inspired me to do so, even without knowing they did. But, I do want to be clear. This is in no way a technical or medical manual explaining any methodology. It is no more than the information given to me through a process I experienced. It's all written from headset sessions. So, if curiosity is truly irresistible, perhaps you will read on, enjoy and be provoked to study what is truly the strangest, most exciting tale I couldn't forget.

First, to be precise, I was abducted into the future three times and came back twice. The people there told me it is only possible to travel into the past. Actually, as I understand the way it works, all the events I recount here did happen in *their* past, so from their perspective, I guess that is correct. They have what they call headsets, quite remarkable little devices. Some fit like old hearing aids, while others fit like police swat-team communicators. Each one carries knowledge in the form of data, recorded up to the moment you put one on. When they activate it, your brain chemistry alters, and you upload any or all information of whatever the subject inquiry is. That is how I was able to recall the events.

My recollection is the journey of several people who became involved in each other's lives because of a remarkable discovery and a threat posed to it by the actions of a power hungry billionaire. It all began in the year 2999, when Dr. Jack Sheldon, Head of Research at the Brock/Swanson Medical Complex was taken to a hospital emergency room. Some time before that, he had discovered something that would change everything, a wonderful medical secret—C.P.T., Chemical Personality Transfer, which he had prepared to introduce to the public that very week. At the same time, billionaire Marion Brock plotted and stopped at nothing to get Jack's secret.

However, unknown to Brock or anyone on Earth's surface, deep below the Complex was a futuristic health-base, Ever-Life, and its leaders wanted Jack's secret too. A catastrophic event occurred, from the conflict between Ever-Life and the Brock Empire, which triggered my time travel to the future.

This book is my written recall of the second headset given to me, while I was under doctor's care at Ever-Life, Post Station 2, Giza, Egypt, in June, year 2999, by surface Earth's calendars. My recording of the first headset can be found in my book, *Ever-Life: The C.P.T Incident*.

೪೮೮ೞೕ

I opened my eyes, after the first headset session, and saw Dr. Luanne Rather smiling at me.

"There you are," she said. "First one done, but you will have to have another session."

"Another? How long was I under?"

"Total transmission time was only two minutes. Amazing, isn't it?"

"I have so many questions about this one. How did I get here? Where am I?"

"Yes, I am sure you do. But it takes time for your mind to accept the information. You are at Time Trust, Ever-Life Post 2."

"Where is that?"

"I have to get back to Arden, New Mexico. You will be in good hands. Try not to worry. Drink this."

I had no idea what that meant or how many headset sessions they would give me.

As Dr LuAnne walked to the door, she turned to me and said, "I enjoyed meeting you. You'll be fine. Just be patient. Someone will be here soon. I hope you enjoy Time Trust. Goodbye for now, Andrew."

Questions haunted me after my first headset experience: *Clones . . . what was Brock saying? Did C.P.T. change everything? What happened to the three fathers and that book? What happened to Brock when the Carrier took him?*

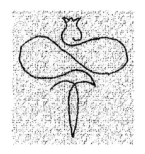

Hope and love abide with all who believe.
May we all believe in the future.
Many people write books to tell a story they imagine.
That is fiction today. But, what if someone writes
a true story that hasn't happened yet?

CHAPTER 1

CONFINED

ONE LONE CARRIER LAY IN A FIXED POSITION, just tangent to Earth's core. There, the magnetic signals generated were so strong that they blocked any communication from the hive mindset of all other Carriers. Inside the beast, a man in a suit lay flat on his back. He opened his eyes and blinked several times before moving. Slowly, he sat up and looked from side to side trying to focus, but all he could see was a blur of white light.

"Where the hell am I?" He wiped his eyes and realized the light radiated directly from the walls and floor.

"You are quite safe," a voice said.

The man stood up and surveyed the empty oval room. He noticed the imprint of his body on the floor disappearing, as if he had slept on an ancient foam mattress. Instinctively, he began frisking himself.

"Everything seems to be here."

Suddenly, before him, out of nowhere, there appeared a chair and table with food.

"Whoa! That's a neat trick."

"It is no trick, my friend; I bring you sustenance and good health. Do you remember anything?"

The man sat down at the table. "A little, I think. I don't know. Some things, I suppose. I certainly remember this: eggs, steak and potatoes, and is this champagne?"

"No, it is not."

"Mmm, different, but good . . . "

He began to eat and talk, "So, am I a prisoner? What is your name?"

"Far from it, as a matter of fact. My name is of no consequence. What is important is that you feel better, and in control."

"How long have I been here?"

"A while . . . months by your time . . . tell me, do you know who you are?"

"Months? Christ!" He grimaced and stood up, wiping his mouth with the napkin. "I am Marion Brock."

"What is your last memory?"

"I remember a large white room, like this; and talking to an old friend of sorts. Am I still there?"

"Not exactly. You are in a stasis mode. It's rather like dreaming, but you are not asleep."

"Interesting . . . "

"You were injured."

"Injured? I am fine. What now?"

"I am going to educate you. Then, we go on an adventure. Will you cooperate?"

"I don't have much of a choice, do I?"

"You perceive the obvious. Good. You are healing."

"Who or what are you, anyway?"

"I am of inner Earth."

"Well, 'of inner Earth', you can cook."

"We have lived far below your kind for thousands of years. We only share ourselves with very few of your better natured species."

Brock giggled, thinking, *Me? Better natured?* "Are you sharing with me now? Is that what this food is?"

For almost two minutes, he sat in dead silence, wondering. Finally, he raised his voice, "Are you still here?"

At that second, it happened. Brock heard a ringing in his ears. Involuntarily, he held his head while at the same time taking deep breaths. Just as he was about to scream, it stopped. His eyes dilated and he relaxed, feeling an overwhelming cathartic, rapturous sensation.

"Yes, I am here . . . what I give you now is against all treaties between your kind and mine. We chartered only to supply you with tangible gifts. What you receive now, we have never shared."

Brock sat unable to move. He began shaking uncontrollably. After a few seconds, it was too much for him and he passed out, flopping on the table. When he awoke, different fresh food was beside his head, his favorite music was playing, and his dog, Buddy, was sitting, panting, looking up at him.

"How did you get here, boy?"

Brock stood up and turned around in wonder. The room was now his old office suite in Hightstown, New Jersey.

"This is my desk, couch, tables, books; it's all here . . . did I go back in time? This building was demolished decades ago." He examined everything in the room. Then, he looked out, through the huge second floor bay window and watched all the people going about their daily lives. "You know, Bud, you would have loved Tom's Café there - best pancakes in town. It's all just as I remember . . . " Brock crossed the room to the door. He flung it open, expecting to run down the stairs and outside. But instead, he stepped into the exact same office suite again. "Christ, what is this? This can't be happening."

He heard the voice again. "Physical laws are quite different here, my friend. You are different. I gave you a few things to think about. Try to concentrate. What you see in your mind's eye; I will project on the wall."

Brock walked back through the door and sat down at the table again. As images began to appear, he rose to look at them closer, but he felt lightheaded, dizzy and bent over holding his knees. "This takes some getting used to . . . I do see something, but it's so strange . . . "

He stood up straight again, opened his eyes and concentrated. His thoughts were playing like a video on the curved wall before him. "My God, they are tunnels, inside the planet . . . and underground dwellings . . . it's blurry . . . there . . . those look like footballs. No, they are fish, swimming. But that can't be. There is no water."

Brock walked toward the wall, rubbing his eyes and reaching out trying to touch the 3-D images.

"I see something else now . . . there and there, and there . . . people, lots of people."

"Do not be impatient, my friend, think. Be clear. Keep trying."

"Cities, many cities; who are they? What am I looking at?"

"All of what you see, my dear Brock, are the Ever-Life colonies. Relax, sit, watch and finish the food."

Brock stared, mesmerized for a time; then he heard Buddy bark and he snapped to his senses. He sat back down, and a clear paper-thin, oval monitor appeared above the table in front of him. He began to watch and listen to everything the voice projected onto the screen.

"Now, Mr. Brock, we begin."

CHAPTER 2

THE EVENT

**It happened at the same time in two locations—
First Location: West Coast, U.S., June 3, 2:00 a.m.**

IN THE NORTHWESTERN UNITED STATES, just south of Seattle, Washington, a night guard sat in a small third floor tower office. Four such towers marked the castle perimeter of O.P.A.S.—Oregon Particle Accelerator Sciences. The guard was dozing off and on with his feet on a desk. Suddenly, he awoke hearing several loud dings from the shiny cylinder lying on a corner table across from his desk. The display on the top blinked out one holographic word: Sidron. From the bottom of the container, a single page printed out. The guard walked over talking to himself, "I've been here two years. This thing has never done anything."

He read the paper and, as protocol dictated, he pushed seven numbers into the keypad on the side of the cylinder.

The paper read,

*Success! Notes retrieved indicate more than expected.
Copy ready to send . . . this is Priority Intel . . . original copy
returned to source . . . awaiting instructions.*

Suddenly, the guard felt a violent tremor that threw him against the wall. The room shook for only a moment. "Holy shit! An earthquake . . ."

But, that would have been good news. When it was over, he got up and stared at his desk. Something impossible had happened. His desk had been cut in half, and one half had completely vanished. The half remaining had no marks of any kind, no clue as to how it happened.

He stood frozen, watching papers pour out all over. When he got over the shock, he took his communicator and pushed a preset emergency number. "Station Two, Tower reporting. Sam, are you there? Sam! Christ, come in! Sam?"

"Yes, keep your pants on! I'm here. What's the problem?"

"Didn't you feel that? Half my desk is gone. It just disappeared . . . I mean, the whole half is gone."

"Christ, Marky, get a grip!"

"It was an earthquake or something. You had to feel it, you're right under me."

"What the hell are you saying? Are you smoking that crap again? Calm down. Nothing happened here."

The phone reception cut out for several seconds, and then the Tower guard heard another voice.

"Hello, Mr. Adams? Is this Sergeant Mark Adams?"

"Hello, hello? Who is this? Yes, this is Adams. Sam, what happened?"

"Sergeant Adams, this isn't Sam; this is Mr. Stevens, from the T.T.I. Lab."

"Mr. Stevens? Yes, sir, but how did you cut into this secure line?"

"Mark, it's very late. I need you to exit the Tower and report to me here, immediately."

As the guard listened to Stevens, the door to his office opened and two armed men, in suits, walked in.

"Mark, listen to me; please accompany the two men. They will bring you here to me. There is no cause for alarm."

∿⋈∿

It happened at the same time in two locations-
Second Location: Cairo, Egypt, June 3, 11:15 a.m.

A main Ever-Life facility, Time Trust, was almost directly on the other side of the globe, deep below the Great Pyramid of Giza, Egypt. Within one of its security rooms, two men sat talking. There were several objects on the table between them. One man picked up a small rectangular item, studied it and said, "This is my old flash drive."

The other man smirked. "Hardly, that term is ancient to us. Let me show you. It attaches to this, like that."

"What do you mean ancient?"

"Actually, it's organic, in nature. Few knew that at the time, by the way . . . first, a few basic pertinent facts . . ."

"Okay?"

"You are from North America, correct?"

"Yes . . ."

"While calendars—up there—record history well into the year 2999 A.D., it is our year 9999.6 . . . in other words, it's June. I suppose you could say we have adopted many of the same terms, but we live by different numbers."

"2999? That's impossible."

"Yes, quite so to you, I am sure. Now, regarding this little jewel, the likes of which I haven't seen in over 10 years, we used it for containing important records. Its organic nature guarantees security, that's another story . . . some of these little buggers have information that dates back more than 700,000 years. I will have to use an old protocol to retrieve inputs. These things were quite reliable in their day. At that time, they were considered . . . how would you put it? Cutting edge. They contained records of all memories from every human within Ever-Life; everything from proofs of man's true genetic origin to the secrets of what you would call time travel. Of most interest to me, though, they had interactive programming for activities and interfaces with all surface creatures. We kept all information regarding every aspect of life within these special little vaults. Of course, we have upgraded now, using software that is much more sophisticated. But, no; this is not your old flash drive."

"Slow down there, mister, I am still trying to absorb the date . . . 2999?"

The two heard the room door open and a guard interrupted their conversation. "Mr. Wheeler, sir, pardon me. We need you a moment."

Wheeler smiled at the man across from him and politely excused himself, "I will be right back." He got up, turned to leave, and then turned back again. "I realize this all may be quite unnerving. Do try to be patient. You are among friends and quite safe."

"What friends? Where am I?"

"You are 10 miles below the bottom of the River Nile. We are part of the Ever-Life Colonies. Please, I will be right back."

As Wheeler walked out the door into the hallway, he saw orderlies running by in both directions.

"Sir, sir, Mr. Wheeler," one said. "Come with me . . . please, hurry!"

"What's going on?"

"Sir, we never really expected anything . . . "

"What? Spit it out."

"The readings, the monitors; there has been a breach in the Sidron highway."

"Christ!"

The two men ran down the hall and into a lab room, just as it exploded. The blast threw them backward against the rock walls. The orderly was blown apart instantly. Wheeler lay bloody and broken, lifeless.

CHAPTER 3

THE QUESTION

EVER-LIFE'S TRANSPORT STATION 606 was located almost a mile beneath Andrews Hospital, which was on the Brock/Swanson campus within the city limits of Arden, New Mexico. Out from the station, various tunnels branched in all directions. All platforms were constructed at the angle of that particular tunnel. Some tunnels pitched as steep 45 to 90 degrees up or down. However, passengers could walk from one platform to another, even if they were perpendicular to one another without fear of falling, because the magnetic field surrounding any individual platform was more powerful than the earth's gravitational pull.

The network of tunnels branched outward into the earth, like the spokes of a bicycle wheel extend from its axis; and they extended hundreds of miles below the campus. Some tunnels leading into Post 3 were a mile wide, and the major cavern in the station was 10 miles below the surface. From that point, the main vertical chasm disappeared straight down, branching out like an upside-down Christmas tree deep into the bowels of the earth. Strangely, though, there had never been any recorded sign of magma or volcanic activity around any inhabited tunnel throughout the Ever-Life colonies.

On the sides of the main cavern, several semicircle ledges protruded, suggestive of mushroom caps growing out from tree trunks. The biggest one was the size of five football fields. It had a large open amphitheater, reminiscent of old Greece. Between and around the remaining circumference of the cavern were huge quartz-like structures. They were many and varied buildings, including business units, malls, hotels, restaurants, healthcare research facilities and countless living quarters.

Looking out over the main ledge's field from a hotel balcony suite, Dr. Jack Sheldon stood, surveying the sights. In the center of the field were several fountains squirting colored water from unfamiliar statuesque shapes and beautiful transparent moving walkways, weaving in, out and around flowers and topiaries. Large, flexible paper-thin monitors of all shapes and sizes, floated above the people. Some had video playing. Others reflected beautiful, artful designs, while playing captivating music. Still others displayed ads regarding the latest in healthcare research. After a time, the monitors would roll up, invisible to any viewer.

Jack watched, mesmerized. "Look at it, strange and wonderful, moving sidewalks, people movers; my, my, how do those things go around corners? What happened to good old-fashioned one foot after the other; and what the hell are those things? People are getting into bubbles—floating vehicles. They do look like bubbles . . . quite an idea for public transportation; no buses, trains, cars or bikes; just bubbles, noiseless bubbles . . . fascinating, to say the least."

He and Rachel had rested and rejuvenated, after the opening festivities some 10 hours earlier, celebrating the transfer of power to take place from GGM Gordon Swanson to Mathew Bellos. Jack stared spellbound.

"What a party. It's all too wild. No one would believe it up there . . . why don't those things crash into each other? They just slide off, change shape . . . " He turned around and raised his voice, "Rachel! Rachel! You know, I just cannot get my head around the fact that all this has been here for thousands of years, not to mention the light. Where does all the damn light come from? How do those, whatever they are, fly around and not crash into anything? Look, there goes one disappearing right into the side of the rock wall . . . shit! Honey?

Rachel, what time does the serious ceremony begin, anyway? God, I have no idea what to say . . . should we even ask what time it is down here?"

Rachel Sheldon walked out of the bath area and down the hall toward Jack. She was dressed and ready to go. "Silly, look at your watch, we have about an hour."

"Well, it's disconcerting, to say the least."

"Stop it. We should feel honored and you know it. Mathew and Gordon have broken all their rules, just so we can be here."

"Rules? Obviously there are no rules. Look at us. We were dead, for God's sake. Don't you ever wonder?"

Rachel froze, wide-eyed, and walked to the window. "Jack, do you remember anything? I mean, anything during the time you were . . . dead?"

Jack walked over and put his hand on her shoulder.

"I remember you, honey. I remember you."

Rachel caressed his hand. "Mmm . . . " Then she turned and faced him. " . . . no; I don't mean in a romantic sense. I mean, did you have an after death experience, like going into a light, you know, anything at all?"

Jack sighed and walked toward the middle of the room. "I don't want to remember."

"Jack Sheldon, look at me! I never asked you because I thought it would come out naturally. But you haven't said one word to me in all these months."

Jack bowed his head and spoke to her softly, "It was nothing like a dream, no light to walk to, and no pearly gate. For me, it was something I never expected or could have imagined. Please, Rach, I don't want to say anymore, not right now. Frankly, I don't know if I ever will. Babe, what is really bothering you? What happened to you?"

Rachel slowly turned with her back to him. "That night, it went so fast. I remember some things, the joy I felt seeing you wake up in that casket. I was so thankful and excited. I remember the sound of the guns, the bullets; staring at you as you jumped out to save us all; but it wasn't really you, was it? I get so confused sometimes . . . I remember feeling the shots go through me so fast; and then, quick as a blink, I felt limp, floating, falling down, tasting blood. For a second, I remember seeing you next to me. I reached for you. I couldn't blink anymore. I was staring at you, when everything went . . . black."

"Oh, darlin', come here . . . "

They embraced, and then Jack gently pushed Rachel off his chest wiping her tears. "Come on, hon, tell me," he said.

"It's just so unbelievable, bordering on silly."

Jack laughed, "Well, that doesn't mean we know a hill of beans about anything important, in this world or the next."

Rachel looked up at him with a tear in her eye. "I saw everything. I know how this sounds, but a guide whisked me up and out of my body, faster than I can explain. It was instantaneous, so real. It wasn't a feeling as much as a knowing, a different consciousness. The guide, or whatever it was, brought me to a place. It was definitely a place . . . I wasn't a body of flesh, obviously. I was more like a body of knowledge and love. I'm not even sure if I should call it love, but that's the only word I can think of to describe it. I wasn't what we would think of as spirit at all, though. It was something else."

"Hmm, very Gnostic, and yet quantum sounding, too . . . okay; so your 'guide' brought you to a place. What place?"

"Jack, that's not my point, and speaking of quantum, I read your new notes."

"My new notes?"

"Yes, sorry, but I wasn't going to have a repeat of the C.P.T. fiasco."

"I had no intention of keeping anything from you. It just evolved from what happened. I never imagined it would lead me into the whole 'Universe' thing," Jack snickered a bit. "Besides, it has nothing to do with us, here and now."

Rachel grabbed his shoulders. "I am a doctor, too, Jack . . . C.P.T. may have led your thinking, but don't deny it. Something happened to you, too . . . the thing is, I remember the moment of death, the moment my eyes fixed and dilated . . . so, was it a last figment of my imagination during which I had this 'out of body' experience? All of your new proofs, everything that is in the C.P.T. manuscript, refers to our knowledge coagulating after 'an hour of death'. Was I not dead, experiencing some mind-blowing euphoria in that last millisecond? Or was I dead in some afterlife and, eventually, the C.P.T. brought me back, perhaps against all that is holy? Jack, did we violate some divine law? Are we here together now, when we really shouldn't be?" Rachel squeezed her husband around his waist and held tight.

"Jesus, honey, it's all right. The fact is, we are here together now. That's all that matters, isn't it? Listen, I don't have the answers. I am in new territory here. We are working with Matt to transfer a lot of information to the campus from both his Time Trust files and my notes. We will analyze it all and make a finding. You know the routine better than anyone."

"Jack, I went through C.P.T., too. I want to be a part of this. Don't shut me out."

"I won't, but you have to be objective about this. Please, try not to get all wrapped up in the emotion and ethereal. Look . . . they are beginning to assemble out there. We should go."

"Christ, Jack."

"It will be all right, babe."

Rachel dried her eyes. "Yes, well, what happened to me cannot be explained away as some ethereal vision, philosophy or religion."

"Yes, dear."

Rachel picked up her shawl and walked by Jack to the front door. As he followed, he chuckled, "Besides, I would like to know what they are doing with it."

"With what?"

"C.P.T . . . What have we been talking about, for God's sake? We are going to have to finish this conversation sometime. I want to know more about that place you went to, and that guide."

Rachel gave him a look. "Really, I expect the answer is in your new notes."

"Ha ha, well, you brought it up. By the way, do you know where we sit, or stand or what we are supposed to do down there?"

Rachel shook her head. "Jesus, Jack, they will tell us if things change. Our seats are in the front row."

CHAPTER 4

THE CEREMONY

IN ANOTHER LARGER SUITE, some distance from Jack and Rachel's, also overlooking the ceremonial park, Dr. Mathew Bellos, his wife, Carla and their daughter, Angie, prepared for the formal GGM ceremony. While Carla engaged in last minute primping in front of the hallway mirror, Angie stood in the main room facing her father, dusting the front of his jacket. Bellos smiled and looked at his daughter as only a father can. "We've come a long way in a very short time, you and I, haven't we, sweetie?"

Angie smiled. "Mmm, my Dad, GGM; it is hard to believe all this is happening."

I know. By the way, I meant to ask you a while ago—are you and Brian an item now?"

"No. Well, maybe . . . I don't know. We'll see."

Bellos kissed her on her forehead. "He is a lucky young man, just be careful."

"I will. There. You look perfect. Are you ever going to tell us what being the GGM really means?"

"Technically, I have to find out at the ceremony. It has all been quite hush, hush; even to me.

"Please, you two," Carla said, "whatever it is, we are staying a family, together. That is all I care about."

"Oh, for goodness sake; it'll be fine. I am the one who is nervous here, and I confess, ignorance is not bliss in this situation. Look at all that, all those gadgets and people. And why do Gordon and I have to walk into the mouth of a beast the size of Manhattan?"

Carla walked over to both of them. "Hmm, why indeed. All I know is, I will not lose either one of you again. Do you understand me, mister? When do we get to see this beast, anyway?"

At that moment, a silent, blinding white light exploded outside the window, and startled the three. They stared, as the light shrunk and defined itself.

"Jesus, Dad, I think it's here."

Bellos grinned a little. "Yes, they like to make a grand entrance. How do you like the way it just hovers there?"

Carla fixed on the spinning head. "It looks like a flying saucer. Is it waiting for people to move? Nobody seems bothered at all."

"I guess I don't rate a whole beast. That is just the head."

The people in the garden moved away without fear. The rotating head landed in the garden area below Bellos' suite, behind the stage and podium.

"How is that possible, Dad? Its head just melded into the field."

"I know, kiddo; nobody has that answer."

"Honey," Carla asked, "where is your friend, Jake Burns? I thought he would be here."

"He is on assignment. I'm sure there are no security issues, or he would be down there right now. I don't understand one thing, though. I've been briefed less about this ceremony than anything else, during all my training years. How does Gordon expect me to handle all this?"

Carla took Bellos' hand. "You'll be fine, my love. You will have plenty to handle after the ceremony. After all, you got us back together. Come on; we had better go. There is Grandpa, waving at us. They have us sitting right in front of that thing."

Within half an hour, the seating in front of the Carrier grew to approximately 700 spectators. Only the GGM's closest friends, the

High Resolve Medical Research Staff of the eight worldwide Posts and their families were invited. The ceremony would then be available, via Knofer, to the general populous.

Once everyone was in place and seated, Gordon Swanson stepped up to the podium and looked out over the crowd. The Carrier Unit's mouth was his backdrop. As he spoke, his image appeared in 3-D on all monitors floating around the field.

"Good health to us all and welcome everyone!" The crowd applauded, and Swanson continued, "Today is a joyous occasion, one that hasn't taken place for over 200 years. While it is somewhat sad for me, I am happy and proud to introduce to you our next Great Grand Master, Dr. Mathew Jeremy Bellos . . . Mathew?"

Everyone cheered. Bellos stepped up, beside Swanson, waved to the crowd and whispered to him, "So now what, Gordon?"

Swanson shook his hand, grinned and turned to the assembly again. "We are also honored and thankful to have with us today, conducting the ceremony, our ambassador from Post 8, Carrier Unit 62712."

The crowd roared, and Bellos again leaned over to Swanson and whispered, "What do you mean conducting?"

Swanson looked at him with a half smile, "This is the last time I can say this, Doctor, be quiet!"

"Ladies and gentlemen, and friends all over Ever-Life, I thank you for giving me the best tenure any GGM could dream of, let alone ask for. I have been proud to serve."

The people shouted accolades and compliments. Swanson turned to Bellos and gestured behind him. "It's time, Mathew . . . come."

Swanson escorted Bellos onto the extended tongue of the beast. It resembled transparent plastic stairs, but it was as solid and sturdy as concrete. They stepped up and stood looking at the crowd. Slowly, the tongue began retracting into the beast's great mouth.

"It's not that I am afraid, you understand," Bellos said. "It's just that we have never entered a Carrier this way, before."

"Mathew, we will be fine. We are doing exactly what was done with me and every GGM, since this started over 10,000 years ago."

"So, that makes me feel better?"

Swanson grinned, as they descended into the Carrier. The great mouth closed behind them, and darkness overcame everything.

"Well, this isn't the usual white, is it?

After their eyes adjusted, they could see only black with a blue glow around themselves.

"Okay, Gordon, this is all very interesting. Remember, years ago, when you told me that I would be asking 'what' a lot? I thought you were crazy. Now, I have so many more questions."

"Ah, good, a sign of wisdom. . . "

Then, the voice of the Carrier filled their minds, "Good health to you, GGM. I bring greetings and good wishes from the Council."

"Thank you, my friend. I introduce to you, my choice, Dr. Mathew J. Bellos, to be our next Great Grand Master."

"Welcome, Doctor. I ask you, Mathew J. Bellos, do you freely accept the responsibility and commit to the tasks before you?"

Bellos raised one eyebrow, looked around at the dim light and replied, "I do . . . but, frankly, I do not comprehend the tasks before me. I hope I have what it takes."

Swanson reached out and squeezed his shoulder. "Not to worry . . . he is ready, my friend."

"Then, let it begin."

There was complete silence. All around them became pitch black and their glow was gone. Bellos squinted, and tried to focus on the void before him. "There, look; it's small, but I see a tiny light flickering, I think. Is that a star?"

One by one, more twinkling lights darted out from the first. Bellos said, softly, "Gordon, it looks like a plasma lamp."

"Yes, it does. Actually, it is all lightening. The life-generating force of the universe . . . enjoy."

"I'm not a physicist. We have all been taught gravity, gasses and particles make up the universe."

"Yes, that, too, but the spark of life, that is electromagnetic energy-electricity in one form or another. That is what Ever-Life is all about—extending the spark of life. Welcome to your first day of school, Mathew."

All of it appeared like a movie fast forwarding, and it all grew, as Bellos watched in awe. Nebulae, Star Clusters, Pulsars and Galaxies, all manner of undefined cosmic wonders populated 360 degrees around them, all appearing in 3-D.

"I'll give you a hint, my boy. Here, time as you understand it, does not exist. We men invented the abstract concept, anyway."

It took Bellos a while before realizing they were no longer on the beast's tongue, they were floating. He was mesmerized, captivated and, at the same time, he concentrated to try to remember it all. Out of the corner of his eye, he noticed that Swanson was floating away, getting smaller in the distance and gesturing adieu with a smile. Bellos could feel a change coming over him. He began to comprehend in a different way. In his mind's eye, he saw different kinds of text characters, each one a story. His comprehension soared in its scope. He understood the construct of atoms, inside and out; their component parts and what they do; what surface Earth called quantum theory. His mind understood the beginning—the Big Bang. He began seeing everything around him in a kind of digital format, and he thought, *These are like the carved characters in my office bed and desk.*

It was the language of the Carriers. Their words and thoughts sucked into Bellos' head like iron filings drawn to a magnet. His mind understood new wondrous information regarding all manner of subjects. He was a limitless hard drive, downloading the secrets of the universe. Swanson was just a speck, far away. Bellos squinted, staring at Swanson and whispered to himself, "Gordon, this isn't just a headset or planetarium moment, is it? The energy and knowledge, they are coming from everywhere?"

Then the Carrier spoke again, "Yes, it all comes from everywhere, my GGM. I am your guide and a provider from this time forward. You are seeing thought, in its purest form. Before anything was created, there was thought.

"I am committed to you and the well-being of all life you represent. By becoming a Great Grand Master, you give up the choices of men, and retain all manner of logic, knowledge and understanding. You are their guide now, and I am yours. Do you accept this responsibility and commitment?"

Bellos listened and stared into the vast timeless beauty before him, "I do."

"My friend, understand me. You may not and must not ever try to explain your experience here today. At no time will anyone understand or accept what you say, and more importantly, there is a penalty associated with this code violation. However, you will have a long life and a destiny of greatness ahead, as well as the wherewithal befitting a Great Grand Master. If there is any circumstance of illness regarding your person, I will see to it that you stay well until that time your species finds a cure."

"I understand."

Bellos remained floating in a trancelike state of learning for an indeterminate time. Then, something disturbed his concentration. He noticed, in the upper right quadrant, a tiny white vortex appeared and grew. Slowly, it began to consume everything and suck Bellos toward it. As he accelerated and got closer, the bright light overwhelmed him. He covered his face and flinched, turning away and closing his eyes tightly just as he shot into it. A rush of wind swirled around him, and then everything stopped, complete silence. He sensed he was standing, firmly balanced.

Involuntarily, he wiped his blinking eyes and focused on a brightly colored transparent figure before him. Definitely a male looking humanoid,he was well-proportioned and over 12 feet tall. The figure bowed, seemed to smile and offered its outstretched arms in welcome. Then, he began speaking in the strange sounding language of the Carriers. Bellos knelt, listened and understood every word.

"By your receiving and acknowledging all we have given to you, and by the authority of our Grand Council and treaty codes, I proclaim you Great Grand Master-GGM-010 over all the Ever-Life colonies. May you reign with honor, peace and wisdom. Never forget life is a gift. Treasure it. Be the scholar, teacher and kindly mind of conscience. Know, on behalf of those who do not. Guide them with the strength and power of Ever-Life."

Bellos' eyes fixed in disbelief and, involuntarily, he began to weep and blink. As he did so, the new GGM felt an ever-so-slight tugging sensation. It was just one or two seconds. He opened his eyes and he was astonished to find himself kneeling beside the podium from where he started. The Carrier was gone. He looked out at the crowd and stood up with tears in his eyes. Swanson put his hand on Bellos' shoulder, turned him toward the people and spoke, "I give you our Great Grand Master, Mathew J. Bellos."

After a few seconds to reorient himself, Bellos shook Swanson's hand and whispered, "Quite a moment, Gordon."

"I know; congratulations. It's a new beginning, a new understanding and a new life for you. Now, say something to your people."

Swanson stepped off the podium and sat next to Carla. Bellos raised his arms to quiet the crowd.

"I am honored today by this appointment and by your trust. I will serve and continue in the traditions of those I follow to bring harmony, peace and better health to us all. Thank you for your display of respect and confidence . . . long life and good health to us all . . . Ever-Life, everywhere!"

The crowd stood up, applauding and shouting, as Bellos' father, Dr. Richard, Carla, Angie, Jack and Rachel joined him on stage. Swanson moved to the podium, raised his arms to quiet the people and then shouted, "Let the celebration continue!"

Over the next few hours, the field filled with dance, food and a great party atmosphere. The floating monitors displayed various entertainments, while small Carriers delivered limitless amounts of food and drink, none of which came from the surface. Eventually, the crowd tired and dispersed. Special Carriers picked up garbage or waste products for disposition. Some disintegrated the unusable waste. Others recycled waste to underground power structures, or for distribution as organic compounds throughout the Post.

As Swanson, the Bellos and Sheldons walked across the field back to their suites, the new GGM shook his head and remarked, "Well, Gordon, you have replaced this job by doing two more, but I'll always think of you as my GGM."

Swanson chuckled a bit. "My boy, I am already forgetting, and it feels quite good, actually. For me, two jobs are better than one, now."

Suddenly, behind them, they heard an explosion from the depths under the field. A blinding bright light exploded all around the great chasm. Bellos reacted just as a GGM should. While everyone else held their ears and crouched, he pressed his Knofer, clicking it into defense mode. A protective aura with an impenetrable shield surrounded each of the group, as he ran to the edge of the ledge. Swanson, Jack and Richard followed. Bellos stared into the abyss and then turned to Swanson.

"This can't be good . . . Dad, get the women inside."

Dr. Richard, Rachel, Carla and Angie ran to a sidewall entrance. Bellos, Jack and Swanson stood watching. From the darkness below, a huge Carrier emerged. The noise was deafening to anyone within hearing distance.

"I didn't invite this one," Swanson murmured.

A magnificent creature soared up the tunnel and stopped, right next to the three men.

"Christ, Gordon, it looks almost albino, a raging albino. Have you ever seen anything like this?"

"Not during my tenure."

The Carrier began to speak. "I am he who has come from the past and future to make right the foul stench of those you call brother and friend. You have no right to what has been given you, or the life-changing abilities you spread like the virus you are."

The Carrier seemed to stare at Jack in particular. Then, it began to spin again, and in an instant, its head became its tails, flailing tentacles all around them. With a loud rush of air, the tentacles quickly entwined like a rope and pointed straight up; then, the creature zoomed back down into the deep. The three men stood frozen, feeling the wind and watching a bluish white light shrink into blackness.

"I don't think he likes me," said Jack.

"Great . . . my first day . . . "

Swanson raised an eyebrow, "Well, here we go."

Bellos sighed, straightened up and pushed his Knofer off defense. "Let's get to work."

Four master guards rushed toward the group, and Jack turned toward them. "Too little, too late, wouldn't you say, fellas?"

The GGM gestured them to stop. "It's all right, men; we are fine . . . Sergeant Parker, right? Arrange for the Sheldons to get back up to Andrews."

There was another click on Bellos' Knofer. It was Carrier Unit 62712's thoughts linking to the GGM. It input the latest information, regarding issues and locations of all known Carriers. Bellos didn't even blink. "Gordon, you brief Jake . . . no time to waste . . . we have to finish transferring those Time Trust records to Brock/Swanson Building 26. I want a virtual meeting with Post Controllers in an hour. Keep in touch."

"Yes, sir." Swanson leaned in toward Bellos and whispered, "Interesting, isn't it, how it all comes to you?"

Bellos smiled, turned and walked with the four guards back into the Ever-Life Complex. Swanson climbed into a small Carrier-Bubble and disappeared down into the chasm.

CHAPTER 5

AN UNEXPECTED GUEST

SOMETIME AFTER THE CEREMONY, Jack and Rachel Sheldon boarded a small Carrier-Bubble, which would take them back to Andrews Hospital. Jack sat on the cushioned bench seat and looked out through the transparent wall, as the Bubble began to move.

"Why is it every time I ride in one of these, and thank heaven, it's rare, I always get the feeling I'm going to fall out?"

Rachel held onto his arm. "Well, one thing is for sure, we will never see anything like that again. Matt was changed, literally changed."

"Not in our lifetime, but we have witnessed stranger things, a lot to reflect on."

Rachel snuggled into him and they seemed content to stare and think. Jack put his arm around her and squeezed her close, assuring her in a private moment of love. The Carrier moved toward the north sidewall of the chasm, accelerating.

"Sorry, I get tense when these things melt into the bedrock." Rachel closed her eyes as the bubble penetrated the rock face, "Are we cutting now?"

Jack watched, mesmerized. "Yes, amazing. It's completely silent. You can see the rock dissolve all around us. Look at the color."

Rachel opened her eyes, and they both stared at the burning orange. "Jack, look closely; that's different; this thing seems to be cooling. It's getting pitch black out there."

"Hmm, you're right; do you feel that? Are we slowing down?"

Neither of them noticed that someone appeared and stood quietly behind them. He was transparent, but clearly a humanoid shape. The stranger spoke calmly, "Excuse me. Yes, we are stopping. I don't mean to alarm you."

Jack turned and reacted, "Oh Jesus! What the hell are you?"

He protected Rachel, backing her into one of the bench seats.

"Please, I don't mean to frighten you. We rarely appear, much less to surface man."

"You scared the shit out of me—us."

"Sorry, forgive me. I am here on behalf of our Council, the Carrier Grand Council. I am a Tyree Master. You need not be afraid." He extended his hand; and, after gaining his composer, Jack shook it, apprehensively.

"Council? You don't look like a Carrier."

Rachel pinched him. "Jack, let's give him a chance."

"Thank you, Mrs. Sheldon. First, I appear before you like this so I can fit in here. Actually, I am a projection, of sorts. We thought you would relate better and feel more comfortable with a familiar image."

Jack was still holding his hand. "You feel solid. How is that possible?"

The stranger smiled and replied, "Well, it is my understanding that you two have some familiarity with the impossible, given your experience with C.P.T."

Jack sat down on the bench with Rachel again and the stranger continued, "I am normally much taller and, a little more glowing, you might say. We have the technology to do different things; subjects for another time."

"So, you are here because of the event at the ceremony?"

"Yes and no; before we can approach anyone of the surface, we must have permission from your GGM. I am here with the approval of all parties."

"Hell if I know what that means."

"Jack, slow down . . . go on."

"Thank you." He sat down, facing the couple.

"To begin with, your transport has stopped, to enable complete privacy. We are insulated by rock for miles all around us. I have come to discuss a very private matter. Mrs. Sheldon, while you are within the colonies, we monitor all communications of any surface being. I do apologize, but it is our policy. Frankly, we prohibit surface man down here. We do not trust his presence."

"Why, for heaven's sake?"

"Because, over the years, you have evolved differently; you react with violent fear, most of the time. You have killed many of your own over the eons, intentionally; not to mention the people from here you've butchered. You two and your family have been allowed here at the request of the GGM. That is a great honor and makes you trustworthy."

"Okay, so what is this about? What do you want?"

"Your question; your conversation, before the ceremony . . . "

"That was private!"

"Yes, and it would have been, had the occurrence not taken place."

"You mean at the ceremony . . . ?"

"Jack, wait." Rachel sat up and stared at the stranger. "What occurrence?"

"I see I tweaked your interest."

"You are not talking about here, down here, are you?"

"What are you saying, Rach? What is this?"

"Doctor, we have been monitoring your work, for a very long time; since before you were at Andrews. You have quite a brilliant mind, and, we respect your evaluations and discoveries, particularly

C.P.T . . . . and, now your latest involvement with particle . . . Particle something; or is it organic microbiology?"

"I never used those terms. How do you know about that, and why does it interest you?"

Rachel took a deep breath, "Stop it, Jack. Do you mean Jack's notes on particle displacement?"

"Mrs. Sheldon, you have read the treatise?"

Rachel looked at Jack. "Yes, I read some of it."

Jack interrupted, "Now tell us what is going on."

"You are aware of the Sidron findings?"

Jack paused and thought a moment, while Rachel reacted. "Sidron? Jack, what is he talking about?"

"Sidron, Sidron, my, my . . . yes. Honey, when science discovered what they thought was the God particle, religious leaders and medical science joined physicists in the investigation to finally prove the so-called Big Bang, you know?"

Rachel got a perplexed look on her face. "Yes, for years we had it crammed into us. The Big Bang created the universe."

"Right, but everyone only talked about the big stuff, galaxies, stars, planets, blah blah blah . . . no one ever looked at how ideas or emotions were born. Everyone was so overwhelmed with the speed of light then. Remember Einstein's ancient E = mc? The speed of light this, the speed of light that; only well into the second millennia did physicists realize light exists within something. Get it? It exists within the body of time and space; therefore, time-space expands faster than light."

"Okay, darling, so what's your point?"

"Well, that is also when another epiphany surfaced: that ideas . . . thoughts, emotions and even power, all of them were individual entities, part of creation, too."

"Jack, I am a doctor, too; don't lose me here."

"The theory was that they were created at the same time with everything else; but each was independent of everything else, riding a subatomic highway called the Sidron. I had been studying the whole concept a while ago, as part of an overall proposal to Brock/Swanson and Matt. But, I did not pull the Sidron files."

The Tyree Master interrupted politely, "Excuse me, Mrs. Sheldon, Sidron is a sort of a magnetic power. Technically, it is true; it is the subatomic highway. And, sometime, after it was discovered on the surface, scientists became afraid of investigating it, rightly so. The Sidron is what connects every subatomic particle to every other one-electron, photon, neutrino, quark . . . it is a network, tying everything together."

Rachel shook her head, rolling her eyes, "So, why do I want to understand all this?"

"The Sidron enables conductivity, sort of. I mean it has its own strange charge. It is self-powering, unlike anything ever discovered before. We labeled it a magnetic charge, but we really had no idea what it was. It allows transfer, movement of anything from one particle to any other."

"Yes, quite so, Dr. Sheldon . . . "

"Okay guys, tell me why I care . . . say so in plain English . . . "

"Honey, listen. First, they thought of using it like a fax or copy machine, only copying over very long distances. It would revolutionize communications, maybe even transportation. Signal frequencies, particle frequencies of any kind, can travel the Sidron, to anywhere, instantaneously. But, they had no idea what experiments to conduct to test the theory. The math worked, but reality-experiments, well, that was something else. The scientific community was stumped. They decided to do nothing until they could put controls in place, which have not been discovered yet."

"For the most part, you are correct, Doctor. However, it is not just transmitting anywhere that is our concern. It is that Sidron can be used to transmit anything to any time. You see, Doctors, C.P.T. was only the door. Through the door lies a whole new misunderstood world; and, that world explains the answer to your question, Mrs. Sheldon."

Rachel perked up. "What? You mean I was right about afterlife?"

"I am here because we need your help. We have known about Sidron, as you call it, for a very long time. If the wrong people get a hold of certain knowledge and try to use it, well, it would be bad for everything."

"But why us?" Jack asked. "My notes are safe. I am giving all the files to the Complex. Matt knows this."

"There has been a breach within the Sidron's time-scope. Someone discovered and used it for personal gain or profit, and the breach has resulted in instability."

"What? What can we do?"

"We want you to investigate. You have contacts at all the particle reactors, Switzerland, Oregon, Africa and China. We believe the initial breach came from one of those locations, or from your Complex. No matter who uses Sidron, even for simple tasks, the threat is too great for us to ignore."

"What are you asking?"

"If Sidron has been used by someone on the surface, he could not understand even a small part of its scope . . . "

Jack shook his head no, "Come on, even scientists up there haven't studied it. Most of the proofs are only on paper. No real experiments were ever conducted."

"We both know the language of mathematics doesn't lie; and you have key contacts. Talk to them, find out all you can. Report back to me using this. It's synchronized to me alone." The Tyree Master handed Rachel a small, peanut-shaped, pliable object.

"What do I do with this?"

"Squeeze it like this, and then like this."

She did and watched as a light appeared inside the stranger's head.

"I will hear you and come. Squeeze it end to end, and it will disintegrate. We can't have that in the wrong hands up there."

"Well, then, don't lose it, honey."

The Tyree Master pointed to the surface and spoke in a worried tone, "I have appeared to you to request your help. There are others down here who are involved, too. You are not alone. Please, we all obviously trust you both. Contact me with any, I say *any* information you may discover."

Jack scratched his head. "Yes, well, I did share some information with one or two colleagues abroad to try and bridge basic hypotheses."

"Your C.P.T. effort related to memory and personality. Whoever breached the Sidron has no idea what he is dealing with."

The stranger paced the Bubble, speaking in a desperate tone, "I will tell you this. The laws of the subatomic world are very different, and with good reason. It is true that ideas, emotions and power are all, in fact, fixed entities. All abstract concepts are just as real as concrete substances. They exist everywhere and ride the Sidron constantly, within what you call the past, present and future. But, it is all the same time, really. Everything is held within space-time, which does expand much faster than light, in order to contain it, as well as everything else. So space-time holds the past, present and future altogether, you see."

Rachel wasn't buying it. "How is that possible? Besides, we are not physicists, certainly not philosophers."

"Well, not to be condescending; but, even your simple communications—your video, audio, all wireless frequencies exist everywhere at the same time. They are all spherical waves. We live within it all, through it, if you will, and, we are given access to it, them, via the Sidron, by function of our ability—our capacity, and our motivation to withdraw whatever we can from it. Understand me, Doctors, we are talking about omniscient and omnipotent forces here."

Jack continued quizzing, "So, my hypotheses were correct. Within the subatomic world, there exist the solutions to cure all ills."

The Tyree Master smiled, "You are way ahead of yourself. Here is a comparison for you. As you are to the totality of existence, a universe, so are ideas to an atom. They are living entities, everywhere at the same time, part of the big picture. Some of us refer to it all as the bloodstream of the Cosmos. Others see it as the synaptic connection linking everything. Some of your kind may call it God."

Jack's medical mind kicked into second gear. "All right, I did not experiment; but, I did not rationalize it, either. My efforts were linked to C.P.T., true. So, I merged medical science with physics. My logic and the math led me. If C.P.T. works, then it followed that humans, animals, insects, anything that has brainpower, can acquire ideas or feelings. It's their capacity to think that governs how much they learn."

"Yes, and not just sentient beings withdraw from the Sidron. Everything in a Universe uses ideas, emotions and power," the Stranger said.

Rachel listened, rose slowly and whispered to herself, "So, we are not simply the result of an organic brain process." She turned and looked the Stranger straight in the face. "You are saying God is truly within us; and, if we hone our abilities and connect in the right way, we can connect with him, or whatever our idea is of him. We can do anything. You're saying there is a Heaven. Are you saying I was in this Sidron and on the road to . . . to . . . God?"

"Mrs. Sheldon, please. There will always be some who have more capacity than others to withdraw ideas, emotions and power from the Sidron; but, who is to say who or what that is, or should be? Certainly, not my kind."

"Rachel, seriously, sit down, will you?" Jack continued, "But proving what is in the Sidron, proving which cars are on the road, well that's something else."

"Exactly, Doctor. Ideas, feelings and power are all alive. In fact, that is why the Sidron is so unstable. They are all pushing and pulling in every direction, competing constantly to be absorbed by life. They are used by all existence. Space-time is a garden, an abundance of everything."

The stranger walked to the middle of the Bubble and looked out at the blackness.

"It is both the answer to the greatest mystery of all, and it is the greatest threat to everything you know. You must help us find the breach."

Jack and Rachel embraced, and then she spoke again, "So, when I asked if we did something unholy, using C.P.T. I mean, I saw something . . . "

"Mrs. Sheldon, organized singular self awareness, which you call souls, may very well exist within Sidron; no one can answer you. But, it's not that simple. These things are most difficult for us to explain, because one has no reference from which to bridge the answers. There is no experiment you can perform to prove this. If there were, you would prove faith. My kind has been here for many eons. It is not since the ancient ancients of your Sumerian culture that your kind has stumbled onto anything of this nature. Both of you experienced a taste of it because of C.P.T.; but that doesn't even scratch the surface."

Rachel kept prodding, "Maybe my education is far too feeble, but there is no way you can just know all this."

The Stranger bowed before them. "Yes, there is; and we do. As I said, I have permission to tell you this. Dr. Sheldon, if someone succeeds in applying your Particle Displacement Treatise and uses the Sidron highway, he or she could travel to and from any time. Who knows how it would disrupt the balance of life? Without the proper controls, we very well would, not could, experience a cataclysm of Galactic proportions."

Jack rolled his eyes. "Jesus, Rachel, maybe you're right about C.P.T."

"But, Jack, we are alive because of your discovery."

"She is right, Doctor. Now, we need your brain power. Your creativity might just help fix this."

"Fix what?"

"We believe the event at the ceremony is tied, somehow, to several time distortions we are sensing. They all connect to the Sidron. We need you to examine everything you have. Be my eyes on the surface. Give us clues; help us find who or what has opened Pandora's Box."

"Christ, why not use your own wherewithal? Go into the future and see what happens . . . "

"I am sorry to say, it doesn't work like that, Mrs. Sheldon. It has to do with free will. Explanations become muddied. I am not here to confuse you any more than you might be already."

Rachel sat back and sighed, "Well, it's not as if you expect us to save the world or anything."

"True, we are only speculating that failure would change the course of existence, perhaps worse. Will you help?"

Rachel looked at Jack, as he said, "Yes, yes; but I don't know where to begin."

"You and your wife have been through something that gives you a sense of how important this could be for every life in the Cosmos. If a lunatic finds out he can be anywhere, or worse, everywhere, at the same time; it would damage the balance structure of the Universe. Thoughts could be permanently damaged, or eliminated; not to mention what would happen to power. Time and space, as you know it, would be altered; and existence itself may cease, perhaps even eliminating this Universe altogether. Do you understand?"

The stranger seemed exhausted, and a little aggravated. "Doctor, don't get caught up in the 'it's all my fault' pity party."

Rachel grabbed Jack's shoulders and looked him in the eye, "Whatever it takes, Jack, right?"

"Right . . . okay . . . Christ."

"Good, when you two get back, search any files. Get a hold of your contacts. We have the cooperation of the GGM data base here . . . agreed?"

"Yes, sure, fine."

The Tyree Master smiled and walked to the far end of the Bubble. "Think positive, you two; we are all still here. That's a good sign."

The couple felt a slight acceleration, as they watched the stranger absorb into the transparent membrane of the wall.

"Hmm, you know, Rach, my mother always told me not to listen to strangers."

"Well, perhaps this is one time, we should."

Rachel squeezed Jack, and they sat arm in arm, looking at the outer rock begin to glow hot orange again.

CHAPTER 6

ALLENFAR

A GOLD CLOUD SURROUNDED THE OBJECT. Jake Burns tried as hard as he could to see it clearly. *Just a little closer,* he thought. He reached out as far as he could to get it, but no matter how hard he tried, it was just out of reach. His face began to turn beet red. *One more inch. Shit! I can get it. That fragrance—roses and gold. It's gold!"*

Then, his eyes popped open. "No! Where did it go?"

Suddenly, a violent jerk threw Jake off the reclining lounge and onto the floor of the Carrier. He woke up, startled, grabbing the back of his head. *Damn dreams! Why do I always wake up at the same part? Christ!"*

The Carrier was just under 75 feet long from its spinning head to the end of the whirling tentacles. It radiated beautiful pulsing green and orange lights as it spun, drilling quickly and gracefully through solid rock and magma. Four sensors that looked like eyes and a mouth rotated clockwise, while the rest of its body rotated in the opposite direction. Each rotation of its exposed razor sharp teeth cut and moved whatever was in front to the side; and then the spinning fins displaced everything, pushing it back to its whirling tentacles, which dissolved or displaced it all onto the tunnel walls. Its speed increased with every foot it dug down through the 30-mile outer crust of the earth into the next lower layer, the outer mantle. Eventually, the hot rock became moving lava; and that became a speeding, burning ocean, hundreds of miles underground.

Carrier 2500 was 1600 years old by surface time, relatively young for the species. It left Ever-Life's transport Station 25, from Post 3, below the Alaskan Bering Straits at precisely 6:15 a.m., Universal Time Zone-9. Jake Burns had been on special assignment, his last given by GGM Gordon Swanson, to monitor negotiations on repairs and age spots in one of the Bering Strait's tunnels. They were constructed long ago by a coalition of European, Asian and American contractors. The tunnels became a worldwide focus decades ago, linking all economic markets and intercontinental trade via rail and truck, reducing dependencies and fuel costs of ocean barges and air flights. One of Mathew Bellos' first duties as GGM was to contact and review that status with Jake Burns.

"Mr. GGM, how are you?" Burns asked.

"Fine. How is it going there?"

"The coalition has prioritized repairs; so, negotiations do continue, and probably will, until they all agree on exactly what the fix will be. I recommend we consider introducing the Carriers."

"Don't you think that's a little radical?"

"Yes, I suppose so; but the truth is, eventually we are going to introduce them to the surface; why not now? They could cut new tunnels within a day."

"I'll think on it. The question is, is the surface culture ready to accept alien life; not to mention, our existence and our politics are very different from anything up there. Besides, recent events dictate our priorities right now."

"You know I disagree with you on this. There were two major tremors during the meetings and everyone thought they were earthquakes. No one knows about Sidron. Some are arguing we should repair the bridges and forget the tunnels. I think that would be a mistake, given the unpredictable weather and seas."

"Understood. I need you to brief Gordon on your meetings. While you are with him, get up to speed on the Sidron breach."

"Yes, fine. By the way, congratulations, Mr. GGM. Sorry I wasn't there."

"I appreciate that."

"I can tell you this: if the damage to these tunnels gets any worse, it'll cause a global economic disaster. All countries will suffer. Goods will stop from Asia to and from the Americas. The world economy will go back to pre-year 2200 recessions."

"Well, then, we will think long and hard about ensuring that connection. Contact me, when you can. Good luck."

Jake had been living more than a dual life over the past eight months. Not only did he still hold the title and responsibilities of Chief Detective Inspector, Arden police; but also, more importantly, he was now officially the Global Chief of Security for all Ever-Life colonies and Special Liaison for the GGM. Time and life marched on after the C.P.T. incident. Two months into his Ever-Life orientation, Jake discovered that he had Carrier motion sickness. Now, only minutes after waking, he began sweating again. No pill helped, sleep was the only relief from symptoms. He knew the Carriers were capable of phenomenal speeds. No one really knew how fast one could go. Truth be told, at depths below 200 miles, they moved like guided missiles.

Today, Carrier 2500 sped west, on a direct line through the earth, to a Post 2's transport station below Giza, Egypt. The station was also home to the main Ever-Life archival resources of Time Trust. There, Jake would meet with Gordon Swanson, now Global Defense Chairman. Swanson's rare genetic illness was no longer in remission; one of the reasons Bellos became GGM sooner than expected. Swanson's capacities had diminished enough that he needed to undergo the new C.P.T. process to rid himself of it. During the last eight months of research, Ever-Life developed a new synthetic catalyst bath and a more reliable, automatic extraction/injection process.

Bellos, on the other hand, would also undergo both duplication and C.P.T. (the two were now performed without the concern of the original DNA requirements). His overall plan was to create eight other C.P.T. duplicates. Each would have the title GGM-010, P-1 thru P-8, respectively, holding the top position of Post Controller for each colony throughout the globe. Each duplicate would report to Bellos, directly, via headset/earplug daily, regarding their individual Post matters. Bellos himself was directly responsible and autonomous over all Post Controllers. In addition, he directly interfaced with the Prime Carriers and the Grand Carrier Council, all of which resided deep within the planet. Additionally, only Bellos navigated all surface contact. In total, there were over three billion people within the Ever-Life colonies. The new C.P.T. duplicates would be upgrades from the older solid holographic models, previously held Post Controller positions.

Over his long tenure, Gordon Swanson had both duplication and transtosis performed five times, using a secret Carrier-Unit process. Unfortunately, symptoms of the "crippling gene," as Ever-Life defined it, continued to reappear. Swanson's primary function, now, was to monitor, direct and coordinate major challenges and threats to any Ever-Life colony. Jake Burns reported directly to him.

One of the first things Jake did, after his initiation, was to restructure every Post's security chain of command. Each Post had a Security Controller, head of the local peace forces, which were much like those within Jake's old New York, Manhattan borough, except for some obvious distinctions. One was the Ever-Life weapons. They were non-fatal, firing bursts of air, which could render a person unconscious up to 50 yards. Another was that since crime in the Ever-Life colonies had been consistently below .001%, they had replaced a prison system with a network of mandatory headset sessions to rehabilitate offenders. Real incarceration or punishment was a last resort, performed by special Carriers. It took place within their temporary sanctuary of solitude. Jake was committed to changing the Carriers having all the authority over rehabilitation. He was in the process of submitting a new treaty, which would enable Ever-Life Security to monitor Carrier rehabs.

Swanson did not anticipate Jake's motion sickness when offering him the job months ago. To complicate matters further, at the time, Jake found it almost impossible to juggle his role of Arden City Chief of Detectives. So, he promoted his co-worker, Forensics Specialist, Dr. James Randolph Watzin. Over the last eight months, Watzin had great success, delegating responsibilities and executing the mayor's policies. Crime over the past six months was down eight points. Caseloads reduced dramatically, and the mayor considered layoffs, to reduce the budget. That didn't sit well with most of the duty officers; so, Watzin convinced the mayor to farm out some officers, as part of the Brock/Swanson security team. Watzin negotiated that each officer would remain on the force, with tenure accumulating, while he acted as security staff for the Complex. Consequently, Jake was able to finish Ever-Life's orientation and begin his duties without the extra pressure.

Today, as Jake lay against the Carrier wall, miserable, a strange ringing began in his head, and he looked up only to see the displays on the wall monitors disappear. The ring became a roar, but he was able to sit up dizzy and shaking. He covered his ears with his palms, and as suddenly as it came, the noise stopped, and the Carrier's voice filled his mind.

"Oh, God, what now?"

"Sir, please be calm. I will not hurt you."

"Well, thanks, I think. This is not my favorite thing to do, anyway. Who are you?"

"We understand you took several special trips within the same Carrier, several months ago?"

"What? Who are you?"

"I am Allenfar . . . there was no provision in your training for Carrier communication. It is prohibited for all practical purposes, part of our agreement with your species. Very few of you, over the years, have been allowed to communicate with us; none of you may share among you any interface . . . according to treaty."

"Yes, I know . . . apparently, we have to make new treaties. Oh, my belly; I am not feeling my best. What was that jolt?"

"We stopped. You should feel better in a few seconds. I must get to the point. We are aware of your initial training sessions, months ago, and the Time Trips you made during your orientation. As you know, only special Carriers control time travel. I represent our entire hive in complimenting and thanking you."

"What? What are you talking about?"

"When you rode with Carrier 1111, A 'Compatibility' took place."

"A compatibility? What is that? And why are you telling me this?"

"A compatibility is a symbiotic fusion, a potent intense mental and emotional sharing, which you provide to us. We tap into your inner being. Your kind have been providers for millennia . . . "

"I don't understand, what is your point?"

" . . . I bring you an invitation—a request really—to use that Carrier again. She is the only vehicle sensitive enough to withdraw so much from you. For us, the fusions are a primary reason we trust and cooperate with your species. In your case, nothing of such intensity, such magnitude, has occurred for centuries; and, we request your assistance in this matter, in view of the recent occurrences, the Sidron breach, as you call it."

"So, it's not really an invitation. Are you saying that Carrier 1111 likes me?"

"It means that she acquired abundant sustenance and vitality from you, when she transported you on your time trips. As a hive mindset, then, we all shared her experience. Average interface with your species provides us with 10 to 60 cretes, per human, on our lansig scale. Your specific interface, alone, rated at 1000 to the 12th lansig. That is for us called a compatibility, and its intensity rating was higher than any in the last 210.25 earth years."

Jake rolled his eyes, "So I'm guessing that's pretty high or good for you, right? Are you acquiring sustenance from me right now?"

"Every human gives us sustenance but nowhere near that of the potency you provided our sister. She is your compatibility vehicle.

Carrier 1111 will contact you to schedule additional travel. It is essential for our species to share in these rare cases. Rare cases like yours enable our species to progress and evolve much faster than we would otherwise. We must take advantage, when one appears. It benefits both our species."

"Why tell me this; why not just take what you want? "

"Be well, Jake Burns."

The Carrier went silent and Jake sat confused; but his nausea had gone, and the video on the monitors reappeared.

"Okay, how could anyone have any kind of pleasurable interaction with a giant glow fish?"

He got up and made it into the lounge chair. The Carrier accelerated, as Jake began to watch the monitors again, trying not to think about the ride.

Allenfar

General Facts Regarding Carriers:

1] Each time a Carrier travels, it burrows through rock, lava or anything in front of it. It can shroud itself within a bubble-like protective shell, and, as it burrows, it displaces anything from in front to behind it, leaving no evidence that it was there. Alternatively, without the bubble shroud, Carriers move through rock like fish swim in water, but their bodies spin, as they reach speeds close to that of a rocket in space. Also, without the shroud bubble, they leave a tunnel behind, rather than displace the rock or lava.

2] Carriers have lived within the earth for millions of years, and those that reach adulthood have grown large enough to burrow tunnels a half mile in diameter. However, there are no records indicating how big they have grown.

3] Carriers and humans share a synergistic relationship. When a Carrier travels with a human passenger, it absorbs an indefinable sustenance, which humans alone contain. After an adult Carrier has accumulated enough human sustenance, it may be stimulated to reproduce, by secreting a gooey jelly from its skin. In that case, they leave tunnels with their offspring glued to the walls. The gel sticks indefinitely, and, those few that grow large find their way to the earth's core, where they prosper as adults in a hive environment by withdrawing magnetic power from the earth's core. The greater the sustenance they derive from humans, the more gel they secrete. The goo contains trillions upon trillions of microscopic offspring, organisms that may or may not grow to become larger Carriers. Carriers mature into many sizes. The rule of thumb is the older, the bigger.

4] Very few tunnels exist without gel, but those that do, remain lifeless and function as vents, allowing magma to reach the surface.

5] Ever-Life negotiates annual treaties, with the Carrier hierarchy, which governs all Carrier behavior with humans, including:

A] To communicate with the Ever-Life GGM, as he requests, via direct mind interface or Knofer. Based on Treaty 91776, called the Michael Plan, Carrier hierarchy agreed to provide instant information to the standing GGM, regarding whereabouts, pertinent events and hive activity. In fact, it is all done in trust. Certain questions have arisen in treaty council meetings, which do remain unanswered, including what the Earth's core is really made of—why don't the great beasts go into it? And why is sunlight supposed to kill Carriers? Fundamentally, it is an accepted fact throughout Ever-Life that the large Carriers are at the top of the food chain, below the earth's surface. New short term agreements can be negotiated as needed with a Carrier ambassador —a Tyree Master, if emergencies dictate; however, these are usually done so within the deepest, hottest known Carrier habitat, the Core Post.

B] To take passengers from any one point within the colonies, to any other, like public transportation on the surface. In return, each Carrier derives sustenance from each passenger and shares it with the hive mindset of their species.

6] Smaller sized Carriers not only engineer and construct their own hive communities, but they also build all the new habitats in the Ever-Life colonies'. They are capable of completing tasks, which might take the surface years to construct, in only a few hours.

7] Carrier offspring supply utility and insulate the colonies from the intense heat and magnetic radiation output of Earth's core. The waste-excrement of the microscopic Carrier gel is what lights, sanitizes, supplies oxygen and a mean temperature of 65 degrees for all life within the colonies. For well over 10,000 years, Ever-Life has endured, prevailed and prospered within the environment provided by Carriers.

8] There are very few Grand Carriers, which are enablers of time travel.

9] All Carriers have a collective, hive mindset. No one in the public knows to what extent the beasts understand humans.

10] The biggest mystery regarding all Carriers is that no colony anywhere has been able to study one. There are no factual estimates of how many offspring exist or why certain ones mature to function in one way while others grow to enormous sizes and function in other ways.

11] The vast majority of Carriers lives and reproduces at the microscopic level. The really big ones reside below five hundred miles, deep within the bowels of the earth.

12] It is an acceptable miracle to all citizens of Ever-Life that each Transport Carrier can provide anything that a human traveler requests, instantaneously.

13] Ever-Life's Post Staff Hierarchy are the only ones who are privy to updated maps of hive locations, and even those are constantly outdated.

14] Except for scheduled transports, no one knows where or how often any Carrier moves within the planet.

CHAPTER 7

BACK TO CAMPUS

JACK AND RACHEL SHELDON arrived back at Andrews Hospital anxious to resolve the mystery of what the stranger in the bubble told them. Rachel went straight home to examine all records in their lab. Marietta, their housemaid of four years, was home to greet her.

"Ah, *Señora*, welcome home."

"Yes, thank you, Marietta, is everything okay?"

"*Sí*, yes; all is fine. Amos is tending the horses, the feed is full, and the mare, she gave a foal, a beautiful brown baby."

"That's wonderful, I have to see."

"They even came to fix the cable lines for *Señor* Jack, you know. I did not know what to show them, but they said they found it."

Rachel did a double take. "Wait, hold on, what are you talking about?"

"The cable lines in the lab downstairs; they came very late, but the man, he was so nice. It was the only time they could come; they did not have to come inside. They just tell me about it. They left a note that said all was done and okay. Why?"

"Where is the note?"

"It was just a little piece of paper; I threw it out. It was only this big."

Rachel had a blank stare on her face . . . *The Lab?* she thought. "Its okay, Marietta; it's all right."

She checked the messages on their computer-pad; nothing from any contractor about cables. Then, she went downstairs to the lab. The door seemed fine; she unlocked it and went to the wall safe. She pushed the sensor control pad and twisted the safe's handle to open the door. There, inside, was the treatise Jack wrote. She took it out and began thumbing through the pages. A few were wrinkled, disheveled here and there; and there were some small notes in the margins, which she didn't recognize, but overall, nothing obvious bothered her. She sighed in relief, and as she returned the manuscript back into the safe, a piece of the black knob on the safe fell off. She picked it up and compared it with the remaining piece. There was a hole through the center, where it broke off.

"Christ, it's a drill mark . . . "

Back at the Brock/Swanson Complex, as Chief of Research, Jack had been locked in meetings, since his return, debriefing for hours regarding a wide variety of issues on the campus. He was unsuccessful in breaking away to search any files or contact any colleagues about Sidron. After one meeting broke up, he took a moment to turn on his computer phone, and it rang immediately.

"Honey, it's me; sorry to interrupt."

"No, it's fine, Rach; I need a break. God knows I need sleep. How is it going there?"

"I don't feel my best, but it will pass, I'm sure. Listen, Jack, I checked the safe in the lab. The knob fell off, and there's a hole in the center of the lock."

"You think it was a break-in?"

"Marietta said we had someone come by in the evening to do some cable work outside. I checked with them and they confirmed. Should I call the police?"

"Anything missing?'

"Not that I can see . . . "

"No, don't call them. We have nothing but a hole as evidence; nothing is missing. I'll let Matt know, though. We'll get his people to check it out. Burns has contacts anyway. We better keep it hush, hush for now."

"I have the book and your notes, right here. There is something written here: it says, 'send to Charlie Rosse' . . . What is that about?"

"Christ! I forgot. I did send notes to Rosse, to justify funding. He is at the conference this week. I sent just enough to tweak his interest.

"Okay, one other thing, I did notice that some of the final pages are out of sequence; I know what a stickler you are for detail; but that's all."

"Hmm, Rosse and I were supposed to meet and discuss money at the conference. I can't go with what's piled up here."

"Speaking of forgetting things, Jack, have you heard from Brian? Wasn't he going to call?"

"Not that I know of. Listen, babe, I have to ask you . . . will you go? It's in D.C."

"What? You are kidding, right? We just got back. We were supposed to meet Brian."

Jack hesitated before he said anything. "I'm sure it's tomorrow or the next day. We were seeing him and Angie sometime after the Marshall thing."

"I thought it was today."

"He is calling us tomorrow. You know what that means. Remember, he was thinking about seeing us. That doesn't mean he will."

"Tomorrow? I'm so turned around. Jet lag from traveling inner Earth is worse than going to the Far East."

"Honey, I am serious. I really need you to help me and go to the conference in my stead. One night, you'll be back before Brian even calls . . . I haven't gone through any files in Building 26 yet, nothing but meetings. Now, more than ever, we need Rosse to commit to funding. He has major construction contracts worldwide. Please, babe?"

"You don't mean that boring Research Finance Fundraiser, do you? When?"

Jack sighed in frustration. "Ah, it started yesterday. I am trapped here."

"Christ, Jack!"

"I know, but, if you hadn't called, I probably would have forgotten completely, and that would have been worse. Charlie Rosse is a major player, and we need his backing for the reconstruction and new edition."

"You have been there a straight 16 hours, not including Matt's ceremony. You are not thinking right; you are going to get sick. You want me to fly to D.C. and wine and dine this Rosse?"

"It's important. We promised the stranger, whoever he was, and you did want to be involved."

"Thanks for throwing that in my face."

"Honey, I need you on this; not to mention, we need the money. Brock is gone. Funding is down. Please? I will meet you there as soon as I can get out of here. Take one of the campus jets. I will make the arrangements. You don't have to pack much. I am supposed to meet him at 7 p.m. tonight, in the lobby of the Hilton in the city."

Jack felt a vibration and the phone quiver ever so slightly against his ear. What is that?

"You owe me big time for this, mister."

"I know; and will you leave a message on Brian's phone? I will call him when I get out of here. Have to go, babe. Thank you so much. Call me when you get there! Love you, mmmmuah!"

"Yeah, love you, too." She hung up . . . "Fine; shit!" In her bedroom at the Sheldon's ranch, Rachel began loading her large purse with women's paraphernalia, muttering to herself, "I called to make dinner arrangements and I get this. Family, what happened to family? Charlie Rosse and the money, that's what's important! Go, go Rachel. Drop everything, right now! Pack up and fly, on some superficial, bullshit jaunt, to see another self-centered, billionaire piece of crap. Oh boy, do you owe me, my darling."

Rachel picked up her phone, grabbed her purse, stomped down the stairs to the front door and opened it. There, in front of her, stood a handsome limo driver, dressed in dark blue, tipping his hat. "Hello, ma'am . . . Dr. Sheldon requested a car for you."

When he saw how upset she was, the driver thought better of saying anything else.

"This does not make it right," Rachel said in an angry tone.

"Sorry, ma'am?"

"Well, let's go; come on. What is your name?"

He opened the car door and gestured her into the limo. "Mike, ma'am, I am Mike Warren."

"Well, Mike Warren, you have me at a disadvantage. I am angry, you see, the freak bitch from hell right now."

"Oh, ah, well, it's all right, ma'am. I have seen worse, believe me. You are catching the jet from the campus airport, right?"

"No, I just got a text directing me to go to the Fargo building's airstrip."

"Yes, ma'am."

Within 15 minutes, Rachel had boarded a single engine, Hush-Jet aircraft, which took off from Fargo Field at 4:15 p.m Mountain time. She sat in the luxury cabin with four comfort chairs facing an oval coffee table. There were two great windows on each side of the plane, no portholes, as in the jets of old. A male attendant approached her from the cockpit area, smiling. "Mrs. Sheldon, perhaps you would enjoy a mimosa or chocolate martini?"

She looked at him sarcastically, "Yes, both, thanks."

"Also, here is an itinerary for the conference and some notes from Dr. Sheldon."

"Ah yes, the conference. Hmm and notes. . . even better; I hate this, you know."

"Yes, ma'am, I am Gabriel, by the way. If you need anything else, just buzz."

He smiled and walked forward to the cockpit just as a voice spoke over the loudspeaker, "Mrs. Sheldon, this is Captain Blake. We are scheduled to land at Dulles International, by 5:45 p.m. Make yourself comfortable; if you need anything, let me know."

Rachel rolled her eyes and pivoted the chair so she could see out the window. "Thanks. Anything I need, huh? I would like a quiet evening with my family." She gulped the mimosa and began reading Jack's notes.

From the cockpit door, the steward looked into the rear cabin, as the captain asked, "Gabe, is she out yet?"

"No, Captain, I don't understand. I slipped her a double dose in each one."

Captain Blake pushed the frequency button to 123.701 and spoke to his ear set microphone, "Brazzie one, this is Hush-Jet 6 . . . Brazzie, come in; come in. Brazzie one; this is Hush-Jet-6 . . . do you copy?"

He flicked at his ear piece twice, repeated the call codes, and then he heard a reply. "InVoy here, InVoy here, read you Brazzie."

"Yes, sir, this is Blake. We have the package, and await instructions."

"Switch to satellite reading 307.1983 . . . follow input directives."

"Understood . . . on our way."

The captain cut the call and turned the plane 30 degrees south, southeast, at an altitude below radar detection.

"Gabe, make yourself comfortable; destination, Rio de Janeiro."

"How long, Captain?"

"This baby is faster than anything I have piloted. Watch how she handles this bank."

"Captain, she has just passed out."

"Good . . . here we go."

The plane banked to the right, while Gabe watched Rachel Sheldon flop, side-to-side, unconscious in the chair.

CHAPTER 8

JAKE'S BRIEFING

AT 4 P.M. CAIRO TIME, Allenfar docked at Transport Station 210, directly below the Giza Pyramid. Jake Burns walked out and onto a people-moving tram, which took him to Carrier-Unit elevators. As he rode down, he pondered the whole concept of compatibility. *It's not enough that this bunch of fish run everything—they are construction engineers, utility and food providers, elevators and transportation. God knows what else. I certainly don't want a date . . . !*

When the elevator door opened, Burns stepped out to see the transport station's grand arcade.

"My God, look at this! There is nothing to compare up there."

He gazed upon the lighted rock walls and splashing waterfalls flowing down into a bottomless chasm. Tube-like crossways bridged the diameter of the vertical tunnel.

"I still can't believe the beasts made all of this."

Jake took one last look at the view, and then turned around and walked to Swanson's office. He loved meandering and examining the priceless healthcare exhibits, paintings and sculptures that filled the foyer. Some of the items were recovered from the surface and had been preserved for centuries.

At the other end of the room was a round door. There was nothing like it anywhere else in the colonies. It was constructed back in 4000 B.C. during one of the dynastic periods in ancient Egypt. No one knows how or why; but it opened and closed like a human iris. Jake remembered his headset session about it.

Originally, this particular Post 2 Station was one of the first medical research facilities in the region, and the door was a security entrance. In those days on the surface, either medical chieftains or shamans diagnosed illnesses based on examining eyes. Ever-Life learned much from the ancient cultures.

Jake liked the fun of moving repeatedly halfway in and out of the door; in, out; in, out; watching the center circle open and close. Through the door, Swanson's assistant, Patty, watched, shaking her head and giggling. "Hello there, Mr. Burns, are we still in kindergarten?"

"Hello, doll. Why can't I get one of these things?"

"You are right on time, as usual. He is ready for you, I think. You may go right in."

"Ah, thanks . . . why don't you let me take you away from all this? You should be my secretary now that the big guy is retired. At least call me Jake."

"In your dreams. Anyway, I have been with the GGM for more than 13 years now. I would never leave, and, if you remember, protocol is protocol. Thanks for sharing, though."

"Yeah, well, I'm too old for you anyway."

"I didn't say that, love." She winked.

Their banter made him forget the morning ride. Jake walked around her desk, and as the buzzer sounded, he strolled between mirrored sliding doors behind her into Swanson's loft office suite. Once inside, wall-to-wall carved bookshelves lined the walls, and, to Jake's surprise, new rustic Adirondack furniture added a feel of the North American wild.

Jake stood pondering the new motif until a familiar voice broke the silence. "Hello, Burns! Is that you down there? Make yourself at home. I'll be right down."

Jake snapped out of his euphoric moment and sat down in the plush leather chair next to Swanson's desk.

"Great! Thank you, sir."

He began watching the eight 60-inch floating monitors, positioned around the room, displaying Ever-Life's news. After having headset sessions, Jake understood all the different languages appearing on videotape texts at the bottom of each screen.

"How did I live without this shit all those years? If only Watzin knew. Christ, if the boys in New York knew, I'd never live any of this down."

One of the text feeds interrupted his nostalgia. Within seconds, all the monitors reported the exact same story: Billionaire Marion Brock returns to buy Time Travel, Inc.

Jake's eyes widened. "Oh, my God!" He tapped his Knofer and it confirmed the authenticity of the reports. Swanson walked down the stairs, staring at the monitors.

"Sir, is this from surface news? The feed is all the same."

"You know we don't get that crap. These are from our resources. It is very strange. Our systems don't work like this, all channels displaying the same video. It is as if someone has hacked into us."

Jake tapped his Knofer again and executed a defense protocol to trace. "I've got nothing . . . "

Swanson stopped for a second at the bottom of the stairs. "All of it says Marion Brock is alive. I have to wonder . . . " He walked to his desk, hesitated, and then he took a book out of the drawer and tossed it in front of Jake. It was titled *EVER-LIFE*.

"I wonder if any of that, or our recent event at the ceremony, has to do with this? Perhaps it is no longer a private matter between you and me . . . ?"

Jake picked up the book, while he listened to Swanson.

" . . . Somehow, we have to fix this, my friend. The book is about all of us down here, and it was written long ago in 2011. There is a stamp on the first page that says NYC Public Library."

Jake took a deep breath, as Swanson turned the pages, annoyed at what he saw.

"This may already have had earth-shattering implications. There are pictures of Carriers in it. Did you read this paragraph?

'Many people write stories they imagine. That is fiction today. But what if someone writes a 'true' story that hasn't happened yet?'

. . . and precisely, what do you think that means?

"You sent this to me via Carrier, so there would be no record in headset files. You must have suspected something . . . ." Swanson gestured to the monitors. " . . . And now, the Brock story? If this book was on the surface for that many years, and Brock, or one of his gofers read it, my God! How many copies were made? Do you know?"

"No, sir."

"The more I think about it, the more I am certain they are related somehow. Put what is on those monitors and in this book together, along with the Carrier episode at Mathew's ceremony, and what story do you come up with, eh?"

"Perhaps, sir, but it is a very interesting story."

"And I know I'll love it. Apparently, it is a story worth writing a book about, eh? Tell me, Jake—we don't have all the time in the world anymore. After all, the book has existed for how long now, centuries. Do give me the who, what, where, when and how of this . . . and, now would be a good time to start." Swanson plopped in his chair. "Puzzling, too, since Brock was taken away by a Carrier, those months ago."

Swanson began fidgeting and staring at a Carrier model, which he kept on the right corner of his desk. In that second of awkward silence, his desktop Knofer ticked. He tapped it and a three-foot holographic image of Marion Brock grew up before their eyes. Swanson's jaw dropped. Jake quickly grabbed his Knofer and pushed buttons to record and send to Bellos. At the same time, he also triggered the next level of Ever-Life's security protocols to 313, which alerted all Post Controllers. Then, both Jake and Swanson fixed on the hologram.

"Hello, Gordon." Brock smiled that arrogant sinister grin. "I can tell by your usual blank expression that I've interrupted nothing.

Long time no see. As I recall, you thought I was swallowed into the Earth's core and gone forever. So, I thought I would call and tell you I'm just fine; never was dead, really. I do hope you are prepared."

"Frankly, Marion, nothing you do surprises me. How did you get my number, by the way?"

"Hah, well, I do love a sense of humor. To put it bluntly, I plan to make some changes, and you are one of them. You see, I just acquired a new Research Complex. You just saw the ads. The point is, we are going to compete. I thought a heads-up, so to speak, was in order."

"Marion, even your laws don't allow you to compete with Brock/Swanson."

"Of course not, I'm talking about your little Ever-Life secret. I'm talking about your time travel operation. You see, I have kept up on what the old staff is doing. My new acquisition will be . . . oh, I'm sorry; I mean, my new acquisition is fully operational, now. Anyway, it's dedicated to stopping your Ever-Life from becoming, well, forever-life . . . I am saving that little jewel for myself. You will have never existed in the first place, when I'm done . . . I just wanted you to know, my foolhardy friend. I told you a long time ago, you didn't have a clue, and I meant it. I wanted you to know the bullet is coming, my dear partner; and it's coming from me, personally, to you. Have a nice day. Oh, one more thing, I would like to compliment you on these little gadgets, they are called Knofers, right? Quite fun, actually."

Brock's hologram disappeared and the monitors went completely black. All went quiet. The two men looked around, as if expecting something else.

"Now that man definitely has issues," Jake quipped.

"Hmm . . . " Swanson rocked back in his chair. " . . . So, either he read this book or, it's something else. And then, there is the issue of the Carrier at the ceremony, the earthquakes in the Bering Straits and the explosion . . . Wheeler?"

"Yes, sir, we shipped his body to Lab 202."

"Any news on him?"

"GGM is handling it, personally. He designated it a priority-one security."

Swanson swiveled his seat, looked at the ceiling and then at Burns. "Okay, you and I run this effort, completely hands-on. You obviously have thought about this book and Brock. You started something here; I trust you will finish it. Use only the best of our team. We need a good plan. Let's start with you telling me everything about this book thing."

"Fine, also I have to tell you about my ride here."

"Priorities, Jake, priorities . . . "

"Yes, well; remember when you first offered me this position and Mathew took me on that tour? I was very attentive, and he did show me a lot, in a relatively short time."

"Yes, go on . . . "

"One area was a Time-Trust pavilion in Arden. I was so impressed, specialists and small Carriers all around. By the way, that was where I thought, in a blink, I would accept your job offer."

"Hmm . . . "

"Anyway, one of my instructors was Time-Trust Specialist, Chelsea Bathwaite."

"Chelsea, isn't that a girl's name?"

"Do you know him?"

"Jake, we have a global population of roughly three billion. So no, I don't; go on."

"Well, we sensed an immediate chemistry, of sorts, much like you and I did the first time we met in D.C. at the weapons conventions."

"Yes?"

"Well, there wasn't enough time on that day. We had to cut it short, because you and Dr. Bellos had to travel to Jerusalem."

"Thank you for reminding me," Swanson sighed, exasperated. "Jake, we have a lot to cover, and I do have other meetings. Do keep that in mind."

"Yes, while you were in Jerusalem, and in several subsequent meetings during my training months, Bathwaite and I got to know each other rather well."

"So are you dating? For God's sakes, man!"

"It's just that I never thought I'd be interested in time travel, never believed in it. Frankly, I thought like most that it was something it isn't. Anyway, my security training took months; and, well, I spent several days with Time-Trust learning its reality and how traveling really works. The short of it is; I was hooked. We didn't do anything wrong, you understand; but, within the confines of rules, of course, Bathwaite allowed me to take several brief trips. I did go back in time."

"I'll bet that was a mouthful, now wasn't it? I see. You realize, now, of course, that there is no such thing as a brief trip in time."

"Um, yes, I suppose that's true."

"And you met this . . . this author?"

Little beads of sweat began appearing on Jake's forehead.

"Yes, sir, I did. I met him four times. Like I said, it's an interesting story. I didn't expect my trips could trigger anything . . . that reminds me . . . there is something else, about this morning . . . "

"Well, none of us expected this, much less something else, now did we?"

"No, sir, it's about the Carriers."

"I certainly realize what time trust means, and its function, as well as the importance of Carrier relations; so, one thing at a time. There is a lot on our plate. It's all quite a bit to follow. Give me the short versions, Jake."

Before Jake could begin again, a priority call clicked on both Swanson's and Jake's Knofers. It was Bellos. "Hello, you two. We have another situation here in Arden City. Two bombs have gone off, blowing up the Fargo Building, completely, and Time Trust-Research Building 26."

"Mathew, I'm sure Marion Brock is involved. It is his way of saying hello and goodbye."

"Brock, hmm . . . I saw the security call from Jake. The bombs just went off . . . didn't we see Brock taken by a Carrier, months ago?"

"There is something very wrong, Mathew. His news about buying Time Travel, Inc. displayed on all my monitors here. He is alive and well."

"Interesting, he has been in hiding all this time. Neither one of us was notified status from Carrier relations?"

"Yes, and more intriguing . . . his timing with the Sidron events is very suspicious. He has vowed revenge toward us, me in particular, for stopping his effort to steal C.P.T. He has a Knofer; very dangerous."

"We have put the colonies on alert. Burns is there with you. Clarify and discuss all the issues, then report to me."

"Yes, we will. You have very big issues right now with the three clergy."

"Yes, but this has top priority."

"It's all related, Mathew."

"I agree."

"Jake is already working on something. I will have him get into all of it. Are you taking all three of the bickering boys back in time with you?"

"That is my plan. Hopefully this will fulfill our obligation to GGM-S. He wouldn't have given them the book if he wasn't sure of something. It couldn't be worse timing, though."

Swanson grinned and replied, "You will handle it. By the way, when do you and I undergo the new C.P.T. procedure?"

"We have a subject for final test today. I should receive results soon, actually. I recommend we schedule ASAP after that. Considering our total population, the Sidron breach and now Brock, Knofer solid holograms don't cut it anymore."

"Yes, big changes. The food budget will have to increase," Swanson smirked. "I will be in Arden day after tomorrow. Mathew, was anyone hurt in the blasts?"

"Fifty people, all from the Complex, no one from below; Jake, are you listening?"

"Yes, sir."

"Mathew, what about Wheeler?"

"I am handling it. Gordon, you and I are scheduled to have a meeting about the Sidron at Carrier-Hive Post 8. Are you prepared?"

"Jake and I are going over some new information, which may implicate Dr. Sheldon or at least his Particle Displacement Treatise.

"Well, we are investigating the bombs. I hope that will tell us more. We have to keep ahead of all this, guys."

"Mathew, how many Carriers will attend?"

"I'm told each ambassador assigned to our Posts and two Primary Adult Time Controllers, so 10."

"I never understood why so many when they have a hive mindset. Good luck with the clergy."

"Yes, thanks . . . be safe."

The Knofer cut the call, and Swanson focused on Jake. "Okay, my friend, back to it. Now tell me, how much does the author of this book know, or think he knows, about us?"

"Sir, will I be going to the hive meeting?"

"You will now. I see no way around it now that you have opened another Pandora's Box. You need to tell me about your time trips."

"It was not that kind of situation; and, besides, it is imperative that I tell you what happened to me during my trip to you this morning."

"Marion Brock is no fool, Jake. You never knew him. He was a billionaire pirate and a killer, but no fool. I don't know how or why he is alive; but, if he finds out, or already knows who this author is, and he can get to him through time travel, then catastrophe! We need to know how much this man knows and where he is."

"He is dead. He died centuries ago."

"Oh, my . . . yes, of course." Swanson thought for several seconds. "So, you think what?"

"I think I agree that this book could motivate Brock. But, I'm not sure he can do much. Remember, since the author is dead, Brock can't change anything in the timeline."

Swanson rolled his eyes, perked up and said, "Hmm, well, I'm sure you learned a lot in your training; but, perhaps one thing you don't know is that by meeting this author, you made yourself part of his timeline. So, if Brock could talk to him and, through him, get to you in that timeline, he could use you to change things here and now. In that case, we would have quite a different game all together, would we not? You are not dead at all, are you?"

Jake pondered, as he listened, and watched Swanson flipping through the pages of the book.

"Also, my friend, there is a lot of information within these pages that reveal our culture. While it only generally describes C.P.T. and Mathew's success transposing the holograms, this could result in dramatic consequences; up on the surface, if read by the wrong people . . . Jake, Jake . . . " Swanson sighed, while Burns got up and paced.

"Sir, I want you to understand. I met the author four different times during his life. I, of course, was the same age I am now."

"I know how old you are."

"Yes, well, the sum total of our time together was only four of his days."

Swanson's eyes widened and he was noticeably annoyed as he listened. "So, four days with you in them are just sitting out there, forever. That is a lot of time and opportunity for Brock to make catastrophic changes. This is a hard way to learn the lesson. He can use that time as a most powerful tool against us. It can't be taken lightly or used frivolously at the whim of the moment. Now, how much can you tell me?"

"Actually, that book was found last week, in the New York Public Library. An old police buddy of mine called me. He read it and noticed my name. He thought it funny, given the date the book was written. He sent it to me at the Arden police station. I read it and sent it to you via Carrier because I wanted strict security. The truth is that the author was a very stimulating man, and I did not resist conversations. But I may have twisted his life a bit, showing up when he was different ages."

"I am certain of that."

"It was during our second meeting that we hit it off so well. He was 40-ish, as I recall. I even thought, 'What a great candidate for Ever-Life, if only it hadn't been a Time-Trust issue. Anyway, we talked at great length about many issues and subjects. I tell you, Gordon, there have been some pretty intelligent average people, living on the surface."

"Hah! No one ever argued that point. So, is that when he wrote the book?"

"I think he started it then; but, later he said he dismissed our first meetings as dreams. I think that was due to the fog that comes from the experience."

"Obviously he was able to overcome it. What were his other ages when you met?"

"The first time was during his college years. He was a first year student, as I recall. It was 1965. We were together around six hours. He was in crisis. I tried to help. Something horrible had happened to him. I felt he needed me, and there was something about him . . . "

"1965, eh? Make a note. Find out if anything significant happened concerning Brock back then."

" . . . Anyway, I left and came back to orientation, but I couldn't get the experience out of my mind."

"He never told you what the crisis was?"

"Not really, I never checked either; but I had to see how he turned out. Bathwaite had no problem letting me go back again. So, I met him in his 40s. He was in crisis again. We talked for a good 15 hours. I was convinced that my help made a difference. Our final two meetings were during his 50s. He was in physical crisis then, heart issues. Looking back, it was all so odd to me. Each time he had gone through a life-changing event just before I arrived. Each time I went, my urge to see him was irresistible. Of course, as part of my orientation, Bathwaite explained I could never repeat a particular trip; so, I could never reconcile my anxiety about the visits and I stopped."

Swanson slowly stood up. "Jake, your irresistible urge? You followed irresistible urges, eh? Really? Good thing you weren't a teenager. What in blazes were you thinking?"

"I realize, now, I was the one in a fog. I was addicted, selfish and a bit stupid. But, I did learn a lot. It was mutual. I thought of him as a son, if that makes any sense. And, another thing you should know, I did give him a headset session."

"You what? Christ, Jake!"

"It just happened."

"I wish I had a nickel for every time I heard 'it just happened'. No wonder he could write the book. What else does he know that Brock could steal? My God, man, you are Chief of Security. This man is a virgin by our standards. Did you think of the domino effect from this, the collateral damage on those who knew him, not to mention the obvious long term affects on Ever-Life? If this is true and Brock succeeds, I won't be sitting here, and we won't have the memories we do right now of anything that has happened. He will wipe us out, and all that we have done, both with the surface and the Carriers."

Jake stood up at attention. "Sir, I have to say, I would go back and be with him again, if I could; or better yet, I would bring him here."

"Well, that is something," Swanson wiped his mouth and returned to his chair. "Relax . . . relax, Jake . . . you look ridiculous."

"I have absolutely no doubts about him, sir. But I am truly sorry about all of it. I realize it may have an effect on us here, now; especially if it had anything to do with what happened this morning."

Swanson sat back with a questioning face. "Well, the book was not that well-written, anyway. Maybe nobody read it, or we would have heard about it. Let us follow this through. Maybe you can keep it a good memory."

"I am talking about something else. Something happened to me, this morning."

Swanson sucked in another deep breath and let out a slow blow. "My plate's pretty full; what do you want to add?"

"We have a Carrier complication. This morning my transport Carrier spoke to me."

"Really?" Swanson sat up again, and with his elbows on the desk, he looked pensively at Burns. "Go on."

"He said his name was Allenfar. He spoke to me, complimented me, actually. Apparently, when the Carrier took me back in time those months ago, she claims to have had a compatibility with me. They want me to take more time trips within her."

Swanson stood up, walked around the desk and sat on its corner. "Did he say anything else?"

"That I was a potent sustenance to her—to them all—more potent than they have experienced in over 200 years. I am sure what happened to me relates to everything else—the explosion here at Time Trust, Sidron, the event at the ceremony. Gordon, there were two tremors at the Bering Straits, too. We all thought it was earthquakes . . . "

Swanson had a blank stare at first, and then he began speaking, as though he remembered something from long ago. "A compatibility, eh? I haven't heard that term in a very long time. Now that I am not GGM, things become foggier with every minute. I almost forgot it was possible. Jake, this could be good for us if it is true. Ever-Life could expand at an accelerated rate, beyond anything we have ever known in modern times. The last compatibility was during the GGM before me. Carriers were not as happy as you'd think to accept my authority." Swanson seemed to strain to remember. "You know, the Carriers live with us symbiotically, sort of, and synergistically of course. Normally, they derive very little from us, only while we travel in them. Even if we could, we are bound by treaty not to calculate readings or amounts. But we know whatever it is they receive from us, it's more than they receive from any other life form. They need us.

Historically, only once in a great while, almost never, someone very special comes along and voila!—a compatibility—a massive link directly into their most stimulating, private being. It's rather confusing to us because we don't sense what we give them. We derive measurable physical benefits from them. Their abilities to travel in this environment, to heal, to control time, to create anything from nothing within their bodies are what we get. But, we really have no idea what it is they get from us."

Swanson sat back down, rocked in his chair, and looked at the ceiling. He rambled on. "We know they derive essential components from our psyche, our emotions and our inner being, things that when enough is accumulated, they propagate, so to speak; you know, the bright goo covering the cave walls. But, it's only in those rare, one in a billion instances, from 'a compatibility', that they can pump offspring out like garden hoses squirt water on the Fourth of July . . . And they can do it for months. Up until now, they have had to accumulate whatever it is slowly and in very small amounts, little by little. If one of us is compatible with even just one of them, all of them share the experience. One compatibility session could generate hundreds of Carriers to breed at the same time. For Ever-Life, a compatibility could motivate them all to create new inhabitable caverns at a rate, well, faster than any effort in centuries."

Swanson seemed obsessed in the moment. Suddenly, he shook it off and looked at Burns. "I am way ahead of myself. There is a lot to think about here; first things first."

"I like first things first," Jake said.

"Let's get back to the author of this book. If he had a headset session, we have a record."

"Yes, probably."

"I want you to check our vaults. We need that file. If nothing else, it will tell us the specifics of your actions in that timeline. We need to monitor and protect you there against a Brock invasion. What a bag of mucky puck."

Swanson took their two Knofers and put them end to end on his desk. Then, they both put headset earplugs on, and Swanson called an emergency meeting of all eight Post Security staff leaders.

CHAPTER 9

FARGO GONE

GGM MATHEW BELLOS JOINED HIS FATHER, Dr. Richard Bellos, and Dr. Jack Sheldon, managing trauma units set up between the two bombed buildings on the Brock/Swanson campus. One exploded in the new Time Research Building –TR-26. The other leveled the Fargo building, where Marion Brock had his primary residence for years. Bellos and Jack had been in the process of transferring data from one of the Time-Trust pavilions below Arden to TR-26. The objective was to influence one of the campus research teams to discover time travel, thereby enabling the Complex to patent, copyright and trademark all aspects of the process. Jack's new Particle Displacement Treatise would play a primary role, as did his C.P.T. with regard to surface medical discoveries made in the last year. It was a new direct approach by the GGM to gain more of a foothold in surface matters. Ever-Life would reap much greater monetary benefits. Of course, that was the plan before the current Sidron events took place.

Mathew broke away from the trauma units to call Swanson and learn of Brock's phone call; then he returned to the bomb scene.

"Dad, what is the status?"

"Most of the wounds were superficial and treatable here."

"Thank God."

"Campus bulldozers should have most of the rubble cleaned up in the next few days."

"What a mess."

"Arden police are over there. They have been interviewing our Security Team . . . hah, their own chaps. I haven't talked to them yet. Detective Watzin did not come . . . Where is my granddaughter, Angie?"

"She is with Dr. Luanne, down under. She said she was going to meet Brian in the morning for the Marshall decision. She is safe for now. What's the latest census?"

"All accounted for but two, Barb Sawyer and Ralph Walker."

"Why would Barb or Ralph be anywhere but Floor Two at Andrews?"

Jack interrupted, "I gave the order. I had them go to TR-26 to get a copy of my treatise. Guards are searching now, but nothing yet."

"Jesus." Bellos turned to Richard. "And that's everyone?"

"Yep . . . "

Bellos then turned his attention to the police detectives searching through the rubble. "Hey, fellas, who is in charge here?"

They all looked up, but Bellos heard a voice behind him. "I am, Doctor."

Bellos turned around to see a young, spry, energetic woman, in her late 20s, wearing a dark purple pantsuit and a grimace.

"And you are?"

"I am Abigail Johnson; Abby, if you like. Your Mr. Burns directed me to report here."

"Ah, well, Jake has good taste."

She surveyed the three doctors briefly, but focused on the GGM. They all heard something ticking and Bellos said, "I think that is you, my dear."

Abby tapped the palm of her hand and then read the display across her fingers.

"Hmm, just what we need, a palm reader," Jack said. "I guess she is not from the police station."

"No," Bellos replied, "and she has a new Knofer accessory, quite impressive."

"Yes, it's new; Mr. Burns authorized my testing it." Johnson began reading from her hand, and after a few seconds, spoke in a determined voice, "Sir, the Fargo building is completely demolished. It was a pro-job. There was minimal damage to surrounding areas— definitely strategic and professional."

"I want them, Johnson. This is the second time in a year that we have been hit. I want it stopped permanently."

"Well, that is why Burns sent me, sir." She reached inside her pocket, recovered a small bundle and handed it to Bellos.

"We found that. It's a remnant of an old type detonator. We also got two fingerprints and fresh footprints off stair planks in the debris. There were five men. We captured one unconscious, outside Fargo, wounded from the blast. He had a concussion and a broken leg. The others fled up to Albuquerque. We ran a dust analysis, trailing the air-path of the blast. Long story short, we searched the Knofer gene pool from the prints on the doorknobs, saliva spray on a glove and stair railings. It all revealed identities. It took longer than we thought; but we found one man at the city train depot and three more at the airport. We know they were Brock's men, Rash InVoy's specifically."

Bellos smiled at her, "Impressive."

"And there is something else. I got word that three Knofers are missing."

"I knew about one. Didn't the defense protocols initiate?"

"Nothing traceable kicked in. The feedback so far is not specific; one tracks Arden to China and back; one tracks Moscow to Seattle; and, the third tracks from Fargo to South America, Rio."

"Organized confusion, sounds like a Brock scenario, a befuddle move. But, how did they get them?" Bellos looked angry. "Something just isn't right, Fargo to Rio? Stream me any exact locations, when you can. Send teams as soon as you know."

"Yes, sir."

"Good job, Johnson." Bellos turned and started walking away. He noticed Jack digging with the others in the rough fragments of

Building 26. "What are you doing, Jack? You are going to cut your hands. You know better than that. Let the detectives work."

"I see something in here. Look at this," Jack lifted the strange transparent fabric. "What is this? It's sparkling but it looks like snakeskin?"

Bellos took the 8- by 10-inch piece, examining and caressing it. "I need to make a call."

As he put it in his pocket, he felt it vibrate, and instinctively, he quickly pulled it out again, up to his Knofer. "Unbelievable . . . " It disintegrated in his hand. "I think Mr. Brock and his team are alive and well . . . and I think, something else . . . damn, no reading on the Knofer."

Jack watched and was noticeably disturbed. "I've only seen glowing like that once before. It's a piece of one of those things —your beasts, isn't it? It has something to do with that bullshit at the ceremony, and what I am working on, your Sidron; doesn't it?"

Suddenly, they heard shouting. "Sir, Ms. Johnson, over here, over here! I've got something!"

They all walked over to him. "Look, an arm," the detective said.

Bellos, Jack and Dr. Richard helped, as they all dug. "My God," said Jack. "It's Barb Sawyer."

They brushed her face off and Jack began CPR. Within a minute, she coughed and opened her eyes. "What happened?"

Jack smiled, as he held her head. "Barb, you'll be fine, stay still. It's me, Dr. Sheldon. Just, don't move."

She coughed again and said, "Dr. Sheldon, what about Ralph? We got your notes; but, just as we left the building, boom . . ."

"My notes . . ."

As the rest of the team reached the two of them, another detective yelled, "I've got another one over here!"

Jack was quick to instruct, "Get her into emergency; check her out, STAT!"

Then, he ran to the other site. Everyone was digging frantically. Jack watched as Bellos and a detective pulled a lifeless body out from the rubble. The GGM brushed the dust and pieces of wreckage off his face. There was a deep gash through the neck, and his inner organs were missing.

"Ralph Walker," Jack said.

"Look at his hand," a detective said. "He is holding something."

Jack went over and pried his hand open. "My notes, my treatise, but some are missing."

Johnson notified the rest of the team to stop looking, while Jack checked the body.

"Matt, he has been dead a while, maybe even before the bombings."

Bellos knelt down, as the ER team arrived with diagnostics. He took a blood smear and put it on his Knofer. "Run genetic analysis."

The two doctors stood up and faced Johnson. "Abby, he did not die from the bombing."

"What?" she said.

"They obviously didn't want Jack's notes, either, or they would have taken them. Ralph died from knife wounds. They gutted him and slit his throat, while he gripped those pages."

One of the ER men whispered into Jack's ear, "Doctor, I found this in his inside coat pocket."

Jack took the crumpled ball of paper, opened it and whispered, "It's the last page of my treatise."

"What are you saying, sir?" Abby asked perplexed.

" . . . I think the bombs may be a cover, just to get our minds off the ball."

"That's a little far fetched, don't you think?" She looked at Ralph. "What diabolic bastard would kill like this?"

Bellos replied, "Marion Brock."

Meanwhile, Jack read the scribbled writing on the crumpled page:

It's incomplete, Jack!
CR

He got a very sick feeling in his stomach. "Jesus, Matt, can't you take Ralph to wherever you do it and duplicate him, clone him, let's give him C.P.T. for Christ's sake?"

"I just checked. He has a defective genetic makeup. It wouldn't take."

Jack shook his head, "God, what was the point?"

One of the ER team spoke to Bellos, "Sir, should we take him to the morgue?"

"Yes," Bellos said, "to the morgue." Bellos bowed his head and gritted his teeth in a moment of respect and anger.

Jack interrupted his concentration in a panic. "Matt! Look here!"

"What is it?"

"Look at this. Christ! And what about Rachel?"

"What about her?"

"She went to D.C. for me, to meet that money backer, Charlie Rosse, look here; CR . . . Rosse? It's Charlie Rosse?"

They looked at each other, realizing, and Bellos spoke into his Knofer, "Charlie Rosse . . . give me all data."

"You can do that with those?"

Bellos shook his head in disgust. "Jack, I gave you Knofers for a reason . . . it says he is a financial mogul. That's all we need, another farking Brock. He and his 14 ghost foundations support a variety of global investments. Most recently, contract negotiations for repairing the Bering Straits . . . Jake just attended the convention there. He said Brock money was all over the place."

"You think Brock and Rosse are connected?"

"Yes, Brock is muddying the water to hide his involvement with Rosse. They all want the contract for fixing the Bering Straits. That would be very bad for us. Johnson, get me all the information you can on the last six months of transactions made by any Rosse or Brock company. Meet me at my office on the 10th floor with it."

"When?"

"Now! Jack, Dad, walk with me."

"Matt, you don't really think this is all Brock's doing too, do you? He is dead. I remember," Jack said.

"If my memory serves me, he set off on a year-long tirade, because of C.P.T., in the first place. Jack, you chose him, right?"

"Come on, Matt, you never understood Marion Brock or what he did for me and C.P.T.," said Jack.

"Your thinking was clouded then; and, obviously, it still is by your obsession to prove your theories. The facts tell us he is alive and up to no good."

"You think he is still after C.P.T.?"

"There is more to it now. He wouldn't have ruined his own home or attacked TR-26, without having a much more elaborate agenda. He is daring us to try to stop him; and he doesn't give a damn who he murders."

"So it's about what? Why is he doing this?"

Bellos stopped and looked Jack in the eye. "It's about C.P.T., your new treatise and time travel. It's about control, Jack; control. He is out of control. He's obsessed. By the way, where is your son, Brian?"

"He is at the law library, I think; then, home, until the Dave Marshall decision."

"Oh, my, Dave Marshall," Dr. Richard said. "Has it been that long? Time passes so quickly and we forget so much, so many important things. That's why I have always supported that time travel should be available to the public."

"Yes, Dad," said Bellos. "I know your views on this. Listen, you two, I am sure Brock is trying to throw off my departure with the three clergy. I cannot miss that because of the Time-Trust parameters and Carrier Treaty commitments. Dad, please stay on campus. Manage the ER efforts and work with the Arden Police. Jack, come with me."

The two got into Bellos' limo for the brief ride back to Andrews.

"Take us to Entrance Five, will you, Mike?"

"Yes, sir. By the way, something I think is important given the immediate circumstances."

"Yes?"

"About Mrs. Sheldon this afternoon, I thought it strange she left from the Fargo airfield."

"I don't understand."

"Dr. Jack called me and asked me to drive her to the campus airstrip. She said I should take her to Fargo. I thought nothing of it and cancelled the other plane reservation. Now, given the bombs, well, I just thought I would mention it; that's all."

Jack exploded, "Christ; you idiot! Why didn't you say something, call me, send up a red flag? Shit!"

Bellos pushed a button, raising the window behind the driver's front seat.

"Calm down, Jack. Take it one step at a time."

Within 10 minutes, they were in Bellos' office on the 10th floor of Andrews. Bellos made a Knofer call to Ever-Life Post 5, Station 120, Peru, South America. "I need surveillance throughout the continent and Post, to trace Knofer numbers 1961 and 1969."

"Yes, sir, it may take a little time. We have to follow Carrier Treaty protocols . . ."

"Do whatever you have to. We need to find those Knofers now!" The GGM cut the call. "Frankly, I'll be glad when the C.P.T. replacements take the hologram's places. At least we will be dealing with emotional beings . . . Abby, first, I want you to start surveillance on both Brian Sheldon and Angie until Jake or I release the security protocols. Take Dr. Sheldon here to Washington, D.C. Use the plane on the main campus runway. I know it's all fueled. Try to trace the plane Rachel Sheldon took, work with the FAA."

"I did, sir. There's no record of a flight plan."

Bellos tapped his Knofer, "Get me Mike Warren."

In a matter of seconds, Bellos' Knofer clicked again.

"Yes, sir, Mike here."

"Mike, did you see the plane Rachel Sheldon took?"

"It was a Hushjet-36. The only noticeable marking was a yellow seagull's silhouette on the tail."

Bellos looked at Abby.

"Got it," she said.

"Thanks, Mike. Call me if you remember anything else."

"One more thing, sir; I found a small bug-recording device, in the limo. I just gave it to Security, Level Six."

"Abby?"

"I'm on it."

"Thanks Mike. Abby, get going with Jack here. Call me en route with updates. Your priority is to see that these two are safely returned, back to Andrews."

"Got it."

"You meet Mr. Charles Rosse, and investigate any possible involvement he may have with Rash InVoy or Brock. Alert your team out there. Be lawful, please?"

Jack was getting more nervous, the more he listened. "Matt, I haven't heard from Rachel at all—no texts, no messages, nothing . . . and she doesn't answer her phone."

"Where are your Knofers, Jack?"

"Jesus, Matt, I don't carry that shit."

Abby replied, "Great, another dinosaur, I'll bet you a dime they're the missing ones."

"Give Dr. Sheldon another one . . . stick it in your pants or up your ass, Jack, but keep it on you. Do you understand? Where the hell are the two we gave you?"

"Home, I think; I don't know."

Johnson whispered under her breath, "How can someone so brilliant be so stupid?"

Jack was quick to challenge, "I heard that. I just don't see them as a priority in my life, young lady."

"What about now?"

"Don't lose it, Jack. Learn it. Now get going. I have to meet with our guests, the three fathers."

Abby gently nudged Jack's arm. "Let's go, Doctor."

Jack and Abby went to Bellos' private elevator and pushed the button to floor 1.

Bellos heard his Knofer again. As he walked, he listened. "Sir, this is Jacque at Time Trust in Post 2, Giza. We need to know how to proceed with our new guests."

Bellos didn't skip a beat, "Make sure they are comfortable but isolated and secure. Contact me if there is a problem." Bellos walked to the oval room and took a call from the Andrews floor two. "Hello, Bellos here."

"Yes, Dr. Bellos, this is Krys in cancer surgery; we need you here . . . STAT."

Chapter 10

Detective / Detective

GORDON SWANSON AND JAKE BURNS finished their conference call with the colonies' Security Managers, and sat thinking about the whirlwind of events. Jake noticed an unusual look on Swanson's face. "Sir . . . Gordon, are you all right?"

"I am just trying to put all the fragments together. I used to do this in less than a minute. You don't miss being GGM, unless you need it."

Jake shrugged. "I have no idea what you mean. It's all a puzzle; I realize that."

"Follow me on this. The Carriers have been the keepers of time travel well over 1200 years, as far as I know. They have taught us the reality of time; that it is more than the abstract concept, which we humans invented and use to measure events or cycles. I accepted that, you see. With great confidence, I have accepted that time travel can only take place within time measured. If there is no measure, there is no time to travel within. That is why we could never go into the future. No event has taken place in time; or so we were convinced to think."

"Yes, basic Time-Trust orientation," Jake scratched his head. "What are you thinking?"

"First, consider the recent discovery made at the particle accelerator within O.P.A.S.—Oregon Particle Acceleration Sciences. They discovered a new atomic sub-particle. It pulses differently than anything else ever detected. Test results showed that it is moving between one time and another with each pulse. They called it the bridge particle. I was supposed to have a meeting with our contact in Seattle about it, but, because of your Bering Straits conference and Mathew's ceremony, I postponed it. I want you to go there, and investigate the whole thing. Second, consider our immediate danger . . . Brock. If he has found a way to travel through time, then how exactly is he doing it?"

Jake thought and offered, "Perhaps he has found a way to use the discovery at O.P.A.S."

"Precisely, but how? I have always found the simple and obvious to be our best guide. Let us consider that Mr. Brock simply bought the technology, bought the findings."

"Sounds like him, that's for sure."

"Yes, but, they wouldn't sell that kind of thing. He must have done something else."

"I know; he bought the man. He paid off an employee."

"Christ, Jake, he hired one of the scientists from O.P.A.S. to run Time Travel, Inc., and then, when he was sure they discovered how to travel in time, he bought the company. By God, that is it!"

"But who?"

"Jake, contact our Post Station in Seattle. See if any records show anyone at Brock's new found treasure, who worked at O.P.A.S . . . now, man, do it now!"

Jake tapped his Knofer and got a security station manager, under Seattle. "Yes, this is Margret Carver; what can I do for you?"

"Carver, this is Jake Burns."

"Yes, sir?"

"Pull up employee records for Oregon Particle Acceleration Sciences, outside Seattle. Also, pull up anything we have on Time Travel, Inc's employee records. Are there any names that match?"

"Let me see, checking now; yes, just one..."

"Name, please?"

"Dr. Hamil G. Stevens . . . Oxford, M.I.T., Randhouse Physics, Group Leader at MicroCern before transferring to O.P.A.S. Last year he accepted the position of Chief Particle Physicist at Time Travel, Inc."

Burns and Swanson looked wide-eyed at each other.

"Thank you, Carver."

Jake cut the call. Swanson sat nodding. His mind was in overdrive. "You see, Jake; look for the simple. Look for the obvious. They stick out for a reason. How soon can we find this, Mr. Stevens?"

"Consider it done."

"Good. Now, next; let me think. Follow me on this one." Swanson triggered his Knofer, "Display fabric residue dated today, # 1035, and results labeled Morgue Cloth, # 909, last year."

"What are you doing?"

"After all these years, I hate to even think of it, but Mathew found a piece of something, a fabric at the Fargo bombings. It disintegrated."

The Knofer displayed two small piles of black soot.

"Look at these, Jake," the Knofer placed the holographic images next to one another above the desk.

"Run comparative analysis: search for carbon tetron.

"So what?"

"Carbon tetron is only found below 100 miles of the earth's surface. Look, they are almost identical readouts."

"So the fabric at Fargo was Carrier skin?"

"Yep, look at that." Swanson pointed to the display. "This is from the shootings at the morgue; and that is from the Fargo bombing." Swanson reached for the Carrier statue on his desk and shook it slightly. "What if there is a rogue Carrier? What if Brock has it? Even worse, what if that Carrier, voluntarily, went to Brock?"

"Why would a Carrier do that?" Jake thought in silence for a moment, and then he stood up, his face blushing. "Brock was in one, remember? I smell something more rotten than I care to believe, Mr. Secretary, and I don't like it."

Swanson looked puzzled. "Really, what?"

"The Carrier that took Brock away, those months ago, we all thought Mr. Brock was gone—dead. What if instead of the Carrier rehabilitating Brock, it had 'a compatibility' with him? Brock has been trying to figure out time travel and he found the vehicle to do it. What if he and the Carrier team up with O.P.A.S.?"

"Well, that would explain quite a bit, now wouldn't it?"

"Ah . . . I sound like a stupid old TV soap opera."

"Yes, you do. Is that what you don't like?"

Jake had a sick feeling in his stomach as he found his way back to the chair.

"What is it? Speak up?"

Jake looked around, rolling his eyes. "All right, I know you hired me because you knew I was a good detective; but, right now, I am not so sure I want to be."

"Tell me, damn it!"

"You said it has been over 200 years since the last compatibility."

"Yes, quite so . . . "

"The Carrier that talked to me this morning said the same thing."

"What are you getting at?"

"If that's true, what are the chances of two different people having a compatibility at the same time? There has to be a connection. It is the obvious simple answer."

"To what, Jake?"

"That your Mr. Brock and I are connected."

Swanson sighed, deflated somehow, and closed his eyes a second, as if he wasn't surprised. Jake saw it in his face and leapt to his feet. "You know! You knew! You have known all along!"

"Now, wait just a minute, Jake."

"No, it was right in front of me, all the time; and I couldn't, I wouldn't see it." Jakes face got beet red. He extended his arm and pointed his finger at Swanson. "What the hell is our connection, Mr.

Secretary? Why would Brock and I both be compatible with Carriers? Tell me, or, so help me, you will never make it to the C.P.T. make-over. You won't make it out of this room."

Swanson stood and raised his hands, trying to diffuse Jake's emotional outburst. "Jake, calm yourself. Everything is fine. Sit down, listen to me."

"I will calm down, if I like what you tell me."

"Well, you are a good detective. I don't know of anyone who has the powers of deduction like you do, except of course me, and our GGM."

"Spit it out, Gordon. The whole truth or I swear . . . "

"Jake, sit down; you look ridiculous. I have been following Brock for years. I traced his money and banking empire from country to country, continent to continent. I needed to keep an eye on every aspect of his empire, to assure his worldwide schemes did not interfere or invade our Ever-Life interests on the surface. Marion Brock comes from a very long lineage of Brocks. They have bought and sold firearms and ammunitions since the mid-1960s."

"So, what has that got to do with me and compatibilities?"

"Jake, you just did a search for an employee with your station security girl, Carver, and look what you came up with in just three lousy minutes. Can you imagine what I came up with, searching Brock's history?"

"What the hell are you talking about?"

Swanson hesitated and then took a deep breath. "Jake, you and Marion Brock are related . . . while it is a distant relation, you are related. You carry several identifiable genetic characteristics."

"Bullshit!"

"I am afraid it is true. There is no doubt."

Jake ran his hands through his hair. "So, did you know this when we met for the first time at the arms convention?"

"Yes."

"Christ! You played me. You have been playing me ever since. Why? For what? Did you think I was in cahoots with Brock? Do you think I am a link to his empire? Why, Gordon? Why?"

Swanson walked around his desk and stood in front of Jake eye to eye. "I don't assume, Jake, I deduce. I was GGM for God's sake. I knew you were a good man, but all of Ever-Life is based on genetics. Everyone here has a genetic record. We do not have records on everyone on the surface. The Carriers insisted that I check your history. They wouldn't say why. I never believed you were part of Brock. Now that the cap of GGM is passed to the next man, my thinking and deductive strengths are getting weaker. With you on the job, we are going to solve this. "

"Candy ass bullshit! That doesn't excuse or explain your deception."

"I have not deceived you, or anyone else. I did my job, and I am doing it now. Stop reacting with emotions. Stick to using your brain," Swanson squeezed Burns shoulders, and then he walked back around the desk, to his chair. "Now let's get back at it. There is something else regarding this that we must consider, and you may be the only one who can do something."

"Jesus, do what? What next?"

"What if during Brock's compatibility, what if it shared its thoughts with Brock?"

Jake blinked and cocked his head. "Is that even possible?"

"That's how we found out about many things down here in the first place, eons ago. In the beginning, compatibilities were two way. We humans are the ones who eventually insisted on one way transmissions. Many of us died from the intensity of the two-way exchanges. Eventually, treaties banned two-ways, and with good reason . . . "

"So, you think Brock and the Carrier are having mind melds."

"It would fit."

Andrew Sarkady

"What if Brock learned how the Carriers move through time, and he has shared enough information with Stevens to give Time Travel, Inc. the boost it needs to succeed?"

"If Brock has a Carrier, he has to keep it out of sunlight. Where would he keep it? Carriers can't be confined . . . plus, our Ever-Life surface contacts would have alerted us. The Carriers would have alerted the GGM, right? And if there is a rogue, wouldn't the hive mindset know and track it?"

"Fair points, unless Brock's compatibility sustenance feeds the Carrier enough to superpower it. If Brock is strong enough, then the question becomes could the Carrier convince others of its kind to rebel against the hive and follow him? Brock's control could spread throughout the Carriers' hive mind, and pervert it, turning them against the Ever-Life colonies. The combination of that, and Brock traveling in time, changing everything, would result in catastrophe. Any way you evaluate this, it's bad for us . . . you have to contact your Carrier 1111. You need to convince her to have a two-way exchange with you. You have to find out if anything we have speculated is fact. Your Carrier will know something."

"Agreed, but when this is over, you and I are going to hash our history out."

"And another thing, have her report on all the interruptions regarding your author's timeline. She took you before. She should have the best time travel recall, if you can get her to tell you. Tell her you want to go back to see him again. I don't care; be creative. Maybe she can sense Brock traveling; and don't forget Stevens, in Seattle."

"But, why don't we just ask the Carriers right now?"

"This treaty/agreement prohibiting two-ways has been in place for over 9000 years. I am not going to let one rogue Carrier with an overzealous sex drive bring Ever-Life to a halt. Let's fight fire with fire and get one on our side, eh? If you have the sustenance Brock has, it may give us an advantage. We have no idea how many other Carriers may have already gone rogue. Considering our situation, how do you know, when you meet her, if it's even her? Without a two-way communication, how do you know anything, Jake?"

"Yes, I never thought of that. I'll leave right away."

"Jake, wait." Swanson unlocked a desk drawer, reached inside and took out what looked like an old pocket watch.

"Here, put this in your pocket. Keep it with you at all times."

Jake studied the watch.

"Thank you, I think; but it's not working."

"That's because it's not a watch. I've had that for decades. I would have given it to Mathew, but he has other means at his disposal, now. Times have changed."

"So, what is it?"

"It'll disable a Carrier; and I never used it. You may have to. You'll know. A friend in the Carrier Council gave it to me, long ago. Keep it handy."

Jake slipped it in his side coat pocket.

"Jake, I know you've got a lot to think about. But hear me out. The center of Earth generates temperatures that rival our Sun. Obviously, we can't go there. Earth's core is the size of the Moon. We don't even know what it's made of. We think the Carriers do. The outer magma surrounding the core is 1500 miles thick and mostly liquid. The earth's rotation creates the movement of this liquid, and that movement generates the planet's magnetic field. That is where we believe the really big Carriers stay and derive most of their power. No one has been able to reach them, unless they invite us. If somehow Brock were to gain control of those Carriers by offering compatibilities through cloning himself, we'd be in a very bad position. He could rule more than the Carriers, or Ever-Life; he could rule time itself."

"Yes, I see, but couldn't we do the same?"

"We could, and it did cross our minds. But, for us, first, there are ethics and morals that humans cling to regarding cloning or duplicating. Second, we haven't had a compatibility like you describe for hundreds of years. Third, we stopped two-way exchanges, because we were dying from the experience."

Jake scratched his head.

"Now come around here. This will only take a minute. I am calling up genetic records."

The Knofer lit a display and created a thin vertical monitor in front of the two men.

"Look, here is your DNA and there is Brock's; now, we overlap them."

"All I see is everything is the same."

"Not quite . . . " Swanson spoke into the Knofer, "Cross check with historic records of last two compatibilities . . . you see, my friend, I never thought of compatibilities when I checked Mr. Brock or his family history. Until you brought it up, I am sure no one has. If you and he do have a gene match, we should see it here . . . overlap the red dashes, please . . . "

"What are the red dashes?"

"Compatibility indicators . . . look at that."

The Knofer compared and listed the characteristics for Brock, Jake and one other person.

"Fascinating."

"What?"

"Translate into numbers please . . . Christ. Brock's numbers are two to three times anyone's in Ever-Life, except . . . there is one here, who lived on the surface. Jake, I want you to get to O.P.A.S.; and stop whatever Mr. Stevens is doing. I suspect the combination of yours and Brock's genetics, coupled with what Stevens is working on, is what triggered the Sidron event. I am sure Brock has figured out how to go back in time with a Carrier; but he does not know about you. I'm afraid this is a time bomb. He has two out of three components to ruin Ever-Life. You have to get Stevens out of the picture. It may make the difference. Jake, you have always been my choice. Please believe that. I will brief GGM. Go now."

Jake turned to leave, but after a few steps, he stopped and turned around.

"Not to add another coal to the fire, but there is another very important component here we haven't discussed."

"What is it?"

"The Bering Straits tunnels."

"Ah, yes."

"There were two keynote speakers from the Brock Companies at the convention. I listened and I found their proposals extremely attractive. Of course, I never expected Brock might be behind the effort, himself."

"Well, he's not a billionaire for nothing. I will tell Mathew. I am sure he will want to get involved, personally." Swanson walked up to Burns and smiled. "I remember when Brock and I first met. I thought, my God, what a combination—brains, money, and charisma. He was the answer to what we needed to complete the campus in New Mexico. He was as brilliant as he was clever. Now, he is a narcissistic, obsessive control freak, without regard for humanity. Jake, remember, he is sick, and he knows it. It all makes sense. He wants to control time, to control Ever-Life. Be careful. He wants to control the planet."

"From what I saw, he's on his way to controlling the Cosmos"

"Let's start with O.P.A.S. Try and find out all you can. Report back to me when you know anything."

Swanson patted his shoulder, and Burns walked out.

CHAPTER 11
WHEELER'S C.P.T.

INSIDE EVER-LIFE LAB 202, below Arden City, a surgical light illuminated the center of the main room. A transparent Carrier bubble had expanded around a gurney to assist Dr. LuAnne and Nurse Angie Bellos, who stood within it, leaning over the body of Tom Wheeler.

Dr. Lu walked to the foot of the gurney and said, "Okay, Angie, help me slide him over on his side, into the body cavity there on the table."

Angie shoved his torso, while Dr. Lu guided his legs. The body flopped into the gel-like mold, and Angie wiped her forehead.

"Boy, things here change so fast. When Dr. Sheldon did this to his wife, he just stuck her in the back of the head and then in the side of her neck."

"That was a first timer, as I recall, and I'm going to say luck, or God, was involved."

"So, who is this guy, anyway?"

"He is Sir Thomas Wheeler, Professor of Particle Phenomenon, Ever-Life Time Trust Physics, Cavern 1017."

"What did he do to deserve C.P.T.?"

"He is an essential. Essentials are genetically capable of duplication and transtosis, repeatedly. Consequently, their DNA will tolerate C.P.T . . . Today, with him, we begin the new C.P.T.

procedure. Among other things, long ago, he helped identify one of what the surface called a God particle. We leaked it to the surface and we all made a lot of money . . . elementary fools . . . our Post 3 here alone got a 5 percent cut of the gross, if I remember correctly. Don't quote me, though. It is in the history headset files, if you want details."

"Is that legal?"

"Standard procedure, when we give knowledge to the surface. Anyway, Wheeler here is a primary controller of our Time Trust records, under Giza in Egypt. I don't know what happened, really, but the GGM put a priority-one security on getting him back."

"Really?"

"Yes, GGM wants to confirm the new C.P.T. for two reasons; first, because Secretary Swanson's health has worsened, and, second, he wants to begin replacing all holographic Post Controllers with C.P.T. duplicates."

"Oh . . . "

"Anyway, Sir Tom here was conducting research on interactive plasma components, which make up different forms of electricity, you know, torsunary anomalies."

"No, I don't have any idea what that is, way beyond my interest and pay grade."

Dr. Lu smiled. "It has to do with combining physics with medicine and genetics. Anyway, we do have his genetic history. The GGM had the body sent here himself."

"Something is up . . . "

"Yes, it has been quite a day, so far."

"Every day is quite a day here," Angie smirked.

"Look over there; hand me that wand; then read me the memory codes and telemetric pools on the monitor."

"I remember this wand."

"This one is a little different."

"Why did my dad want me to be here, anyway?"

Dr. LuAnne focused and placed the wand tip against the base of Dr. Wheeler's skull. Then, she let go. The 10-inch wizard wand stuck to his neck, wiggled, and then it morphed completely, shrinking to a tiny, half-inflated transparent balloon, two inches in length. It stayed in that fixed position, while Dr. Lu announced to the room, "Please initiate program. You see, my dear, the bubble around us is really a Carrier, and it will control the procedure now. We will monitor."

"Fascinating . . . "

The procedure took only minutes, but precise in every detail. The small wand-balloon sucked a small glob out of Wheeler's head and mixed it with the new synthetic catalyst, already inside. The two women watched, as the combined mixture burst into a blue carbonated liquid. After the balloon inflated, it disintegrated the needle. Then it rolled around his neck to the right side and injected a new needle into his carotid artery. It squeezed the sparkling liquid back into the patient, and then both the needle and deflated residue of the balloon disintegrated.

"Unbelievable!" said Angie.

"Yes, it really is. The wand is organic, controlled by the Carrier. Now we wait . . . "

"How long?"

"Look!"

Dr. Lu grabbed her Knofer, used it to scan Wheeler from head to toe, and then spoke into it, "Please note and record movement, normal brain liaison and body coordination observed at 7:17.5, Post 3, Ever-Life Lab 202, Universal Time Zone 7 . . . well, we are done here, Angie. Please take Dr. Wheeler to Module 10 down the hall and to the left for recovery. You can go after that. Thank you."

Dr. LuAnne walked through the bubble membrane, out of the lab. Angie covered her patient, tucked the sheet into the mattress, and felt a hand on her sleeve.

"Hello there. Thank you, for whatever you did."

Angie smiled, "I am your nurse, Mr. Wheeler. Welcome back. You are going to be fine."

Wheeler looked around the room. "Where am I?"

"Lab 202."

"How long?"

"The procedure took only a few minutes. I was told you were here almost 12 hours."

Wheeler instinctively studied everything he could see. "I love these floating beds. What is your name?"

"Angie, Angie Bellos."

"Oh, Bellos? You're his daughter; I must see your father, right away.

Angie cocked her head. "How do you know me?"

"Please, get me a pillow, will you? I need to sit up a little . . . I am Dr. Thomas Madeline Wheeler. Don't let the middle name fool you. It seems your dad has intuitive powers, regarding safety. You are here because it's the safest place to be right now. And I believe we should find your dad, right away."

"First, you recover, then you see Dad. Doctor's orders! Now this is just a little something to help. Drink it and rest."

"Angie, do you have any idea who I am?"

"No, not really."

"What is your schedule?"

"I am leaving for the surface, soon. I have an early appointment with a friend."

"Don't go. Stay here until your dad arrives. You are in danger."

Angie sat on the bed and took his hand. "Don't be so paranoid. It's probably side effects of the new procedure you just had. Go on, drink. It's good for you."

While he swallowed his cocktail, Angie tapped her Knofer, and within seconds, a lab nurse came through the door. She was a majestic woman, who you couldn't miss in a crowd.

"Hello, you two! How is our patient?"

"I am fine, Madam. I do not require your condescending tone. What I do require is the presence of our GGM."

Angie spoke quickly, as she moved to the door, "I have to leave. Can you take over?"

"Yes, miss, certainly. We will all be just fine."

Angie opened the door and turned to Wheeler. "I hope I'll see you soon."

Wheeler began to get out of bed. "Angie, you must not leave. Just believe me, please."

"Sir," the nurse snapped, "protocol is solitude and rest, to guarantee all functions."

"Poppycrap! And, you are not my mother."

"It looks like I'll have to be."

The nurse quickly injected Wheeler with a fast acting muscle relaxant and he fell back on the bed. He couldn't move, but he was fully awake and watched the nurse smiling, as she tucked him in and whispered, "Night-night . . . "

CHAPTER 12

THREE FATHERS

THERE WAS NO MOON that evening, and the campus lighting was strategic enough so no one looking out the Ever-Life limo saw any bomb wreckage. The car stopped at the hospital's main entrance, and driver Mr. Mike Warren told the three passengers to take off their blindfolds. Then, he escorted Pappas Kristos Alieri, representing the Christian faith; Rabbi James Yeshua the Jewish and Imam Ahmir Udera the Islamic, up to the Bellos office suite. The three fathers had just spent the last two hours riding in a Carrier from Jerusalem to Andrews, without saying a word to each other. They agreed to blindfolds only because it gave them all an excuse not to talk to each other. Once inside the suite's foyer, Mike said, "Thank you for your patience, gentlemen. I must leave you now. I trust youwill play nicely until Dr. Bellos arrives. Please look around and make yourselves at home. There are pastries on that table, if you like. The doctor should be here soon. Good day . . . "

He tipped his hat, turned and walked out the door. The three fathers looked at each other and shrugged.

Kristos finally broke the silence, "My brothers, this is ridiculous. Please consider our history together. We are not enemies."

Ahmir scowled, "I was reprimanded, indignantly, repeatedly. If only you had just given me the book those months ago. You knew this would happen. Why have you done this, even now?"

"You two must stop bickering," James interrupted. "What did it say, Kristos? We know you read it."

Kristos moved down the stairs into the oval room, ignoring their baited words, and looked at the books and artwork. He noticed an entire row of what looked like the same book he was holding; except each of those had different initials inlaid on the back of its binding. He turned to address James, when he heard footsteps in the back hallway on the other side of the room, and in walked Mathew Bellos.

"Hello, gentlemen. Just for the record, all those books say pretty much the same thing. It is the people that change."

Kristos looked at Bellos with a questioning expression and extended his hand, "How do you do, again? I believe we met on the villa steps."

"Yes, quite a while ago . . . it is my honor to receive you all. How was the ride?"

"As for me," James said, "I'm still in shock at how fast we made it, quite comfortable, actually."

The fathers nodded in agreement.

"Please sit down, my friends. Make yourselves at home. I have a little story to tell you. First, would you like anything, perhaps light refreshment, pastries?"

All three nodded yes, so Bellos went to the far corner of the oval room, while his guests picked up cakes from the coffee table tray. He opened a small compartment door and took out four wine glasses, filled with a sparkling white liquid. As he withdrew the tray, Ahmir saw it and remembered, "Is that what I think?"

"It is an old traditional drink." Bellos handed out the goblets. We should toast this auspicious occasion. I welcome you to my home and to your friend, S's gift."

With an apprehensive look, Kristos said, "To the gift of truth?"

The four men sipped.

"This is it, isn't it?" Ahmir giggled and looked at the other three.

"He's right," James said.

"My goodness . . . " Kristos studied the glass.

"Yes, he is right," Bellos said. "Perhaps you three can remember this moment of agreement and sustain that thought, throughout our meeting."

"Please, Dr. Bellos, will you explain. Tell us what we are doing here. I was contacted by the guard, whom we all met at the villa when S passed away. He invited me to witness S's heritage presentation. It's been a long time, but, of course, I would not refuse his dying wish. But, it's time we all know why we are here."

"Sit down, gentlemen, please. Yes, that is correct, and I have the honor of presenting it.

"Whatever does that mean?" Kristos asked.

"It means S charged me with explaining that book you hold. Hopefully, you will stop bickering about the silliest of trivia, and understand the cooperative effort that you plotted in the first place. Don't you remember his last request to you? He looked at you three and softly but resolutely said, 'My friends, you can be at peace and do not let what appears to be my pain or anyone else's euphoric promises cloud your thinking or deaden your ears and minds to what you must understand'."

The three clergy looked bewildered at each other. They sat up ridged in shock at what Bellos quoted.

"But how could you know those words?" James said. "He spoke to us alone."

The other two nodded, agreeing. Bellos walked to the chair next to their couch, sat down and looked at all three. "The truth is that this is somewhat of a challenge for me . . . my first time. The important thing is that you three realize you are in this together. You committed, not only to uniting your faiths, but also to the patience it will take to do such a thing. S had faith enough in you three to give you that book, and he charged me with taking you to where you can find the answers you seek."

The fathers looked a bit puzzled, sat back on the couch, again, and Kristos gestured to Bellos, "We are all ears, Doctor."

"Well, thank you," Bellos walked to the bay window facing the Atrium.

"What is this brew, Doctor? Do you know?" James asked.

"It is an old healing elixir. Some said, eons ago, that it was a magic recipe. Huh, maybe it is."

"I'm afraid I'm at a loss, Dr. Bellos. We have many questions," Ahmir said.

"I recall, you three had been preoccupied, even obsessed, with the concept that your diversified faiths have brought confusion, hypocrisy, even heresy and terrorism to worship. We are aware of your effort with Mr. Marion Brock."

Kristos was the first to react, "It is just fact. Our three religions have been at odds, even warring off and on, for thousands of years. S was more than a friend; he was a peacemaker and confidant to each of us. But, who are you, Doctor? You have no right or authority over us."

Bellos put his glass on the coffee table. "I am Chief of Hospital here; that is true. But also, I represent a culture, just like each of you three do. Unlike yours, however, our culture does not live on the surface of planet Earth. We have evolved and prospered within the planet, miles below the surface.

"I realize how that may sound . . . I represent your friend, Master S, too, who asked us—in particular me—to contact you and brief you regarding your effort to unite the faiths. That is why he gave you that book, so that you would gain a better understanding of all faiths, to help humanity love one another and live in peace and cooperation; ever better ourselves. We discovered long ago that no individual or group could do that if anyone is unhealthy. Whether it is physical, mental, emotional or spiritual, one has to be healthy before one can think and choose correctly. So, our culture is based on healthcare, and every other aspect of life stems from that. S charged me with offering you the care you need to bridge your unhealthy bickering behavior."

The three clergy sat stiff, appearing not to react disrespectfully. After a moment, Kristos spoke, "You judge us, Doctor? While I feel a bit foolish in some respects listening to your speech, and we do appreciate your concern, the fact is that we each live in a free society, in which, whether we agree or not, we respect each other's right to disagree."

"My society respects and supports that concept, too; so, why do you bicker? Why are you not happy and healthy with your disagreements, your diversity? Is it not because one of you has something the other two insist on having, as well? Hasn't that been the problem between your faiths all along? Look at you, in particular, Father. You refuse to share that book. You just said you live in a free society, yet you deny these others, what your beloved S said was theirs too."

"It's our nature as humans," Kristos interrupted. "Our job includes helping and guiding humanity back to God, and, yes, to be better people, to live in harmony, according to the teachings of our Lord and Savior. Each of us has different components to our faith . . . we guide our flocks."

"Wait, my brother," Rabbi James said. "Excuse me. My faith is strong and unyielding, but we do believe our God wants us to live the best life we can, and obey his commands, while your path simply requires a belief that God's grace will save man's iniquities. There is a difference. And we should remember our Brothers in Islam . . . "

Ahmir stood and lifted his arms, "We already believe there is only one God, and Mohammed is his messenger. We agree with the unity you seek."

Kristos rattled a quick reply, "Please, need I quote our effort was to address and bring a common good to as many as we could, and to stop the spread of modern terrorism, which plagued us all for decades? It would bring solace to every Catholic, Jew and Muslim, solace to all religious flavors, even to the agnostic and atheist. Uniting so many will fill us with the peace of the Holy Spirit."

Bellos interrupted, "You quote the words, my friend, but when was the last time you and the Dalai Lama worshipped together, or you, James, with a Pagan priest? Where is the unity you seek in the bickering you do and the deception you pose with that book? What about your brothers right here, Kristos? They have been waiting for some word from you, and you sent nothing. Your debate rages on in your own mind, Father. Eventually, it oversteps boundaries, which must be maintained for the health of all life. Marion Brock had no answers . . . you three are very privileged this day. I am going to take you on the trip you could only dream of."

"And where would that be, my friend?" Ahmir asked.

"Gentlemen, we leave for Jerusalem to meet the man who will reconcile your quest."

"But, Doctor," James said. "We just came from there. What purpose could it serve to return tonight?"

"We are not going there tonight. S's heritage presentation is a trip for you three to bridge over 6000 years of confusion and misinformation. It will enable you to understand the true meaning of unifying the faiths."

"I don't see your point, Doctor." Kristos was noticeably annoyed. "We all have churches throughout Jerusalem."

"It has always been our holy city," James said.

"Your home is the foundation of your confusion, and the beginning of your bickering" said Bellos. "It is not a distance we travel; rather, we will pass through time, my friends, to meet your master."

The three looked in disbelief. Kristos chuckled and gestured for Bellos to sit down. "I am not proud to say that I have read this book I hold. I have withheld its contents from the others for a reason. You do speak a truth. I have been afraid that what it describes would be misinterpreted. My heart says to share it with the world, but my mind says I should bury it, and never reveal the contents." Kristos looked at his brothers. "I am sorry, my friends, that is my truth. I see other books like this right up there. This book gives no answers we seek. I should give it back to you now, Doctor, and be done with it. It will promote discord."

Bellos stood and placed his hand on Kristos' shoulder. "Father, you promote the conflict you seek to unify. You must each choose freely, but you must all decide what it is you want, the truth, or what you have now, the ongoing debate of your ancestors. After all, you have had millennia to try to reconcile your differences. I will leave you to decide. If you cannot, we will part, and you may go back to your lives, knowing your beloved S thought enough of you to trust you this much. You may leave the book on the table."

Bellos turned to go to the foyer and the elevator, when Ahmir stood up. "Wait, Doctor, I for one will not argue, and I believe we should see what S wanted us to see." Ahmir looked at Kristos, begging.

"I agree," said James.

"My brothers," Kristos pleaded, "you do not understand. Perhaps we are to unite in faith, not in proof. I believe, and therefore I am with him. Blessed be those who do not see and yet believe. Please, think my brothers!"

Ahmir turned to Kristos with love in his tone, "My friend, let us unite here. We all committed to this, under your leadership. Let us finish it. We do this for God and him, who we loved. The doctor is right. S loved us enough to give us that book and charge us, all of us, to decide if it should be made public. It's not just your decision. Our faith is not in question here. We must find a way to give the people the understanding and peace they deserve."

Ahmir and James looked at Bellos, nodding, and James said, "Yes, Doctor, we two will go with you."

Bellos looked at Kristos. "And you, Father?"

Kristos sighed, closed his eyes and then, looking up to heaven, he said, "God be with us all, Doctor. We go."

"Then come, follow me. Leave the book on the table. You won't need it. You can have it or read it after the journey."

Bellos led the men through the hallway to his office's computer room. Kristos gestured nervously. "Doctor, we understood we would complete our stay here tonight and then return to Jerusalem. We all have matters to attend to at home."

"I have had to make some changes, due to events here at the hospital. Lives are at stake, and after all, life before trips. But, do not fret, my friends, you will have plenty of time, and you will each be on time for your separate schedules. Now, there, further down the hall, you will find three suites. Pick a room, make yourselves comfortable and meet me here at 8 a.m. sharp, tomorrow morning. We leave promptly, so no stragglers."

Bellos turned and walked slowly back to the oval room. "If you need anything, just push the red buzzer on the night table in your rooms. See you in the morning."

CHAPTER 13

BELLOS AND WHEELER

WHILE THE THREE FATHERS FOUND their sleeping quarters, the GGM stood in the front oval room talking to Jacque at Wheeler's lab in Giza.

"Sir, the new C.P.T. went well. Mr. Wheeler is in recovery, in Arden. He is in Module 10."

"I am going to see him now." Bellos stepped into his private elevator and rode it down, below Andrews, while listening.

"Sir, I also have details on the time event itself . . . as you know, three guests from the past have appeared. They are all the same person, three different ages. They trace back to 1965, 1983 and 2010."

"Do we know the source of the event?"

"Well, that is the odd part. Our readings indicate one of two familiar imprints. One is Jake Burns."

"What?"

"Yes, sir, no doubt, the other is an imprint not part of Ever-Life, also from the surface.

"Are you sure?"

"Yes, the Sidron transported our three visitors here and that triggered a delayed explosion in the lab. We do not know how Mr. Burns and the other person are involved; but their imprints are unmistakable, along with something else."

"What?"

"The Sidron moves everything in a balance. We only have three visitors; there were four events."

"You are saying four causes; therefore, we can expect another effect?"

"Yes, sir, there should be another person involved, another transport, perhaps not to here. We need more information. Nevertheless, the combination of all individuals, together with something at Giza, triggered the transport and the explosion."

"Something at Giza?"

"We speculate, whatever it is, it's on the surface."

"Thank you, Jacque. Keep on it; keep me and Mr. Burns, only, updated, understand?"

"Yes, sir."

"And do me a favor; contact and set up Controller Three for the fathers' trip tomorrow."

"Right away."

Bellos cut the call, closed his eyes in a moment of quiet and then, he looked up with an expression of clarity. "A *compatibility*. Christ, it is the Carriers!"

He walked out of the sixth floor elevator below Andrews and down the hallway into Module 10. "Tom, how are you feeling?"

"Hello, Matt, quite good actually; it's good to see you . . . I could not keep your daughter here."

"She is quite the charmer, my friend. It's all right; just relax. Think, can you tell me what happened?"

"It was unprecedented really; regardless of the magnetic alignments within the region, I have no explanation for any of it yet."

"I talked to Jacque. I want your details, Tom." "Yes, of course, I was alone in a cell, preparing inputs for vault storage. Monitors registered frequency vibrations I have never seen, completely alien. While I was tracking them, a force yet unknown to me hit directly above us at Giza. Wave frequencies registered off the charts. God only knows what the wave echoes did."

"Go on."

"After the initial tremor, I got a call from Module Control. 'It appears we have three new guests,' they said.

"Each person appeared in one of our separate sealed cells. While I was questioning one, a guard called me out. The orderly and I ran into the Frequency Lab, and *boom*! How are the others who were in the lab?"

"Gone."

Bellos turned his back to Wheeler and paced. "Matt, one other important thing . . ."

"Yes?"

"Our visitors, they are the same person from three different ages in his life."

"Jacque said the same thing . . . " Bellos crossed his hands behind him and whispered to himself, " . . . the Carriers."

"May I go back to work, sir?"

"Yes, Tom, we are both going back, together. I need to meet our visitor."

Bellos' Knofer ticked on, registering an upgrade in his defense protocol, and he spoke into it, "Play video of Time Trust Giza visitor on Module 10 wall."

His Knofer projected video of a young man sitting in a lounge chair watching wall monitors. After a brief moment, everything Bellos looked at began to blink, distort and blur dramatically. The GGM spoke sternly into his Knofer, "What is happening? Reply, reply!"

"Sir," Wheeler said, "he is one, the young one. I believe you are witnessing another Sidron event, right now. Look at him!"

"My God, all the rooms are secure, right?"

"Yes, completely."

"Tom, get dressed . . . repeat the video . . . "

"Look at him . . ."

The man began to blur again. "He is dissolving, disintegrating."

"He is gone."

"We need to go there now, Tom. No telling what will come next. I need to talk to the other two, before something else happens.

Whatever these events are, we have to stop them. I need you on this, Tom, right now. The Sidron has been breached. It's being used, stimulated and even controlled. We need to find the cause and stop it, correct it."

"Then, you do believe it to be a time displacement?"

"More than one. They are a direct result of multiple particle displacements. This is a violation of nature. I need to talk to this man and the Carrier Council."

"What are we going to do with him—them?"

"I just hope we get to them before another frequency wave hits."

Bellos stared at Wheeler and then the monitor with a very worried look. He tapped his Knofer and briefed the colonies' controllers. Then both men walked out of the Lab Module to the station's boarding platform. A Carrier awaited, and they walked into its standard travel room. After getting situated, the GGM began interacting with Post Controllers via Knofer regarding a multitude of colony issues.

Suddenly, he alone heard the voice of the Carrier in his mind, *"Good day, my GGM; I am Allenfar."*

"Hello," Bellos replied through thought exchange. "Your species has been full of surprises today. Report, please."

"I have been assigned to you, strictly speaking, sir, until we sort out the Sidron situation."

"What can you tell me?"

"The Carrier high council has instructed me to replace your Carrier 62712, and to directly interface with you and Mr. Burns as you instruct."

"Take us to Post 2, Giza Station 1, as fast as you can."

The Carrier went silent and Bellos went back to meetings with various commanders. After a time, he heard a voice behind him, which sounded like a man but it spoke in the language of the Carriers. He turned around and saw a humanoid figure like the one at his ceremony. But, this one did not have his arms out in friendship.

"GGM, we must talk, in private." The stranger gestured to a door, which appeared instantly. They both walked into a different room. Once inside, he began, *"I have come to help resolve the threat."*

Bellos replied, "Our situation is the result of a combination of variables."

"We agree. I have, within me, all information from the council ready and available to you. We confirmed that one of our Carriers is, in fact, involved . . . you rode within him months ago, during the C.P.T. incident. We instructed him to rehabilitate Marion Brock. However, we have been unable to communicate with him. He has acquired much sustenance from Brock. He has enough power to block sharing with the hive."

"Why would your Carrier do such a thing?"

"We know he had a friend; you would say she was family for him. She was the Carrier killed in your hospital morgue."

"Why would he wage a battle against his own kind or mine?"

"We are not sure what he is doing. We have traced the events to 1965. Carriers are the only species who can travel through time. Now, we believe he has breached the Sidron, without authorization. That is a crime.

"We also believe there is something within Dr. Sheldon's treatise, which will prove most valuable and give us answers."

"Well, Jack is a treasure of ideas, that is for sure." Bellos thought a moment. "Interesting . . .now, I need to know any history you have, very quickly. Tell me about the lineage of Marion Brock."

"We will transfer what we have, but we doubt it is more detailed than that which is available to you already."

The Tyree Master began inputting facts into the mind of Bellos.

"Marion Brock, IV inherited his money . . . centuries ago, in 1965, Nicolas Edward Brock negotiated the largest ammunition trade in United States history during the Vietnam conflict. He played both sides of the war, selling to the Chinese and Western powers. Both sides killed each other using ammunition from the same source. Over the next 175 years, Brock Finance grew

overwhelmingly, evolving and profiting again by supporting the first drone warfare during the surface worldwide terrorist engagements. Then, something unforeseen happened within the family. Power and leadership shifted from male to female, as global politics changed. In 2160, Marisa Brock invested the family fortune to support the new Nazi movement, which overthrew the genocide of extremist Muslims in Pakistan. She had a son, Marion Brock, I, who eventually arranged for her assassination. He stopped selling arms to Pakistan and backed the world movement to wipe out the Nazis. It was a global bloodbath, but the Brocks' gained political and financial power in almost every country."

"Some things never change."

"That success gave the Brocks the power and monetary support they needed to become the global leader in high tech arms and ammunition sales.

Today, we believe your Marion Brock, IV has decided to invest substantial financial support in an effort to control events in time, by purchasing Time Travel Research, Inc."

"How does Jake Burns relate to Brock?"

"After the power shift in 2160, the matriarch's sister, Ellen Brock, moved from North America to England. She married Zachery Burns, the direct descendant to your Jake Burns."

"That's why Jake and Marion have more than similar genetic make-ups."

"We believe GGM Gordon Swanson found out, quite by chance, some time ago, after he met Burns at a weapons convention."

"So, Swanson hired Burns knowing he was related to Brock?"

"Some have said, keeping your enemy close is a wise choice."

"But Burns is not our enemy. He is an Ever-Life citizen, not to mention our colonies' Security Chief."

"Correct, and as it turns out, he, like Brock, is compatible with us. Ages ago, before our treaties, our kind rebelled, because of the power compatibilities brought."

"We don't have those records; and I wasn't made aware of that. If true, all of Ever-Life is in danger from your rogue Carrier. We could have a war for the first time in our history, and a timeline shift."

"Correct. That is why I am here."

"I need to get to the Great Pyramid in Giza before we go to the Post 2 station drop. You need to get me inside. Is that a problem?"

"The entire pyramid is still quite insulated. We should have no problem."

"You know as well as I that the entire pyramid was a battery, eons ago. I am counting on it to have preserved certain magnetic frequency echoes. That may give us some clues. Tell me why have you allowed yourself to be seen like this? My friend in the other room will not forget you."

"It is time; and, he is witness to our sincerity. We could not prevent this. Our Grand Council acknowledges the surface wherewithal has evolved. We must postpone our meeting with you until this matter is resolved. I will interface with you and the surface as is appropriate. Trust remains a great issue. We recognize the need to approach the surface; and, regardless of their constant warlike behavior, they are progressing to the point of space-time and interplanetary travel. We need to educate and establish boundaries. We have much to investigate. The Sidron events are very disturbing, especially if one of us has used surface men in a compatibility. It generates many questions."

The Tyree Master then turned and absorbed into the Carrier's wall. Allenfar swam, faster than a missile, across inner earth's ocean of heat, to the great pyramids of Egypt.

CHAPTER 14

THE MARSHALL DECISION

EARLY THE NEXT MORNING, at the Arden City courthouse, Brian Sheldon sat with Angie Bellos in the right side back row of courtroom 210. The jury began seating to read the verdict for David Marshall, who was arrested regarding the murder in the Andrews' morgue months ago. The charges against him included one count of conspiracy to commit murder, another count of conspiracy to commit a terrorist attack against the Brock/Swanson Complex and five counts of aggravated battery during his stay in the Arden City jail.

"I thought your dad didn't want you here, Angie," said Brian.

"I had to come. You know I hate this guy. Besides, I wanted to be with you. I only wish your mom could be here."

"Yeah, me, too. I got a message from her that she went to Washington, D.C. on some last minute jaunt—a convention or something. I guess my dad couldn't go . . . "

"Shhh, it's the bailiff.

"Hear ye, hear ye; all rise . . . "

"Okay, Brian, here we go."

"This 3rd District Court of Arden Township is now in session . . . the Honorable Pamela Wills, presiding."

The judge walked into the courtroom from her chambers behind her elevated mahogany bench. She stepped up, sat down and looked out over the courtroom. "You may all be seated. Today, after much time and effort, I would like to thank both the prosecution and the defense for their exhaustive and thorough handling of this case. Madame Forewoman, has the jury reached its verdict?"

A woman in her mid-50s stood up from the jury box and replied, "Yes, we have, your honor."

She handed an envelope to the bailiff, who gave it to the judge. Judge Wills read it, and then handed it back to the bailiff.

"I never understood this part," Brian whispered to Angie. "Why doesn't she just read the damn thing out loud?"

Angie placed her hand on his. "Protocol, Brian, you know about that. Be patient."

"Madame Forewoman," said Wills, "you may read the verdict."

"We, the jury, in the matter of case 51269, The State of New Mexico vs. David J. Marshall, on this fourth day of June, do hereby unanimously declare: regarding count one of conspiracy to commit the murder of Dr. Jack Avuar Sheldon, we find in favor of the State and we do judge Mr. David J. Marshall guilty, as charged. Regarding count two . . . "

At that instant, Brian Sheldon leapt to his feet and screamed, "Yes! You son-of-a-bitch! . . . Yes! Woohoo!"

Brian's outburst stopped the reading. All eyes focused on his rant. Angie pulled at him, trying to get him to sit down.

"Order in the court! Order in the court!" the judge yelled. "Bailiff, remove that man!"

"Wait! No!" Brian suddenly realized his wrongful behavior. "I have to hear the rest. Angie, no!"

Two police guards grabbed and forcibly escorted Brian out through the courtroom's double doors. Angie followed behind them, watching the guards push and prod him out the building and down onto the concrete steps. She ran to Brian and grabbed his arm, helpfully. "What did you think you were doing, for heaven's sake?"

He got up, brushing himself off. "Releasing months of cooped-up anger and satisfying my need to kill that bastard."

"Well, that worked, didn't it? Now what?"

"Now we celebrate, if you're up to it. What do you say?"

"It is 10 o'clock in the morning. How do you plan on celebrating?"

"Hmm, right, I guess. But, that felt so great."

Brian rolled his eyes and sat back down on the steps. Angie started to sit down next to him, when it happened. Brian stared wide-eyed at her and blinked in disbelief. He shook his head, trying to focus. He grabbed at her but, just as they made eye contact, Angie cried out, "Brian, my God, what is happening?"

Her whole body appeared to flicker, her image blurred, and then, she was gone, just vanished. Brian jumped up, twisting and turning, reaching for her. "What the f . . . ?"

As he looked around, he saw someone running out of the courthouse and yelled to him, "Hey, you! Help me here! It's an emergency!"

The man stopped and yelled back, "I can't! Something just happened in the courtroom . . . wait a minute, I remember you. You are the ranting idiot they kicked out."

They both started walking toward each other, talking at the same time.

"I'm Randy Farrell, reporter for the Daily Gazette. I know you. Your friend the convict, he just vanished in the courtroom, not two minutes ago, gone; just like that. I have never seen anything like it! It was unbelievable. They are all in a panic in there, everyone, including the judge. And she's holding everybody until it's sorted out. I was in the back and slipped out before they noticed. You were lucky."

Farrell turned to go, but Brian grabbed his shoulders. "My girlfriend just vanished out here, right before my eyes on these steps, right there . . ."

"Holy shit! Both of them at the same time . . ." Farrell collected his thoughts. "I videoed the whole scene in there. I've got to get back to the office to study it."

"We should take it to the police."

"Bullshit! They have cameras all over the courthouse . . . good luck!" Farrell turned and ran across the street. Brian tried to call his father, but the phone displayed, *no signal*; so, he ran to the parking garage and his car.

༄༅༅ఠఙ❦

And where was Angie? In a blink, it was hours earlier . . . the rising sun was beginning to burn the haze away from the Arden morning sky. Angie Bellos rustled in her bed, fighting off the covers. She popped up, throwing the covers back onto Brian, who was naked next to her, snoring. She was drenched in sweaty wet clothes that clung to her body.

"Oh, my God!" she yelled in a whisper, feeling and pulling at her clothing. "What the hell just happened?

She ran to the bathroom, threw cold water on her face and looked in the mirror. "Yes, it's me . . . these are the clothes I wore to the courthouse."

She turned around and looked at her bed. "Brian? Why are you here? Christ, how did I get here? This is insane!"

She tiptoed to the window, drew back the curtains and looked out at the rising sun. Then, she looked at the clock on the nightstand. At the same time, she pulled a Knofer out of her pant pocket. "Shit, that can't be right. The clock says 4 a.m."

She brought the Knofer close to her lips and whispered, "Confirm time and day."

The Knofer immediately displayed a 3-D model, which read 9 a.m., U.S.A. Mountain Time, Ever-Life record, Tuesday, November 12, Arden, New Mexico. She also noticed something else. At the bottom of the Knofer display, red letters blinked the words, *Defensive Mode.*

"That can't be good." Then, Angie began to shake involuntarily. She sat down in the chair next to the window and placed her hands over her face, sobbing, disoriented and trying to gather herself, when she felt two hands on her shoulders lifting her.

"Hey, you, what's wrong? Are you okay?"

She looked up to see a naked Brian Sheldon standing before her. He took her in his arms and hugged her. "Come on, babe, don't cry. You're so cold, and why are you shaking?" Brian rubbed her back. "Why are you dressed in these wet clothes?"

Then, he released her enough that they could see each other face to face. Angie looked deeply into his eyes and felt paralyzed in the moment. Brian caressed her cheek, and as they fixed on each other, he kissed her tenderly. They both felt the warmth of the moment and each held on to the other. Angie felt the shaking stop, replaced by her heart rate pounding. Brian pulled her into him. He opened his eyes and held her chin as they separated. Then, he took her hand and led her over to the bed. She was shocked to him naked, but she followed him and sat beside him.

"Brian, I . . . "

"No," he said. "Not a word this time. Let's get you out of these wet things."

Angie was numb and limp. She didn't speak, as Brian peeled off her top, then her skirt and shoes. "There, that's better. You're not shaking anymore."

"Brian, is it really you?"

He giggled and kissed her, again, passionately pulling her back down on the bed. "Yes, darlin', I'm the same guy you made love with last night."

"What? Wait a minute . . . " Angie pushed back and stood up.

"You know, babe, naked and serious somehow don't quite go together. Look at me," he gestured with a smile.

Angie stared and shook her head. She felt the shaking start again and turned her back to him. "Brian, something is wrong—dead wrong! Something has happened. We have to talk."

She went to the closet and opened the door. There were two white bathrobes, so she threw one at Brian and put on the other.

"Turn on the TV, will you? Put on the news."

"Okay . . . "

They both watched the monitor as local newscaster Parker Phillips announced, "Good morning, Arden, its 4:16 a.m. and our skies look like they are going to clear nicely for the Marshall verdict today."

"Brian, do you have a Knofer?"

"What, my phone is on the table?"

"Oh, my God, look at the time on the screen." Angie grabbed Brian's phone on the nightstand and studied it. Shit, it says 4:18 a.m., too, same time . . . Brian, we have to get to the courthouse!"

"Why? What are you talking about? Ah, we should be asleep. The verdict is hours from now."

Angie stood fixed. "Brian, it's really after 9 a.m.; and we already saw and heard the verdict . . . oh, my God!"

She pushed Brian on the bed again. "Listen, something is not right—all this. Here, look at my Knofer."

"This thing says 9:08 a.m. How could that be? It must be on Ever-Life time. Who cares?"

Angie stood and paced. "Tell me, what is our relationship?"

Brian chuckled, "Come on, babe. We love each other. We've been living together for four months."

"Brian, I hate to tell you this, don't freak out . . . I don't think I am your Angie."

❧❦☙❧

At precisely the same time, across town in the Arden City jail, prisoner Dave Marshall awoke on his cot in a 6- x 9-foot jail cell. He was soaked in sweat and shaking in his green prison night garb.

"My God, my God," he cried. Rushing to the small mirror hanging on the concrete wall, he studied his reflection for a moment. "It works! Shit, it really works . . . son-of-a-bitch!"

He gathered his senses and turned, examining the room. "This isn't right. It's my jail cell . . . I'm supposed to be out, not in here."

He stumbled to the jail bars and grabbed on tight, screaming, " . . . *Brock!*"

☙❧❦☙❧

Back in Angie's apartment, Brian showered and Angie recounted her morning to him as she sat in her bathrobe on the toilet. When he shut the water off, she reached inside, handed him his robe and he stepped out.

"Your turn, girl, go on. You need it more than I do."

The shower's warmth calmed and soothed her. While Brian dried, he talked, "So, what do you suggest, my sweet?"

"At a time like this, I wish I had more headset sessions. Ever-Life taught me that the more I have, the more memories lock. There has got to be something explaining a situation like this."

"What are you talking about? I was never an Ever-Life candidate. You know that. It was the C.P.T. and our dads' friendship that brought us together. So, I don't understand headset this, headset that . . ."

Angie turned the off the shower, put her robe on again and stepped out. She plopped on the edge of the bed. "Shit, shit, shit!"

"That sounds very productive. I know this might sound silly, but you say that Knofer is in *defensive mode*, do you remember any of the protocols?"

She rolled her eyes and shook her head, "I think we have to get back to the courthouse."

"Why?"

"I'm not sure. I had a conversation with a man, in a hospital bed last night, or whenever. He said things that seemed ridiculous to me then, that I was in danger. They didn't really register . . . then this?"

"Who? You're very confusing. You are not in Oz. What you need is an attitude adjustment."

"I need to talk to Mr. Wheeler."

"And if anything you say is true, where is my Angie? God, as if we haven't been through enough. Anyone else would say you are a raving lunatic."

"No! Brian, listen. Something or someone has done this. I don't know why or how. "

Brian saw the determination in her eyes. He cupped her face and kissed her on the cheek. "You are not even dressed . . . .fine. I'll do anything you say, just calm down. You're going to have a heart attack."

They hugged, and after a few seconds, Brian spoke softly, "Angie, do you think I'm a ghost, or maybe a figment of your imagination?"

"No . . . I don't know." She talked as she quickly dressed. "What I've told you is the truth. You know I am the daughter of a GGM. I am not crazy. You know what both of us went through before for God's sake."

"Yes, I remember. You don't think anything like that is happening again, do you?"

They fixed on each other's gaze.

"I don't know . . . what if? Brian, I think the sooner we get the Knofer to trigger, the better off we are all going to be."

Just then, Angie startled from hearing a squeaky beep.

"Speak of the Devil, it's coming from your Knofer over there."

Angie picked it up, only to feel intense heat; instinctively, she threw it on the bed. "Jesus, that hurt; maybe it's over-charged or something. It shouldn't be that hot."

Then, the Knofer bellowed a very low-pitched noise and the couple watched, as the shiny silver unit began projecting a blue triangular light up to the ceiling. Within seconds, it sculpted a life-sized hologram of Sir Thomas Wheeler.

"That's the guy . . . that's the man I talked to last night!"

When the Knofer finished, Wheeler's image stood by the bed. He was wearing an Ever-Life doctor's coat, glasses, pants and shoes. But the Knofer wasn't done. It began to fill in the 3-D image, and Wheeler became a solid model. After several minutes, it released the model, enabling him to move and speak as any normal person.

"Hello, child."

"Oh, my God," Brian said. "What are you? How did you get here?"

Angie grabbed his arm. "No, Brian, wait! He is a friend . . . I remember my mom was like you. Hi, hello, Mr. Wheeler, I just saw you last night, remember?"

"Yes, Angie, hi, except he was flesh and bone. I am here, as your defense guide. At present, your protocol only requires me to advise, and see if we can't remedy your situation."

"Yes, well, thank you. Can you tell us, exactly, what is my situation? What did happen?"

Wheeler turned, examining the room closely. "You two better sit down for this."

Angie leaned onto the bed and picked up her Knofer. "Do I have to leave this out?" she asked.

Wheeler looked out the window at the sunrise. "There is no more beautiful sight . . . no, that's all right, no need . . . "

He turned around and began to describe the event.

"I remind you that your Knofer has a record of all knowledge, Angie. Your father has authorized these defense protocols. I am your link to those protocols." He smiled kindly. "There is no reason to fear anything yet. So, relax, we will fix this."

Angie and Brian looked at one another.

"But," Brian said, "if this isn't my Angie, where is she? Who is this? And, where am I?"

"Brian, you are you and she is she—Angie is Angie. We are all who we seem to be but split. Consider her a sort of mirror image, if that helps, but not a reverse image."

"You mean I'm a reflection?"

Brian stood up and walked several steps. "Or, are you both reflections, or am I?"

Angie sat up disturbed and uncomfortable. "What? I know I am real . . . "

She and Brian locked eyes as Wheeler spoke, "Listen carefully, you two. Reflection is just a word to help you. You are both very real. The laws of physics regarding space-time and matter can be easily understood, or very complicated. Let's just say, Angie, you ran into something that bumped you into a different room."

"So, where's my Angie. She has got to be freaking out?" said Brian.

Wheeler didn't skip a beat with his reply, "She is in the other room."

"Whoa!" Brian said. "So, we are in an alternate universe or something?"

Wheeler watched, as a confused Brian sat on the bed; so, he tried to explain again, "No, not at all . . . are you both familiar with the phrase, 'My heart skipped a beat'?"

"Yes," they nodded.

"Well, you are between beats of time. You are not moving in time. You are stuck in a *time anomaly*. This particular one is an event out of control . . . "

Both Angie and Brian wore blank expressions.

"I know, it is technical. I am here to help you correct this and to prevent you from staying here any longer than you have to. We have to prevent you from causing the Knofer to advance to the next defense level. That could cause a permanent separation in the physics of it all."

Brian wasn't impressed, "Oh, that's clear, thanks. What the hell are you saying?"

"It appears someone has decided to try to use time travel, but doesn't understand the ramifications. You are both equally real, and you can be as you were, if you follow my instructions."

"Yes, of course," Angie said.

"Yeah, fine, but it sounds stupid," scoffed Brian.

"That is because you want me to explain things." Wheeler smiled and said calmly, "Now, you have to return to the point of origin, where the anomaly triggered, to prevent it in the first place . . . "

Angie asked nervously, "You want us—me—to go back to the courthouse?"

"Yes, to the point of origin, the doorway out of the anomaly."

"And I should do what?"

"You must find the specific place, and go back through the door."

"Well, that certainly sounds simple enough, right, Angie?"

"What? How do I do that, and what if I can't?"

"In that case, *I* will return you to your father."

Brian cocked his head, "What is the catch?"

"The catch is I am your Knofer, Angie. I am in *defense mode,* Level 2. Therefore, my priority is you, no one else . . . no one here. If I initiate the next level protocol, the response has no regard for others, and it may leave a scar on the time anomaly.

"What will happen to Brian?"

"No one can say. No one can come back here to find out. If I were Brian's Knofer, no one could say what would happen to you."

"My God," Brian said. "Where is my Angie? Is she in the same situation somewhere else? Is her Knofer telling her the same thing?

"Wheeler nodded slightly, "Actually, it does not work that way. Angie is fine. My explanations may leave you more confused than I intend. The mirror analogy is merely to enable you to have some sort of comprehension of the concept that all things exist at the same time. Truth be told, there are countless possibilities of where your Angie could be. Perhaps this may help. If I say something to five people, what I said is now in five new places—five new heads. Think of the anomaly as a new place, one of many, a new head, so to speak."

"Oh, yeah, I got it now; that makes it much clearer . . . " Brian rolled his eyes.

"I am instructing you on understanding this. I am coaching you about what to do. My interference is a last resort. It is necessary to bring Ms. Bellos home and correct the anomaly."

Brian and Angie let out a slow nervous sigh. Angie looked at the clock and then Wheeler. "How do we do this, when court isn't even at the same time it was where I came from?"

"Get into the courthouse. Use your Knofer—me. I can do many things, including opening locks. Command it to sense the point of origin. The fact that I am in *defense mode,* Level 2 has activated many security features, but you have to be within the correct distance. I have reset to try to sense the anomaly's vibration. You must use me to examine the room in which it occurred."

"I don't know which room to find in the first place. The last thing I remember is the stairs outside."

"That is the challenge. I function within a specific range. Your Knofer will find the *sweet spot* – the door, if within range. You simply dive in."

"*Sweet spot,* what exactly is a *sweet spot*?"

"Look for a moving blur perhaps, or a sphere, something out of the ordinary in a familiar landscape."

Angie raised her eyebrows. "So, I see it, or don't see what I should, the Knofer confirms, I dive in, and everything is fixed."

"Yes, well, there is one thing," Wheeler squinted a bit. "If anything else, or anyone else touches the *sweet spot,* even inadvertently, before you get to it, it will close. They will be caught in their own separate new anomaly, and you will be here, indefinitely, cycling repeatedly, and so on. It will go on and on, repeating the same time period, over and over. New anomalies can continue to appear, outside your original timeline, from anything or anyone, other than you. Unfortunately, this one has triggered because of compatible genetics. Regardless, the domino effect is quite unfathomable."

"Give me an example of a trigger."

"Even if the trigger were a bug, or a large enough dust particle, an anomaly can reproduce. You are the key, Angie. With your input alone the anomaly will reverse, eliminating the perversion."

"Huh. Well that sounds simple, right?" Angie looked at Brian, taking it all in. Then, she tapped her Knofer and Wheeler disappeared. She picked it up and threw Brian his coat.

"Let's go . . . "

"Yeah, no time like the present," said Brian. Piece of cake. Who cares what happens to me . . . ?"

᯼•ᔓᗢᑕᔓ•᯼

While all that was happening within the anomaly—

Outside the anomaly, back at the Arden City courthouse, Brian Sheldon made it to his car, shocked and scared about what happened to Angie and Marshall. While driving, he turned on the radio and heard the news confirming Marshall had disappeared; but the media were broadcasting that it was an escape from jail. There was a three-state alert, roadblocks and he heard helicopter engines in the sky. Brian repeatedly called his father, but got no answer. Finally, after countless times, Jack answered. He and Johnson were in midflight on another private jet to D.C. to find Rachel.

"Hello, Brian, where are you?"

"Dad, thank God!"

"What's wrong?"

"Dad, Angie is gone, vanished! And Dave Marshall escaped from jail."

"Just slow down, son. What are you talking about?"

"Angie and I were at the courthouse. They found Marshall guilty!As we were leaving, walking down the stairs outside, I watched her—Angie just disappeared.   She just quivered, blurred and vanished. That's it . . . I talked to some news guy and he said that Marshall disappeared inside, too. Dad, what do we do?"

"Put your phone on speaker . . . disappeared, that's silly, son. People do not just disappear. Where are you?"

"In my car."

"This all happened at the courthouse?"

"Yes, about a half hour ago . . ."

Jack put his hand over the phone because Johnson began talking. "Jack, I bet your son is describing a Sidron event. Can he tell us specifically where it happened?"

Jack spoke into his phone, "Brian, I have Abby Johnson here from security at the Complex."

"Hi, Brian."

"Hello."

"Can you tell me where this took place?"

"I saw her disappear on the steps outside. We were talking and then . . . poof! I talked to a reporter, who ran out of the courthouse a few seconds after. He said the same thing happened to Marshall inside Room 210."

Abby thought a moment and then said, "Listen, Brian, I need you to do me a favor. Can you go back into the courthouse and ask one of the courthouse staff? Or, if you find a court reporter, find someone who witnessed the event? I need to know precisely where both events happened, specifically to within the inch, if that is possible. Can you do that?"

"Christ, Johnson, he is my son, not a trained cop."

Abby was quick and whispered to Jack, "This could be the break we need to find out the cause of the Sidron events. Trust me, Jack."

Jack spoke into the phone, "Brian, I know this is asking a lot, but I need you to try and do this."

"Fine, I'll get back to you."

"I love you, son; good luck."

"Yeah, thanks, love you, too."

CHAPTER 15
HELLO, MARION

A LONE KNOFER TICKED on the desk, in a small plush office setting, and the long fingers of a brilliant billionaire tapped it to answer. As a life-sized holographic image grew before his eyes, Marion Brock marveled at the technology it took to create such a masterpiece of communication.

"Hello, Marion,' the image said, "Did you forget about me?"

Brock smiled in his sinister way and, with an evil twinkle in his eye, spoke calmly and eloquently, "Mr. David Marshall, my connoisseur of the Arden jail; no, I don't forget the most important people in my life. But, I didn't know you had one of these little toys, too."

"Yes, it's an insurance policy of sorts. I still have friends down below. I have several of these toys, including the ones I gave you. They can't trace any calls. Yours and mine are special. They are linked."

"Fascinating. What can I do for you?"

"For starters, you can tell me why I'm still in jail? The time-boost was supposed to push me forward out of here. I am still at the courthouse and it's this morning again."

"Yes, well, frankly, we don't know yet. You see, everything was properly programmed, but it took you back. I hope you didn't suffer side effects."

"Thank you for restating the obvious . . . side effects? I have been sweating like a faucet. I was unable to speak for over an hour."

"Hmm . . . David, David, do keep calm. We knew there was something wrong when you didn't show up in the chamber. Our people are on it. We will talk later. Just bear with all of this for just a little while longer. You can do that, David . . . I have the utmost confidence in you."

"Don't patronize me, Brock. I have no intention of sitting in a six by nine cell for the rest of my life. I mean it!"

"My, my, I'll chalk that comment up to side effects. Remember, my friend, I am more interested in the time travel working correctly than I am in keeping you in jail. You are my proof that Time Travel, Inc. is a success. So, relax, be patient. Enjoy the free food and solace."

Brock smiled sarcastically. Then, he cut the communiqué and looked at the Knofer, "I'm going to prove time can conquer you and your Mr. GGM, himself."

His cell phone, next to the Knofer, rang.

"Yes, hello."

"Mr. Brock, hello. This is Stevens at the Time Travel Lab . . . "

"Yes, Stevens, I was just going to call you about the Marshall test this morning."

"That's why I'm calling you, sir. There was an event . . . we think . . . sort of."

"You mean he didn't go forward? He went back in time? I know."

"No, I mean Mr. Marshall didn't go forward or back in time. He shifted off the timeline completely, something to do with the equipment, I think. There is now a separate anomaly just hanging out there. It was quite by accident. We are gathering data. I have no explanation for the cause yet. Our readings indicate it is a net of repeating time, operating much like an old merry-go-round. Also, there was another person affected when we triggered the test."

"Oh, for God's sake, Stevens! Can you speak English? Can we get Marshall out or not?"

"Frankly, I'm not sure. There is another variable now—the other person."

"Who is it?"

"We are trying to get a fix, but the person is not stationary. We cannot identify who it is until he or she stays put long enough. Sir, this changes a few perceptions."

"*Perceptions*? What the hell are you talking about?"

"It means the cycle of time within that anomaly will repeat, but the events may change. Time may have taken on a mind of its own."

"For God's sake, Stevens! Damn it, tell me so I understand!"

"Sir, there are two people from our time stuck in the anomaly—Marshall and one other person from the courthouse. Each went back several hours. They are stuck repeating that period; but the events within that timeframe may be different. The people may not even realize they are living the same hours. The longer they are caught in it, the stronger the likelihood they won't get out. They will live the two to three hours over and over again . . . never moving into the future or living with anyone else but those they are with during those hours."

"Shit!"

Brock sat for a moment and his expression changed. He thought, *Why, what a fabulous place for Mr. Marshall!*

Stevens broke Brock's concentration, "The fact is, this couldn't have happened if Marshall was captured alone. We think it's the other person attached to the program who overloaded it, causing the anomaly."

"Okay, I think. Can you fix it?"

"I am not sure. It would be a lot simpler if I could talk to David directly, but that would be impossible."

"Can we set up a new test? Would that be faster?"

"Probably, but we can't just leave two people in a time anomaly lost forever."

"Wait a minute, Stevens, if what you say is true, how is it possible that I got a call from Mr. Marshall not 10 minutes ago? He described the event and his side effects!"

Brock listened to silence, and then Stevens spoke urgently, "Sir, there is no way Marshall can communicate with anyone outside the anomaly. It is physics, sir, impossible! Unless, that is . . . "

"Unless, that is, what?"

" . . . Unless you, sir, are somehow also linked to the event."

Brock's eyes bulged and he thought, *Marshall said the same word, linked.*

"Fine, Stevens, just shut up a minute. Let me think . . . have you heard from InVoy? Does he have the rest of the notes yet?" As he held the cell phone to his ear, Brock looked back down at the Knofer, and then suddenly stood up nervously, whispering to himself, "*It can't be.*"

"Sir . . . Mr. Brock . . . are you there?"

Brock regained his composure and listened to Stevens.

"Sir, we have to address this immediately. If you talked to David, we need to examine you right away. Is there anything unusual happening, particularly electronic or magnetic where you are?"

Brock could not stop staring at the Knofer. He squinted and shrugged, "Just the phone. Other than that? No, not really. I'm not sure."

"Well, good. The link triggers by some electrical impulse, so first I advise that you discontinue use of anything that requires an impulse, including this phone. You should turn it off and come here to me, *immediately.*"

Brock looked at his cell phone, and with a fearful frown, he reached and picked up the Knofer, turning and examining it, thinking, *How do I turn you off, my little jewel?*

"Stevens, what you are saying is unavoidable. Everything from car batteries to my airplanes generates electrical impulses." He raised his head and spoke softly to himself, "Marshall, you son of a bitch."

"Sir, I don't want to frighten you, but that is why you need to be here. I can only secure you, here . . . "

"Yes, fine."

" . . . and one other matter, sir. I received a call from the guard at the warehouse, south of Seattle. Something very strange has appeared in the silo. I instructed the men to secure it until I talked to you."

"What! And?"

"It appears to be a very large fish, sir."

Brock grinned a bit and thought to himself, *Well, Mr. GGM, I guess we have one of your little pets.* "Who knows about this, Stevens?"

"The men at the warehouse, me, and now you . . . I really must insist. Come to me, immediately, sir."

"Send me the coordinates of the warehouse."

Brock cut the call. He had been in deep seclusion for over eight months, careful whom he saw, and disciplined to travel only with his most trusted bodyguards. They were confidants, counselors really, and handled most of his private affairs, while he controlled top priorities from his underground hideaway in Vancouver.

He developed many new interests as a ghost investor, buying huge land bundles and sea rights from foreign countries. He limited his travel, only flying to Time Travel, Inc. when necessary. Brock's pet investment was supporting O.P.A.S. through a shadow foundation to keep his name off their books. He secretly bought their old accelerator landscape, south of Seattle and, when his team had reached its intelligent limit, he pirated Hamil Stevens from O.P.A.S. to complete his time project. Rash InVoy, his Chief of Staff, managed most of his other worldwide affairs.

So, that morning, after talking to Marshall and Stevens, Brock called his trusted bodyguard to make flight arrangements. He turned off his cell phone, picked up the Knofer and walked out of his office, wearing aninconspicuous tan suit and dark glasses. He proceeded down the private staircase, four floors to the parking garage. As he opened the stairwell door, his guard, Briggs, escorted him into the black stretch limo and drove him to one of five corporate special airlifts for the short flight to Seattle.

CHAPTER 16

SEMITRI

INSIDE A REMOTE WAREHOUSE some 50 miles south of Seattle, two special service guards crouched in front of the double door entrance which connected the warehouse to an old missile silo. An unbearably loud screeching continued to render them helpless. When it stopped, they took their hands from their ears, got up and rushed through the doors into the silo. They froze on the ledge, looking at a 100-foot tall Carrier beast transforming before their eyes. The wet looking fish-like creature, which they had tied against the silo's walls an hour ago, was no longer passive and quiet. It was alert and obviously mad. They watched it morphing into a horrific thick snake, some 15 feet in diameter. As the Carrier reduced in thickness, the chains around it fell to the floor.

"Holy shit! What the hell is going on?"

"Damn if I know . . . "

"Get the chain extender!"

"Screw you! I'm out of here!"

Guard One turned and began running back through the doors and down the hallway, leaving his partner stunned. Guard Two heard a hiss behind him and wrenched around to see the animal was almost directly above him. In that instant, he reached for his revolver. He stepped backwards, but the snake was very fast. It slithered up through the doorway, darting past Guard Two and splintering the double doors after Guard One. It stopped right in front of the running guard who froze in terror. He stood shaking, red-faced and unable to move.

The snake reared its head back, and with one sweeping motion, its huge mouth engulfed and swallowed the screaming man. Then, out of the corner of its eye, the animal saw sunlight shining, creeping toward him through the windows, which lined the outer walls of the main warehouse. It snapped back and recoiled. In one unbelievably fast move, it raced back through the doors and swallowed up Guard Two on its way back down into the dark bottom of the silo.

❦❧☙❧❦

20 minutes passed before a gray stretch limousine pulled up to the warehouse and parked. A driver got out, opened the rear door and Marion Brock stepped from the dark interior onto the sidewalk. He placed his hand on the driver's shoulder, "Thanks, Briggs. Quiet here, isn't it?"

"Yes, sir, that it is . . . should I wait for you?"

"Yes, please. And Briggs, notify InVoy that I've arrived at the site. Tell him I'm surprised . . . it appears I am the only one here."

"Yes, sir."

Brock walked some 100 feet, up to the old brick building. Thirty years ago this was his family's Pacific coast ammunition site. As he unlocked the front door, his phone rang. "Yes . . . ?"

"Sir, Stevens here. I beg your pardon. I thought you were coming directly here . . . to me."

"Stevens, you can be a pain in my ass. I am going to make sure all is well. I don't see any guards by the way."

"Sir, there were two assigned. Perhaps they are in the silo. Regardless, you need to come here!"

"Well, that's not going to happen. You work for me, you know. I'll check this out and get there when I can . . . "

Brock cut the call and walked onto the huge warehouse. "Hello . . . hello!" His voice echoed. "Christ, what's next? Hello!"

He walked inside, some 100 yards, and stepped over the splintered double doors at the other end of the building. In the entry hallway to the silo, he saw a cap and shoe. When he reached to pick them up, he heard a loud, strange squeal coming from within the silo. As he bent down, a snakehead, at least 10 feet wide, slithered up to him, and its eyes focused on his. He was terrified yet unable to move or speak. Some force, he never felt before, was holding him frozen. *"Mother of God,"* he said. *"What are you?"*

The snake moved around the perimeter of the hallway and coiled, wrapping himself so Brock was in the center of the circle. The snake opened his dragon-like mouth and Brock smelled the darting tongue and winced at the razor sharp orange teeth. Then, it lowered its head and calmly closed its mouth. Staring at Brock's terrified face, and with a nod, the snake released Brock's invisible binding and watched as Brock lifted his foot, but there was nowhere to run.

"Christ, what the hell are you, you sick viper?"

The snake looked deeply into Brock's eyes and seemed to smile, *"Hello Marion, it was wrong of you to think you could bind me here. Do you not know what you see?"*

"No, I do not know what I see." Brock turned, spinning in a panic, studying the great beast and looking to escape. "How is it that you speak? I don't see your mouth move . . . shit!"

The snake seemed to chuckle, *"I am Semitri. You want me to help you . . . ?"*

Brock gasped and seemed to recognize the voice. He squinted and began to relax, "You mean you are the beast . . . "

"I am Semitri. You knew I was not to be tied or restrained in any way."

Brock watched as the snake's coils began to change. Semitri's head retreated slowly into the coils as they solidified into pearl white walls surrounding him. Within seconds, the billionaire was no longer in the hallway. He was inside the Carrier, Semitri.

"Now Mr. Brock, meet you . . . "

"What are you talking about? Where am I?"

As he stood in the middle of the white room, Brock watched a door appear and open. The clone of Marion Brock walked toward him.

"Jesus . . . and what the hell are you, for God's sake?"

"Hello Marion . . . I am he who you sent to get the vials of C.P.T. months ago. Don't you remember?"

"What is this? You are mine, then, and just a clone."

"Just a clone? Hah! Frankly, it's all very simple." The Clone-Brock [C-Brock] paced around Brock. "I have been trapped within this thing for all that time, apparently feeding it. But, in return, it fed me. I have learned a great deal. Have you ever heard of a *compatibility?*"

"You work for me, you know. Christ, you *are* me!"

"No, actually, I work for me. I have negotiated with our friend here that he can have as much of us as he wants. In return, I run the Brock empire. You see, by cloning yourself, you opened up a completely new world for both our friend here and me. If I clone more of us—you—and let him hold the clones within him, he will gain unlimited power, and give us—me—whatever I want, or, something like that . . . hah! So, he and I have agreed not to kill you."

"What do you mean, *whatever we want?*"

"Watch . . . Semitri, please supply standard furniture, monitors, bath suite and food . . . my favorites, please?"

Everything appeared, magically from nothing; and all of a sudden, C-Brock was wearing the same clothes as Brock.

"You see? Sit. Enjoy."

"Christ, how?"

"First, the most important thing you must remember is that Semitri here and his buddies suck sustenance out of us, which they consider more than food. You and I have something that, if he can keep or get more of it, well, he will be all-powerful to his own kind. So, you see, he will do anything we ask—I ask, that is. You—well, all you have to do is just sit here and they'll give you anything you want."

Brock snarled at him. "So you think I'm just going to stay here. I'll make my own deal."

"Well, that's the catch, I'm afraid. You see, your strength is much more intense than mine, or any clone's, for that matter. Now that you are here, I am afraid he has no intention of letting you go, especially, since you tried to imprison him. Think of it this way, my brother. You can have as much of whatever you want. You will find it is not all bad. I know how much possessions and money mean to you. Count all the money you want, imagine whatever you will, and he will make it appear. Our friend here will take good care of you."

"Why, you twit! You think I will let this happen? I don't control my empire because I'm stupid."

Clone Brock walked briskly toward the door. He waved and said, "He will keep you fat and happy. That is the least I owe you for what you did to me, my brother."

Brock turned, looking around the white room and yelled, "Release me!"

C-Brock snickered, turned, and walked out of the Carrier into the warehouse.

Semitri moved into the bottom of the silo and spoke calmly to his new visitor, *"So you are, in fact, the great Marion Brock. Welcome! I have gotten to know your brother quite well over the last few months . . . impressive, your refusal to quit. We have many things to discuss. Sit, eat and we will talk."*

Meanwhile, Clone Brock found his way to the limousine, where Briggs waited. "Sir, I was beginning to worry."

C-Brock smiled as Briggs opened the door.

"All is as it should be."

"Should I take you to Stevens now, sir?"

"Yes, to Stevens . . . and update me on all issues that you know of."

Briggs closed the doors, started the limo, and sped off to Brock's Time Travel research base.

CHAPTER 17

JAKE'S MATE

JAKE BURNS SAT WITHIN A CARRIER as it sped through the volcanic ocean of inner Earth toward the northwestern United States and Oregon Particle Accelerator Sciences. He tried not to think about the ride. Rather, he concentrated on the labyrinth of challenges before him. As he studied a few notes, a voice spoke distinctly and, at the same time, the image of a young woman's face appeared on the Carrier wall.

"Hello, Jake Burns. We meet again."

"Well, then, hello again."

"I am Carrier 1111."

Burns did a slight double take and replied, "All right, yes, our friend, Alinflavor, said . . . "

"You mean Allenfar."

"Yes, that's it. He told me we may meet again. He said you and I are *compatible*, that you have a crush on me or something."

"How flattering, but not quite; you may call me Miriam . . . a compatibility is quite different from a crush."

"Well, are you and I? You know . . . having a thing right now . . . I mean . . . ?"

"Yes, whenever you ride within me, we share."

"Well, you see, funny you should say 'share'. I did want to talk with you about that. I mean, we really aren't, are we?"

"I am not sure I understand."

"And, I am not sure how to ask this. I don't mean to be rude. It's just that I need to know what you know. That is to say, I am requesting a *two-way compatibility*, a real sharing—a two-way communication, between us."

"We reserve that experience for GGMs alone, as stated in our treaties. In addition, there is the issue of genetic code. I may harm you, permanently."

"I have been told I have quite an unusual genetic sequence. I will be okay."

After a moment of silence, Jake noticed part of the Carrier's wall began to play 3-D video of his childhood, family and early career experiences.

"How did you get these? They are events that had no videos recorded. This is impossible."

"The video you see is your own thoughts. I can show you some of mine like this."

"There is a great sense of urgency about what I ask. The fact is; I need to know what you know and understand, as you do. I am charged with finding a solution to our mystery about the Sidron and the man named Marion Brock."

"If I input directly into your brain, it would be a great stress, you would most likely die . . . "

"I have no choice in this. I am willing to take the chance."

When we traveled in time months ago, I experienced our compatibility and notified our Grand Council Tyree Master. He visited your GGM recently and has conveyed much to him. Our council approved our further interactions with limits. Beyond their set of boundaries would violate synergistic treaties."

"We both want the same thing, to correct the Sidron and stop Marion Brock."

"My assignment is to stop one of our own kind, Semitri, and to return him to the Grand Council. I must find out how and why he is using the Sidron, and why he has allied with a surface man. He has already found a way to prevent our hive mentality from knowing

what he is doing. You may ask your questions, Jake Burns, and watch the walls. That is our offer."

The wall video began playing a detail of the shooting in the Andrews morgue from eight months ago.

"I investigated this murder. If I hadn't, I wouldn't be here now."

"Months ago, three of your doctors and a girl were inside Carrier Room 2210. She lined the walls of the morgue room. The bullets from the guns fired killed that Carrier. Afterward, Carrier 2211-Semitri had taken Marion Brock and a clone of Angela Bellos for rehabilitation. The girl expired. Semitri dropped off our tracking ability and he hasn't communicated since. It is not unusual that we rehabilitate members of colonies in solitude. However, it has been much too long. Our kind are very comfortable with periods of solitude, and right now we have 263 Ever-Life convicts undergoing rehabilitation within correctional Carriers."

"Why haven't you shared that fact with us before now?"

"We do, with the GGM, when it's appropriate. In your case, you don't share every human discourse with us, either. By treaty, we were responsible for rehabilitating Marion Brock. You are to be notified, only if the rehabilitation is successful. If it is not, we would dispose Mr. Brock. We have no further responsibility to notify your kind, in any regard."

"I am hoping to change that . . . "

"Regardless, after the female clone expired, we did not hear from Semitri. We never knew what happened to Brock. We had no contact. Only through working with the new GGM in the last 24 hours did we confirm the breech in the Sidron; and, only within the last hour, have we recorded unexplained signal waves from Semitri."

"How did you receive signals, only now?"

"He acquired ability to time travel; something he did not have before. We have all records of any Carrier that travels in time. Each gives off an unmistakable wave frequency."

"My God, this video shows so much detail of the murders. I could have used this that day. How do you get the camera angles?"

"Everything within a Carrier is recorded from all angles. It is standard procedure for us. By treaty, we give all pertinent inputs to GGM for processing."

"No wonder Gordon knew everything. We could use that for judicial purposes on the surface. Well, first things first, then. I have to find a man named Hamil Stevens. His last location was the Oregon Particle Acceleration Sciences Lab in Seattle. We think he may have caused the Sidron breach. How fast can you get me there?"

"Twenty-six minutes, 22 seconds."

"Meantime, do you have a history file on him? And please play everything you have on Brock, too."

"Displaying now . . . "

Burns sat, watching and comprehending all he saw, while, at the same time, he wore an earplug and listened to various Knofer inputs regarding many Ever-Life security matters.

CHAPTER 18

THE FATHERS' TRIP

AFTER A GOOD NIGHT'S SLEEP, the three fathers met outside Bellos' private lab at Andrews Hospital, and waited for his arrival. Twenty minutes passed without a word from him, so they entered cautiously one by one.

"Dr. Bellos," James called out. "Dr. Bellos, are you there?"

"Look at all this," Kristos said. "The miracle of science, my brothers. I guess we should be thankful."

"Then they fixed on the floor to ceiling statue in the far corner. It was a Carrier.

"Okay," James said. "What is that?"

"Is it glowing?" Ahmir asked.

Each of the statue's long tentacles was shaped into a lounge chair." Mathew Bellos entered the lab. "Good morning, gentlemen. I brought traveling supplies."

Bellos reached into his bag and took out an extraction syringe and three Knofers.

"What do you mean?" Ahmir asked.

"First, here. These are handheld computers, sort of. Just press this and speak into it there. They will answer any questions if we are separated. Please, hold them up and look into the red spot on the front . . . that's it. Now, you are securely linked to our time period . . . and each one has a *Defense Mode*, which would kick in as a fail-safe if there is a threat."

"What do you mean?" James asked

"Please, think clearly," said Bellos.

"Sorry, what?" asked Kristos.

"Those little gadgets run on pure knowledge, and each is now programmed to your individual thoughts. In some cases, emotions can override thoughts, as you know. Therefore, it is important to try to focus, concentrate, if you have a problem. Don't let your emotions cloud your thinking. That is what *S* was trying to tell you. Anyway, if Defense Mode does kick in, that little unit should read your imprint, and the Carrier will return you back to itself."

"I see," said Kristos, a bit confused.

Bellos continued, "Also, pay attention. In this syringe is an immunity shot to protect you against viral or bacterial infections of the time. The delivery system is just air."

Bellos took each syringe and injected the contents into the right wrist of each man.

"Lastly, here is a canteen for each of you."

"Okay." James took his and remarked, "It looks like a baby bottle. Apparently, we are not going to be gone long."

Bellos smiled. "It doesn't need refilling. It won't run out. It's pretty nifty."

"Nifty?" James giggled.

"Sorry, I'm a lover of ancient clichés . . . and it's not filled with water. That is your wine."

"Wine? The stuff we drank?" Kristos asked.

"It will feed us and quench our thirst. Unfortunately, we cannot eat solid food on the journey. Remember, this is very important, no matter what. Do not eat anything solid, even if you are so tempted by look or fragrance. It would be very bad. It's a rule that you must not break."

"So, Doctor, this little phone thingy, you call it a unit?"

"Actually, we call it a Knofer,"

"Okay, Knofer you say, it will protect us and bring us back in case of an emergency. And this little bottle of wine will nourish and sustain us throughout the trip . . . we don't need any food and we are safe from harm?"

"Yes," Bellos smiled. "One more thing, please place this on your right underarms.

"It looks like a quarter."

"It is self-adhesive, you won't feel it. It records body functions while you travel."

Then, the doctor looked at the statue, and the three fathers turned and saw it begin to change.

"And may we ask, Doctor, what exactly is that?"

"That, my friends, is our ride."

"What is it?" asked Ahmir.

"Actually, it's not an it. She is a time controller."

"I'm afraid you have us at a complete loss," Kristos said.

"There are many new things that you will experience with me today. She is one of a species that lives within our planet, unknown to the surface population."

"Praise be to Allah," Ahmir whispered.

"Dr. Bellos," James raised an eyebrow. "How are we able to travel in time?"

"Come this way," Bellos extended his arm, pointing toward the Carrier. "Please position yourselves around her and lean back onto her arms. She could explain it much better, if she chose to; but, summarily, the earth's core has an ocean of molten magma rotating around it. That flowing motion, combined with the rotation of earth and orbit around the sun, is what creates the magnetic field around the planet. That field surrounds us all and holds us within it. By harnessing the energy of that magnetic field and focusing in a certain way, our girlfriend here creates a time vibration—a particular frequency. Then, she can ride the frequency wave, like a surfer on a surfboard, to almost any event in time. But, there is a catch. Once *you* have been to that time and stayed for whatever period, you can never duplicate the trip again. The second trip's frequency vibrations would cause your cells to confuse and divide, to accommodate the two timelines you had visited. Unfortunately, the result is that each of your cells would separate from itself, break apart—disintegrate. You would become cell dust."

"Well," Kristos added, "we don't want to be cell dust, do we?"

"Good. Now does anyone have to do anything before we start?"

The three nodded no with thankful smiles. Bellos turned his complete attention to the Carrier statue and bowed respectfully to it. He began speaking out loud in the Carrier's language, "Dear Sister, in the name of Time Trust Treaty 120856, we ask that you take us in safety and peace . . . our respect and admiration, always."

"Do you recognize the speech, Kristos?"

"No, it's nothing I've ever heard or studied."

"Nor I . . . " said Ahmir.

"It's not Latin, Greek, Hebrew or Aramaic," said Kristos. "Could it be some derivation or of Coptic origin?"

As Bellos finished, they all spoke at once and Bellos gestured and answered, "It's a combination of many languages really. You three remember the Tower of Babel story, right? Everyone spoke the same, until God scrambled their languages. Well, think of it as the original native tongue, everyone spoke . . . "

The three fathers did a double take.

" . . . and remember, we humans have different vocal capabilities now. We could never duplicate the original tones, anyway."

Kristos rolled his eyes, as the Carrier began to hiss. Slowly, she changed, appearing transparent, pliable and wet. Her cloudy glow became brighter. The men leaned back onto what at first appeared to be razor sharp metal, but in fact, the tentacles felt cushiony and comfortable as they wrapped around each rider.

"Surprisingly comfortable," James said nervously.

"Don't be alarmed."

"Excuse me, Doctor, if we knew what was happening, we wouldn't be so anxious."

"She is beginning her search for the right frequency."

The membrane inside the room began to shrink, tighten and pull away from the walls and furniture, toward the Carrier. It was turning into a protective bubble outer layer. The four lounges began to rotate in a counter clockwise rotation. From the apex of the creature, the tongue was flailing, generating short popping sounds. To the men watching, everything in the office began to spin. Then, after a moment, the room's movement changed, and everything moved from side to side. The popping stopped and, strangely, there was absolutely no sound at all.

"So, Doctor," James asked, "what is happening now?"

"She has started the vibration. See how things seem to move quicker and quicker? As the vibration increases, the bubble around us will change. It will seem like all has stopped. Watch when the bubble becomes shiny, it means she's vibrating very fast, searching space-time, for the right wave. Soon after that, you will all sense a feeling of euphoria and drift into a very light trance . . . it is hard to explain before you experience it. Take deep breaths and try to relax, as much as you can."

"But how can we travel anywhere?" asked Ahmir.

Bellos was sensitive to their tension. "Actually, it's to any *when*, really. As I said, the Carrier is searching for a certain frequency. All life, in space-time, exists at a particular frequency of existence. She will find the frequency of our destination—that time we chose, you see. When she finds it, we go. The bubble around us can only exist, if we all stay at a certain level of comfort, though. The less you know, in this case, the more apt you are to stay within the correct comfort range. The coins you wear tell her that you are all okay, so she can trigger the next phase, providing our monitors approve your vital signs. The process will move much faster if you try to relax."

The three fathers nodded and watched the balloon bubble constrict.

"My goodness, it is quite something," Kristos said. "But there is no sense of movement. I am not dizzy at all."

"This will be like nothing you have ever experienced before; and yet, it will be just another moment in your day. The trip should cause no pain. We will be able to move as we do normally. Have no fear, gentlemen; we will be fine."

The three were mesmerized as the bubble turned an opaque mauve color. Flashes of light sparkled; and within seconds, she was spinning so fast, no one could see anything in the room.

Kristos looked at the others wide-eyed, "I think the fact that there is absolutely no sound makes it most unnerving . . . Doctor, how long does it take to . . . ?"

A blinding light from the beast made them all involuntarily close their eyes, and within the short time they blinked, they transported. When they opened their eyes again, the bubble had begun to dissipate, and the tentacle lounges gently pushed each of the riders up to a standing position. They were inside a shallow, dark cave, about six feet high, 20 feet wide. Bellos looked at his wristband and Knofer, quickly checking to make sure the fathers made it without any physical problems. He tapped his Knofer and it became a small flashlight.

"Come this way."

"Wait," Kristos said. "Look around. This is a burial chamber." He walked over to one of several small rocklike containers. "This is a Jewish ossuary, a burial box carved out of limestone. It's fresh . . . new."

"Yes, I've seen them before . . . " Bellos said.

"What a sight," James said. "Look, more of them."

"Over there," Ahmir pointed. "It's a side tunnel, light is coming from it."

The three men looked at each other and then at Bellos. "Doctor, we must see," Kristos said.

"Go then, we have time."

The three chuckled and walked single file to the light. It seemed brighter as they got closer.

First, James, then Ahmirand then Kristos crouched to walk through the side cave's entrance. What they saw staggered them. Light seemed to radiate from the walls, and a man sat before them on a rock bench wiping himself with pieces of clothing, which were scattered on the bench. He noticed them and smiled. Each of the three clergy heard him speak in a different tongue, Ahmir heard an Arab dialect, Kristos heard Greek and James heard Hebrew.

"Greetings, my brothers. Forgive me, I am not at my best."

Ahmir was the first to react. He fell to his knees, closed his eyes tightly and bowed reciting, "There is only one God, and Mohammed is his Prophet. My Master, forgive me!"

James knelt, fixed and staring. "My Lord, Moses, it is you . . . "

Kristos watched and listened to the other two. He tried to stand straight, but the cave's ceiling was not high enough.

"Who are you? What have you done? This is some trickery, and I shall not be the fool."

The man spoke with reverence, "Believing is seeing, seeing is not believing. Be not afraid. I will not harm you. Please, all of you come closer. As with all things, you see what you will. I am true and will help you."

None of the three fathers noticed that the tunnel seemed to enlarge. Kristos realized he could stand up tall without hitting his head.

The three priests moved slowly over to the bench.

"Come now, you three came to me. Do not be bashful."

"Where are we?" asked Kristos.

The man said, "It is my birthday. Behold, my clothes are my gifts."

There, next to him, was a disheveled pile of clothes. Kristos reached down and felt it, he picked a loincloth up, and, as he did so, he saw, "Your wrists, your feet, you are hurt."

Kristos studied the garments for a few more seconds, and then he realized they were soaked in blood. He clutched them to his chest and began to sob, "What have I done?" He fell to his knees before the man. "I am just a stupid man. I am so sorry," Kristos bowed into the dirt and caressed the man's feet.

"My Lord, forgive me, forgive me."

"Stop, stop," the man said.

As he spoke, the three stared at his face. His image changed before their eyes. They each now saw the same face. However, each one continued to hear him speak and pronounce words in their individual native language.

"Be calm and thank you for coming. You three have forgotten something. Customs and interpretations change over time, and so must the law. It is alive, too. You three twisted your thinking to justify dealing with a demon, because you rationalized a euphoric end. Your idea did not justify your perverted behavior. Every generation studies, refines and interprets texts, to their own time. But, be careful. Original meanings can become clouded, or even lost. Stop it . . . for many people, to follow in the path of sacrifice is impossible. Your Father, in Heaven, gives you the grace of his love in those cases. Every son or daughter is pressured to think conformity. It is your job to teach clarity, and to invite your brethren and children onto a right path to God. By living God's will, one can find the kingdom of heaven within him. Then he can see by my deeds, it is not just a personal experience, it is the next step in life's wonder . . . but each of you has to find his own path. Your Father has created a grand variety of life and thought. I came to show you that humans can have a personal relationship with your Father through doing His will and sharing in brotherhood. Every one of you sees, in his own way, based on one's capacity to understand teaching and revelation. No one should force another to see as he does . . . invite, yes; teach, yes; and coach, certainly."

Then, the man stared eye to eye with Kristos. "Each of you has two eyes, and each one of them sees the same thing from a different perspective. Why do you conspire and insist that others should see as you do, or think as you think? Every true religion has its own language and tells stories inviting followers to travel along a righteous path to God and inner peace. Even when the way and the truth stand as a path before you, you have the choice of whether to take the first step. Let your people choose for themselves on what road to walk. Your Father created the universe. Could he not rescind free will if he wished? Do not complicate the simple truth, or think you can prove something that is a matter of choice."

Then the man leaned in, put his hand on Kristos' shoulder and said, "That which is not yours is not yours to keep."

The man sighed, smiled and slapped his knees, asking, "Now, will you three help me?"

"Help you?" Ahmir said.

"Yes, will you?"

Kristos stood and spoke assuredly, "What can we do? Yes, of course."

"Come, I will show you."

The four walked out of the lighted room and back into the larger cave. No one noticed Bellos, anywhere.

"There, you see that stone that covers the entrance to this darkness? I am hurt. Will you help me move it, so I may leave?"

The three men looked at each other, filled with a refreshed enthusiasm. All four of them went to the stone. Placing their hands upon it, they positioned themselves.

"Now push!" the man said. "Push!"

They all strained and shoved again and again; but it would not budge. Kristos, James and Ahmir backed away, looking at their hands beginning to bleed from pressing on the prickly, jagged rock.

"We are sorry. It is too heavy," said Ahmir.

The man looked at them all, "Nonsense, we try again. I must leave before first light."

The three looked at each other, and each picked another spot to push.

"On three, agreed?"

"Yes," they all said, taking a deep breath.

"1 . . . 2 . . . 3 . . . PUSH!"

The stone inched to one side, but hardly moved. They let go.

"I think it moved," Kristos said.

Their hands dripped red with blood. They took several deep breaths again, and even more determined this time, they set themselves against the stone.

*"Come on!"*Kristos yelled.

They pushed again, and again and again. Inch by inch, the rock slowly moved to the side. Finally, the entrance was open far enough for the man to squeeze out. The three fathers fell back onto the dirt. Exhausted and panting, James asked, "Now what?"

Kristos was smiling with tears of joy. The man was still leaning against the stone out of breath.

"Thank you . . . you three are very smart. Try to bring your thoughts back to basics. You see, my friends? Teach others to unite in a good, right purpose. Invite them to a better life through worship. With the right sacrifice and faith, you can accomplish anything, perhaps even a happy ending. Of course, patience helps, too."

The man stood up straight, taller and more muscular than he seemed before. He turned toward them briefly, wiping his hands on his garment. Then, he smiled at them, turned around and carefully stepped out of the cave.

The three fathers sat, spellbound. Each began to laugh and cry at the same time. James reached over and wiped his bloody index finger on Ahmir's cheek giggling with tears. Slowly, they helped each other up, and began hugging together.

Kristos whispered, "Bellos?"

Only a few seconds went by when they all heard a strange ringing in their ears. It seemed to come from a back corner of the cave. They turned and saw a blinding bright light. A Carrier appeared, however, it looked different from the one in which they arrived. It was one pulsing color—a beautiful steel blue, and it had a silver halo glowing around it. Across from the Carrier, some 15-feet away, the figure of Mathew Bellos stepped out of the shadows. He stood fearlessly, facing the beast. A door opened in front of Bellos, and out stepped the figure of Marion Brock.

"Interesting place for a meeting. I followed your trail, Mr. new GGM. I expect you will come voluntarily, or not, it makes no difference to me."

Bellos simply said, "You have made a mistake."

The GGM reached for his Knofer, but Brock was faster, moving with the help of Semitri. He lunged, diving onto Bellos, but he went completely through the GGM, falling to the ground. The three fathers froze in shock. Bellos looked down at Brock. "You see, my dear Brock, I am but a Post Controller. Our GGM is quite safe."

The 3-D hologram clicked his Knofer, and in an instant, he and the three fathers disappeared from the cave.

Brock stood up and brushed himself off. "Christ, you bastard. Well, this is just the beginning, anyway."

"That is correct," Semitri said, "Mr. Brock, nothing can stop it. Come. We go on."

"To where?"

"To gather the power."

Brock stepped back into Semitri, and with a quick glow and quiver, the steel blue beast disappeared, and the cave was dark, empty and quiet again.

CHAPTER 19

BRAZIL

THE BRAKING ROAR OF THE AIRPLANE ENGINE and bounce of the wheels on the runway signaled the landing of the Hush-Jet on a private airfield outside Rio de Janeiro. Rachel Sheldon wiggled and awoke without side effects from the drug slipped into her drink. She felt her head and looked out the window.

"This is not D.C."

The steward, Gabriel, was quick to enter the cabin and spoke politely, "That is true . . . we detoured, ma'am."

"I can see that. My God, there is Christ's statue on the mountain."

"Yes, ma'am, we are in Rio."

"Jesus, why? What is going on? Who are you people?"

"If you will be patient, ma'am, Captain Blake himself will be with you, after taxiing."

"Not going to happen. I am not in the mood."

Rachel reached for the seatbelt release, but it would not release. She yanked repeatedly. "What the hell! Let me out of this, you bastard!"

"Ma'am, just relax. No one is going to harm you."

The plane taxied to a private hanger and stopped. Rachel was steaming by the time the captain walked to her. He sat in the couch opposite to her.

"Mrs. Sheldon, I am Captain Michael Blake. I am sorry for the inconvenience; but, as you can imagine, in this case, I cannot have you wreaking havoc throughout my airplane. Now, if you calm down, we can talk civilly. How does that sound?"

She took a deep breath, closed her eyes and appeared quiet and subdued. "All right, Mr. Blake, may I ask why we are in Rio?"

"I was paid to bring you here."

As the captain finished his sentence, the entry door at the front of the cabin opened and a short, trim East Indian man walked inside to behind the Captain.

"Good afternoon, Mrs. Sheldon. I'll take it from here, Captain."

Blake got up, walked to the plane's entry door and turned toward Rachel. "Nice meeting you, ma'am."

Rachel focused on the small man in front of her with disdain. "So, can you tell me what is going on?"

"Actually, yes I can. I am Rash InVoy. How do you do?"

"I do very well when I'm not tied up or kidnapped, thank you."

"I do apologize for this, Mrs. Sheldon; it was necessary, believe me."

"I don't believe anything you say."

"Well, perhaps this will help . . . " InVoy undid her seat buckle and offered, "There, if you would like to leave, be my guest . . . "

Rachel got up and started walking to the door.

"Mrs. Sheldon, have you ever been to this side of Rio before? I find it most interesting, if you like the gangland or terrorist elements. Please, stay and learn why we brought you here. I doubt your Mr. Rosse is going to miss you."

At that point, another man walked in through the plane's door and almost bumped into Rachel. "Hello, Mrs. Sheldon, we haven't met. I am Charlie Rosse."

As he extended his hand to shake, Rachel walked backward to her seat and sat in silent shock. "Okay, fellas, what the hell is this?"

Rosse sat down, took a thick bound manuscript out of his briefcase and handed it to her. InVoy stood up, waving Rosse away. "Do you know what that is, Mrs. Sheldon?"

"It looks like my husband's manuscript on particle displacements . . . you bastards!"

"Good guess, but not quite. Your husband is quite the clever man, you know."

"What do you mean?"

"Look at the date, there, on the second page."

"2102 . . . what is this?"

"That's a copy of the original Sidron papers. Now look at this." InVoy took another manuscript out of his own briefcase. "Open it."

Rachel did and gasped. She took the other book, set them side-by-side and began opening the pages in sync.

"Christ! Where did you get these?"

"It's a long story, believe me. I work for Marion Brock, Mrs. Sheldon, not Gordon Swanson, or his Ever-Life monsters. We have been working to recover those papers for decades, ever since they surfaced in 2855."

"That's 144 years?"

"Yes, the Brock family owns them."

"What do you mean? My husband wrote this one!"

"Yes, but how much is really his? When Mr. Brock and your husband collaborated to develop C.P.T., Mr. Brock showed Jack those files on the Sidron. Your husband, being as brilliant as he is, applied everything to his own discovery. Mr. Brock negotiated a long-term contract with Jack to bind the C.P.T. effort with his own interests. The plan was to compare the complete historical records of Sidron with testing the C.P.T. formulation. But, the catalyst bath was the challenge. We couldn't test anything without preserving the formulation in the bath."

"So, you tried to steal it with clones and murder."

InVoy smiled and replied confidently, "Not really. It was your husband who figured the more clones the more formulas. Your Gordon Swanson made a deal to get the very same thing from your husband. The only difference was; if he failed, his precious colonies would not burn up in Hell. If we failed, a big part of Brock's empire would stop. What would you do?"

"Screw you!"

Rachel stood up as an armed guard appeared from the flight attendant cubical. InVoy grinned and gestured to her. "Please, Doctor, sit down?"

"Where did you get my husband's papers?"

"He gave them to us; however, as you can see, they are incomplete."

Rachel opened it to the back, "What happened? Where are they?"

"Precisely, and so, you are here."

"You think Jack has the missing pages?"

"Mrs. Sheldon, we know he does. We gave them to him in the first place. You see, he was supposed to return them, but he never did. He broke the agreement, and now we are compelled to recover the papers."

"So, you broke into our home?"

Rachel sat back in shock for a moment. She glanced out the window with a tear in her eye, and then she took a deep breath and wiped her cheek. "Christ, you almost had me. For just a second, you almost had me . . . bullshit, Mr. Whatever-your-name-is! You think you can brainwash me, justify breaking into our home and blackmail my husband? Never, you bastard!"

"Does it really matter what the truth is, Doctor? You know it's what you believe that counts," InVoy snickered. "And, in fact, it is what you perceive from your point of view, really, isn't it?"

"You are a very bad man."

"Well, that may be your point of view, but it doesn't concern us here, now does it? You are going to be my advantage—my bait—to get those notes. I was hoping you would cooperate."

"Not on my life."

"Mrs. Sheldon, it will happen, or you will have no life. Guards, take her away."

"This isn't going to work, you little shit!"

Two guards grabbed her by her shoulders and forced her down the aisle.

"You little weasel, why don't you fight like a man? Let go of me, you assholes!"

InVoy stuffed a cloth in her mouth and instructed the guards. Then, he called Marion Brock. He had no idea he was really calling a clone.

"Brock here."

"Sir, InVoy here, we have the wife."

"Well, get on with it . . . have Rosse contact Jack. We will have a nice reception waiting. Don't screw this one up."

"I'll handle it . . . "

Chapter 20

Giza

ALLENFAR BEGAN HIS ASCENT from Earth's fiery ocean up to the Great Pyramid of Giza. "We will be docking at the subterranean chamber, sir."

"Can you get me closer to the Grand Gallery?" asked Bellos.

Allenfar slowly rose to the exact point where the ascending passage meets the Grand gallery. Bellos and Wheeler walked out into the dimly lit hallway. Wheeler looked around in awe at the rock walls, "Quite claustrophobic, isn't it?"

"Nothing like the spacious feeling in the colonies, that's for sure."

"Maybe it's just that we are used to the dark, but I see something that reflects . . . and why are we here?"

"One step at a time, Tom . . . ."

Bellos took out his Knofer, tapped it and laid it on the floor, and spoke, "Display detail rendering and analysis of limestone values and impulse readings."

"What's the plan?"

A triangular scale model of the pyramid grew out from the Knofer, as Bellos continued. "Examine both the walls and apex. Then, compare readings with particle displacements or Sidron events. Check findings and compare with all pyramids around the globe."

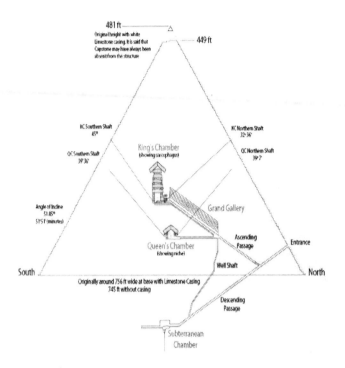

"You think there is a power base here to run a particle displacement test?"

"In ancient times, all the major pyramids around the world were linked. We know the builders had common construction materials, and we know some were conductive. Some historians even recorded electrical impulses at many of the sites. Records imply they were battery capable."

"A world network of power?"

"Exactly. Altogether, a global output and input of electrical energy, but no one knows to what extent. If Brock has found a way to harness or focus that energy, how much power would that be? And, could it generate a frequency field big enough to trigger the Sidron?"

Wheeler witnessed a strange inquisitive look on the GGM's face, as he received input from the Knofer. Bellos looked as though he had an epiphany and said, "Even after thousands of years, it's more powerful than anything we imagined."

"Well, don't keep me waiting?"

"Its combined focus *is* sensitive to the Sidron. This has to be their power source, or somehow they focus power here. They network it from Time Travel, Inc. What a brilliant plan! Who is going to check the pyramids? No one would consider destroying any of them!"

Bellos turned to the Knofer's model again. "Display any frequency echoes within the last 24 hours."

The hologram reset and displayed five twinkling lights. Each radiated waves, pulsing outward to the boundary of the model.

"Mathew, are those locations of the Sidron events?"

"They are the echoes recorded. This is the archive of the exact positions and moments."

"Why would they be in here, of all places?"

"The apex of this pyramid received the displacement signal, and then it projected the particles to Time Trust below. The ancients had many secrets, yet to be uncovered, even in our time. They didn't define things as we do. They used their knowledge, in many ways, beyond what we do."

"So, our visitors in Time Trust now, were transported via the Sidron through the apex up there, down to us?"

"I am sure of it. This pyramid is somehow the passageway for the displacements. The Sidron zapped one man at three different times in his life—from his time to ours. But how? And why? What was the trigger? We always thought the Carriers were the hourglass of time. It looks like Brock has found a different way. Tom, look! One of the lights . . . that one . . . it's fading. I need to question our visitors."

"Mathew, look over there, a new light just appeared. There were five stars—now there are six."

"If each is tied to an event . . . five stars, five events . . . that means another event just happened?"

"Yes, let's go." Bellos spoke to his Knofer, "Transmit all data and findings to Jake Burns, STAT!"

The two men ran back to Allenfar, and Bellos spoke quickly, "Take us to Time Trust security Area 36, of Post 2 . . . Tom, search the vaults and the headset files. Check everything you can think of. There has to be something—a clue, to tell us what happened to our first young visitor."

"Fine, but if a new event just occurred, why haven't we heard something?"

"I don't know. I am going to see our friend, in Room 8. Perhaps that will give us some answers."

"Are you interviewing both of them—him?"

"Yep, that is the plan, the younger first. Let me know anything you find."

"I will. It may take time."

"Unfortunately, we don't have that."

It took Allenfar only a few minutes to dock at Time Trust. The two men exited, each going in a different direction.

Meantime, within a Time Trust unit, one of the remaining two visitors, the 40-year-old, sat watching the walls broadcast 3-D video. He had been studying how different life was below the surface. There were educational displays and exotic agricultural programs. The huge caverns on the screen were far from dark and dank. The man marveled at the bubble Carriers taking passengers back and forth in any direction. At one point, he studied historical information regarding Ever-Life's origins. All that he saw always had a common thread—health care. And every program had interruptions, advertisements about better living through the Ever-Life foods and genetic medicine.

It was early the prior morning, when the first Sidron event occurred that brought three copies of the same man from his lifetime to Post 2's facility, each one a different age. Unfortunately, the youngest of the three already vanished, and there was no way of telling if or when the other two might also. For hours now, the 43-year-old man sat, trying not to upset himself with the stress of where he was. Finally, his room's door opened, and GGM Mathew Bellos walked in. The man got up and looked with professional kindness at Bellos, who immediately extended his hand.

"Hello, I am Mathew Bellos."

"I am Andrew. Frankly, I'm not sure what to say." The man shook Bellos' hand cautiously. "Nice place here. Clean and very white. Different, but interesting."

"That it is. Please, be as comfortable as you can."

"What happened to the other guy, Wheeler, who was here before?"

"I'm sure you have many questions, and I would spend time answering them all, if we had time; but we don't. I assure you I have no hostile intent. I know you must be uneasy . . . "

"*Uneasy* . . . that is the understatement of the day."

"The best thing I can do is tell you everything in an instant." Bellos grinned. "This is very unusual for both of us. I ask that you trust me, even though there is no reason to."

"I don't see a choice. I'm obviously a prisoner."

Bellos walked around the man over to the wall, and a small door appeared at his shoulder height. He took out a headset and turned around.

"This will give you some perspective and answers. It's a brief program. You open the clip, like this; fit it on your ear, comfortably, like this. Then, just sit for a moment. It won't hurt."

The man took the set and studied it. "Is this some audio device? There are no wires."

"Not exactly, but it won't hurt."

The man clipped the device on his ear as Bellos said, "You might want to sit down."

The man went to the lounge and Bellos took what looked like a small 3-inch by ½-inch remote out of his pocket and handed it to the man.

"This is similar to what your Mr. Wheeler showed me. You want me to trust you?"

Bellos pointed and said, "You see the black button there? Push it and then try to relax."

"Right," the man laid his head back on the lounge and pushed. Within seconds he reacted, "Oh, Christ!" Then he shut up and gripped the chair's arms, squeezing tightly. Involuntarily, he closed his eyes.

Bellos sat in the chair beside the lounge, quietly waiting. After a few seconds, the man opened his eyes widely and stared at the GGM. Bellos raised his hand gesturing for him not to speak. "Just push the dot again and remove the earpiece before you say anything."

The man did so and blinked several times, as though clearing his mind. He looked at Bellos as if there was something familiar. "You know, I remember doing that before, in college, a long time ago. Odd, but it was more like a dream then. Did I? I mean . . . did I dream it?"

"No. In fact, you did meet Jake Burns here on three other occasions in your life; but the other two are yet to come. I believe that is why you were involved in the particle displacement today."

"Particle displacement? Considering I have been stuck in this room with a wall size 3-D TV, what I just saw is hard to accept, much less particle displacement."

"I know, but it's all true."

"So, this Sidron is the highway of knowledge and power, and somebody used it to. . . for what?"

"For his own benefit, to capture power and change what is, or has been, to what he wants it to be."

"What year is it, exactly?"

"It is our year 9999.96. By your calendar, June is the month and the year is 2999.6

The man sighed with a serious look, "It's mind blowing that I am still back there, with my life going on and, at the same time, here. But, I have a hard time believing I am really, in fact, dead."

Then he looked at Bellos eye to eye, "Can or will I go back?"

"I'm not sure. Nobody has answers. We believe that time travel cannot change a timeline of someone who died. If that's true, even if you did go back, what you know now should make no difference."

Bellos felt his Knofer vibrate. As he took it out, he smiled at the man and heard Wheeler. "Sir, are you there?"

"Yes, Tom."

"Sir, we have activity on the equipment; intense, immeasurable."

Bellos looked, wide-eyed at Andrew, who began to flicker, like the first young visitor. He reached for Bellos; but before either one could touch the other, the man was gone—disappeared. Bellos stood alone in the room and replied to Wheeler, "Yes Tom, I know. You better get me those readings right away."

"What happened, sir?"

"Just get me the readings . . ."

Bellos cut the call, and sat in the lounge waiting only a few minutes. Wheeler came through the door and said, "Done, sir. They're on your Knofer."

Bellos played the Knofer hologram. "I better have them for our last visitor."

"What do you think, Mathew?"

Bellos lifted his head, "I think Brock is succeeding. Get this information to both Burns and Swanson. Tell Burns to initiate highest Defense Mode. Oh, and Tom, did we retrieve anything on Angie's status?"

"We got a reading from her Knofer. We are trying to trace it through the same efforts we are using to track the Sidron vibrations. When this last event occurred, we registered her Knofer as active, but only during the event. After that, the readings went dead."

Bellos and Wheeler walked out the door and turned in different directions again. Bellos entered Room 9, which held the eldest of the three visitors. Both men looked at each other and shook hands. The man said, "My God, you haven't changed a day. Hello again. Mathew, isn't it?"

Bellos was a bit shocked, but he quickly replied, "Andrew, you remember?"

"Yes, I guess I am about 15 years older than the last time we met. I thought it was a dream, again; nevertheless, I began talking it out and writing what I saw last time. Why am I here again now? Did you ever find out what happened those years ago?"

Bellos looked him over from head to toe. "You should sit down for this, I think."

Bellos sat beside him. "The last time we met, we were across the hall. It was 15 years ago for you, but I just came from that room not five minutes ago for me. I walked directly from our meeting there to here."

"I woke up in my bed, thinking I dreamed it all, until I found this." He pulled out the flash-drive headset vault, which looked like a flash drive from when he sat on the lounge with Bellos. "I couldn't use it of course in any way. I thought about having it analyzed, but what good would that do? It would have been destroyed. I told parts of the story to a close friend, but we drank a lot together, so it was easy to brush off as bullshit. I carried that with me almost every day, everywhere, knowing somehow I would write about it; but I never did, that I know of anyway."

"Well, you did later, and your book has become a prime element in a mystery here, which we are now trying to solve."

Bellos accepted the file back and sat, praying the man wouldn't disappear.

"Mystery?"

"Yes, it looks like the wrong people read your book. Ultimately, we think that's why you are here."

Bellos opened the room's door and the guard handed him something. "Is this your book?"

Andrew took it and began reading. "These are my words, my name, the copyright is dated . . . Jesus!" He sat down, shaking a bit. "You were right about Mr. Burns. I did meet him before, I think. He was a new hire, right, bragging that he could time travel? I showed him that flash drive thingy too. At first, he refused to comment. Finally, he studied it enough to confirm that it came from you, here. I told him things he couldn't discredit that I saw last time. After that, he was very informative. We shared many thoughts and ideas.

Eventually, he gave me a headset session, and everything became so clear to me. Déjà vu became real memory. I remember crying for a week or so, after he left. It affected me in so many ways."

"I am sorry. We don't make it a practice to interfere in people's lives on the surface, much less in a case such as yours. I thought giving you the headset next door would trigger your memory of a man named Marion Brock."

"No, not familiar . . . "

"How about anyone named Brock?"

Andrew shook his head no. Then he hesitated for a second. "Wait, a long time ago, I think; it was when I was in college. I remember the Vietnam War was a big deal to us kids . . . "

"Long ago is right."

" . . . Something about weapons, or ammunition, but it wasn't Marion. It was another name, and, it was the first time I met your Mr. Burns, too."

"Was it Nicolas?"

Just then, Bellos'Knofer clicked again. However, this time it was Jake Burns. "Sir, I have important news. I need to speak to you right away."

"Go ahead," Bellos turned and remarked to Andrew, "speak of the devil! It's your friend, Jake Burns."

Andrew froze as Bellos tapped the Knofer and Burns appeared as a hologram in the center of the room.

"Go ahead, Jake."

"Sir, we have traced the Sidron waves back to an event in 1965. It seems there was a great intensity— an inflation—a small Big Bang. In this case, a time anomaly resulted. A pozzit of time separated from our timeline."

"Not an explosion?"

"Of sorts. Of course, there was no sound, but it was a great disturbance; and it was within the Sidron. I believe it was a result of two or more people having compatibility with a Carrier, an overload.

Apparently, another person was the catalyst in some way. The combination of so many triggered the event."

"Catalyst. I hate that word now. I wonder . . . "

"You don't think Ms. Angie, do you, sir? I mean she was the catalyst needed for C.P.T. Perhaps . . . "

For a second Bellos had a blank stare. Then, he stepped to the side of the hologram, revealing Andrew.

"Jake, say hello . . . do you remember Mr. Andrew, here?"

Bellos gestured toward his visitor. Jake startled and then he bowed respectfully, saying, "Ah, uh yes, interesting! Good to see you again, my friend."

"Well, I wish I could say the same," Andrew replied.

Bellos began again, "Jake, I think there may be two possibilities for that catalyst you mentioned."

"Ah, yes; I see what you mean. I'll have the lab run comparative tests if our visitor there will consent."

"Good idea," Bellos smiled. "Well, Mr. Andrew, what do you say? Care to help solve our little mystery?"

Andrew looked at the book and around the room. "Will I be allowed to see more than just this room?"

"I think I can arrange that."

Burns began to rant, "Sir, I am reading a new event. We have another problem."

Wheeler burst through the door. "Matt, we have another problem."

"Well, one of you spit it out!"

Jake blurted out, "I just got word that Secretary Swanson has disappeared."

"What? Christ! Wheeler, take Mr. Andrew here to the lab. Run comparative tests on his DNA with our records. Get everything on a genetic profile. See if we have any matches or similarities in any of the colony vaults . . . Jake, where are you?"

Bellos tapped his Knofer and ordered up a holographic map of inner Earth.

"I am at X-1500 miles east of core, Y-angle 30 degrees north, northeast linear."

Bellos pinpointed Burns's location. "Do we have any intel on what happened?"

"Sir, we need to talk in the same room. I suspect our communiqué is contaminated."

"Do you have a fix on the suspect's location?"

"My Carrier does, yes."

"Then follow the signal and keep in touch. I want to know location and source."

The Knofer cut the call and Wheeler spoke to Bellos quickly, "Mathew, Gordon was in his office. Patty says he disappeared right in front of her."

Bellos squinted and whispered to himself, "Brock and a Carrier . . . " Then, he looked back at Tom. "I have to go. I have a meeting with the Bering Strait Commission. Keep digging. Get me anything you find out. Test Mr. Andrew and get me the results."

CHAPTER 21

ROSSE

BOTH JACK SHELDON AND ABBY JOHNSON seemed very uneasy during the plane ride to D.C.

Jack had been in a zone looking out the window, and then turned to Abby. "I feel like I should be three places at once. There's so much back at the Complex, too, and now, Brian and Angie."

"They will be all right, the GGM is on it."

"How soon before we land?"

"Same as two minutes ago, try to relax a little. The pilot will tell us when we approach landing."

"Relax? Are you married, Johnson?"

"No, not yet."

"Well, I am, and not just married. I married the love of my life. She is the love of my death, too."

"Interesting choice of words."

"Yes, because we did die, sort of anyway. Regardless; you wouldn't understand."

"Well, you may be right . . . look, down there, the ancient nuclear power plant outside Harrisburg, Pennsylvania. I read about nuclear power on the surface. Some thought for a long time that it was the energy saving messiah; stupid people."

"Yes, electromagnetic energy wasn't taken seriously at that time. What is that sound?"

"It's coming from your pocket."

"Oh, it's my phone." Jack fumbled and answered, "Hello, Rach, is that you?"

"No, Dr. Sheldon, this is Charlie Rosse."

"Rosse?" Jack was befuddled, for a few seconds. "Hello, Mr. Rosse, how coincidental, I am on my way to see you. Has my wife contacted you yet?"

Johnson looked on, pensively, and she tapped her Knofer to trace the call. "He's not in D.C. at all, Jack."

"Yes, I met your wife, briefly. That is why I am calling, in fact. She is with me. We are on a little trip together, and we would like you to join us."

"Jack," Abby whispered, "he is calling from Rio de Janeiro."

Jack rolled his eyes, and then he spoke into the phone, "You mean you kidnapped my wife?"

"Strong word, kidnapped. Let's just say, you two have been invited to a meeting, and if I were you, I'd bring the last part of the notes on your treatise, my friend."

"I am not your friend. If you harm her in any way, it will be the last thng you ever do!"

"Oh, she won't be harmed, rest assured. We only want those pages. You know that."

"Where?"

"Write these coordinates down. We will call you when you are within a half hour of landing. And Doctor, do I have to tell you to come alone?"

"I'll be there." Rosse hung up, and Jack looked at Johnson, "Did you get all that?"

"Yes, it's on its way to GGM. I'll give this to the pilot. Jack, one of the Knofers we tracked came from Rio. Does your wife have one?"

"Frankly, I'm not sure."

"I'll be back. Try not to get too upset. We need your brains working, not your emotions running wild."

The plane turned southeast, toward Rio.

CHAPTER 22

BACK TO THE COURTHOUSE

ANGIE AND BRIAN finally made it back to the steps of the courthouse. They stood looking up at the clock tower.

"Guess we are early."

"Brian, you can't trust that time. You heard Mr. Wheeler."

"Jesus, he was a hologram! And why should I believe any of this? Time anomaly? The whole thing is ridiculous. It's bad science fiction."

"Yeah, well, I believe him. I'm living it. Let's go."

"Wait! Didn't you tell me you were outside on these steps when it happened?"

Angie stopped cold. "You are right. We need to look right here. Let's see . . . you, I mean the other Brian, and I came out of the doors up there. We walked down the steps, over there . . . come on . . . yes, about here. Look around. See if you notice anything strange . . . "

"Strange? This whole thing is strange."

"Yes, well, blurry then, or something in the air that shouldn't be there . . . "

"This is nuts. Okay, I am looking for blurry. Nope, everything seems in focus . . . now what?"

Angie sat on the steps, frustrated. "Hmm, maybe it's something else or somewhere else."

"Good thinking, babe; brilliant."

"Maybe we are approaching this from the wrong angle."

"Why don't we go inside, and get a cup of coffee at least? Better yet, I could use some food."

"Inside! That's it, Brian!" She grabbed his head and kissed him hard on the mouth. "I love you. Come on."

"Where?"

"To Room 210, where it must have started, it has to be there."

"Are we going inside?" Brian rose slowly and followed her. "Yeah, that makes perfect sense. You can't find anything out here, so it must be in there. Great deduction, Sherlylocks! Oh, my God!"

Angie turned at the top of the steps and said, "We have to search where the event actually took place. The only other place with people was Room 210. We start there. Come on, slowpoke."

"I find your reasoning difficult to accept."

"Think about it: was I the event or collateral damage? That means . . . the main event was someone else!"

"Well, how do we find out what or who?"

"Simple, nothing has happened to me. I am just with you. We search, a slow, laborious search. Now come on!"

"Your reasoning is woman's thinking, not deductive."

"Come on, anyway; I'm not a lawyer."

"Well, I am. Or I will be, once I pass the bar exam."

They walked quickly up the stairs, opened the double doors and hurried to Room 210.

"Okay, Inspector Angie," Brian opened the courtroom door. "Please, after you, miss."

"Thank you, sir."

Brian stopped, as the door closed. "Boy, it's a different place without the commotion, isn't it?"

Angie had already walked to the judge's bench. "My guess is, if the event took place in here, it was in the jury box or around the judge's area over there. We'll each take a side. You look over there. Be thorough; examine everything, inch by inch. But don't touch anything, especially, if you see something that doesn't belong."

"What the hell does that mean? I have no idea what to look for."

"Wheeler said we will know it when we find it. Just take your time."

"Fine . . . "

After a time, Angie stood up straight, as though she had an epiphany.

"Brian, you hate this guy, right? I mean Marshall, you hate him, right?"

"Yes, I hate him. I'd have him dead, if I could. He arranged to have my parents killed. Wouldn't you?"

"He's here, in here somewhere, isn't he?'

"I guess so, in the jail cell. I don't know; so what?"

"I want to meet him. Maybe he knows something. Let's find him. I am sure he is somehow involved with all this."

"What about our search, here?"

"I just want to talk to him."

"The holding cells are right under us. Why would they let us in? It's sentencing day."

"Come on, you know your way around here. You are the lawyer for God's sake. Get me in there, think of something."

"Jesus, well, you're not boring, I'll give you that. Follow me."

They walked out and down the hall to the stairwell. At the bottom, a jail guard saw them and stood up from his desk. "I am sorry, you two, we are not open to the public and it's not visiting hours. You have to leave."

CHAPTER 23

OREGON PARTICLE ACCELERATOR SCIENCES— O.P.A.S.

JAKE BURNS WALKED into the main lobby of the O.P.A.S. Corporate Offices in downtown Seattle, Washington, and stood in front of the main receptionist.

"May I help you, sir?" she asked.

"I'd like to see Mr. Oscar Randall. I believe he is expecting me."

"Your name, sir?"

"Jake Burns. Detective Inspector, Jake Burns . . . "

"Oh, yes, I see it here . . . Mr. Burns, you may go up. Take elevator 10, down the hall up to the 30th floor. His office is straight out the elevator."

Burns did so, and walked into Randall's reception area. The secretary bade him sit, and within a few moments, a 5'8" gray-haired man, in a dark, well-tailored suit, walked out to meet Jake.

"Mr. Burns, I am Oscar Randall. Please come in."

They shook hands and Jake followed him into his huge office. It was 40 feet wide by 100 feet long, bound on two sides by windows overlooking the Pacific Ocean. One wall was jagged rock, to remind everyone of the glorious mountains surrounding the skyline and port.

At one end were a couch, several lounge chairs and a 15-foot bar with a well-stocked refrigerator behind it. Randall walked behind the bar and called to Jake, "Please, make yourself comfortable. Would you like something to drink?"

"Allright, yes, do you have any potato vodka?"

"You speak my language, straight up or rocks?"

"Rocks, please."

"I'll make it two."

Jake meandered along the glass cabinets that lead to the bar. They displayed the history of O.P.A.S. and described its product lines.

"Mr. Randall, I thought you were only into particle science."

"We don't advertise anymore. I often wonder if the public thinks so, too. We started as one of the Brock Companies. As you can see, we have been involved for centuries, and those are just the highlights. They had to diversify long ago due to monopoly laws. Then, those changed. It all was highly controversial for a long time. A lot of underhanded political negotiating took place, as you can imagine. Brock bought and sold us several times. We became one of his business units, so we could maintain a foothold and stay the premier scientific developer of particle phenomena in North America."

Jake was captivated as he read each of the captions on the displays.

♦ 1965: Nicholas Brock Founds the Brock Ammunition Company.

♦ 2040: Brock Finance Develops Revolutionary Drone Warfare Modules to Fight Global Terrorism.

♦ 2160: Dark History—New Family Leader of Brock Finance, Marissa Ann Brock, Invests in New Nazi Movement to Rid World of Terrorism. Pakistan Falls to Nazis.

♦ 2196: Marissa's Son, Marion Brock I, Stops Selling Arms to Pakistan, Instrumental in Wiping Out Nazis. He Re-directed Brock Finance Investing in Commercial Industries.

♦ 2199: Marissa Brock Assassinated in London. Brock Companies Golden Age Begins.

- 2302: Brock Companies and Germany Collaborate to Develop New Gyroscopic Technology.
- 2306: Particle Accelerator Galaxy, Desera 59, Discovered by Brock Company and German Military Research.
- 2570: Two Generations: Marion Brock II and III Founded and Developed Oregon Particle Acceleration Sciences—O.P.A.S.
- 2666: Gyroscopic Gravitational Expanse Satellite Constructed by Brock Universal, O.P.A.S.—The First Orbital Space Probe That Can Measure One Planet's Gravitational Plane Relative to Another and to the Sun.
- 2797: O.P.A.S. Photo Laser Imagery Offered to Public. First Used to Map the Moon for Mining Fuels to Be Used in Space Travel.
- 2855: O.P.A.S. Constructs Commercial Fuel Inventory Module and Distribution Port Orbiting Moon.
- 2933: Transportation Acquisition—Personal Vehicle Stellar model 75, Operated by Electric Motors, Guided by O.P.A.S. Gyroscopic Technology.
- 2983: Marion Brock IV Commits to Communication Research and Development of Video/Audio Device—V.A.D.—Technology.
- 2988: Brock Research Develops New Global Satellite Internet for All Communicative Devices.
- 2966: Brock Research Partners with Swanson Developers to Expand Medical Reseach in Arden, New Mexico.

"I didn't realize the magnitude of it all," Jake said

"Yes, it's really something, isn't it? Like I said, those are just highlights. Now tell me, Mr. Burns, what is a police detective from Arden, New Mexico doing in Seattle, and why see me?"

"I'm on a case involving one of your companies, Time Travel, Inc."

"I wish it was ours. But, no, several angel investors came up with capital to buy it."

"Angel investors?"

"Silent trillionaires . . . at least, that's my understanding. We didn't know it was to be a Brock enterprise until the announcement yesterday."

Randall handed Jake a drink and offered a toast, "To your success, sir . . . "

Jake chuckled, and they sipped.

"Please, make yourself comfortable. How can I help you?"

"O.P.A.S. . . . I always wanted to visit here, and understand physics, but I don't think I ever will, really. I became a flatfoot in New York, you know. I worked my way up through the five boroughs."

Jake noticed the words etched on the rock wall, up to the right of the bar behind Randall and walked closer to read them.

"Interesting motto, *Hope and Love abide with all who believe. May we all believe in the future.* Is that your logo?"

"No, actually, that's quite an ancient art design. I think it was a family logo at one time. I just like the way it makes a rose from one continuous line. It reminds me of how successful and beautiful our efforts can be, if we just push on, step-by-step, steadfast. The words and flower were created almost a thousand years ago . . ." Randall walked over and stood beside Burns . . . "I had it etched there when I got this job. It's sort of my daily mantra."

"I see . . . Mr. Randall, how long have you been C.E.O. of O.P.A.S.?"

"A little over a year, now; why?"

"Do you remember an employee, Dr. Hamil G. Stevens?"

"Yes, he was quite favored, before he quit. He was pirated—stolen —by Time Travel, Inc. when they bought one of our old facilities, an older warehouse, really, with a smaller particle accelerator below it. The deal closed the first quarter I started."

"Smaller accelerator?"

"Mr. Burns, do you have any idea what we do?"

"Somewhat. You came from the famous Switzerland Complex, right? Company assets are roughly $160 trillion, up 12 percent in one year. You have invested heavily, not only in man's effort to find the answer to what makes up matter, but also in practical space exploration, fuel to run space stations and vehicular gyroscopes. The company also collaborated to keep our intercontinental transportation in tune, indirectly, of course. You yourself have published two dissertations in the last five years, each focusing on Brock's space mining—supplying fuels from the moon to Mars, as well as private sector travel. Of late, your investment firms, excuse me, angel investors, have collaborated with Mr. Charles Rosse to address and hopefully contract fixing the Bering Strait tunnel systems. You are quite the busy man, Mr. Randall."

"Well, thank you. Impressive knowledge to say the least, Inspector. You obviously know more about me than I do you. But I am still waiting for you to get to the point."

"To start with, I want to know about Marion Brock. How exactly are you and Mr. Rosse involved with him?"

Randall stood in front of the etched words, took a breath and then he turned, put his glass down and lit a cigar.

"Would you like one?"

"No, thanks."

"Mr. Burns, I first read those two sentences in a book that Charlie Rosse gave me long before I started here. Everything had been going wonderfully in my life. I am a very lucky man, so far. At the time, I had been involved with the two greatest discoveries mankind had ever made, The Sidron Examination and now here The Bridge Particle."

Jake interrupted, "Believe it or not, I know what Sidron is, go on."

"Ah, well then, the Sidron was first discovered centuries ago in, of all places, here in the United States . . . Who would have thought? Unfortunately, at that time, neither the mindset nor the technology were advanced enough to investigate it, so they suppressed the discovery and filed it for a later date. Recently, you must have heard, we found a new subatomic particle. We labeled it the Bridge because it pulses back and forth from one time to another. We are certain time travel is within our reach. Can you imagine? Anyway, Rosse and his group of companies offered me this position, specifically, to lead this company into the next great adventure, time travel."

"So Rosse owns controlling shares in O.P.A.S.?"

"It's a public company, but most shares are split between governments and some very powerful private sectors. Rosse is one of those, on the Board of Boards, you might say."

"Back to Stevens, please."

"Unfortunately, the man who had the hands-on experience in the research of time travel was, in fact, Stevens. He is a brilliant mind. Anyway, Rosse's interests pumped money into O.P.A.S. and the funding is building us the largest particle accelerator in the world, only 20 miles north of here. Also, we started constructing one in orbit, around Earth, to support our time travel efforts. We are one of only eight locations around the world that continues to investigate and proof particles, deep within the atom. Over centuries, particle accelerators have evolved from the linear to our new paddle design. It includes some rather plush living quarters.

"We are tweaking the finished construction; and plan to be on line within six months. We will change the world and our future."

"Very interesting, to say the least. I just need to ask you a few more questions, if you don't mind."

"Anyway, through merger and buyouts—the usual big money deals, O.P.A.S. sold the older local accelerator . . . "

"Can you tell me to whom and where it is?"

" . . . to the same outfit that pirated Stevens—Time Travel, Inc. That accelerator is located about 30-35 miles south of the city. Their research is supposed to be local, but I'm not sure of the specific address."

"Can you find out for me?"

"Randall pushed a button on the coffee table's display and his secretary answered, "Yes, sir?"

"Kate, do we have any old files on Hamil Stevens?"

"Perhaps, sir. You need a password, though."

"Send it to me."

"Yes, sir, on its way."

Jake's eyes perked up, "Your secretary has passwords?"

"Not quite. She has one to get into where I enter mine. Quite secure, I assure you."

Randall tapped a section of the tabletop, and it displayed a 3-D screen on his lap.

"There, now I do this, enter hers and then, here, mine and voila, Hamil Stevens."

A bust size model of Stevens appeared along with a flat display of his history and personnel file.

"There, Mr. Burns, read for yourself."

Burns did, "There is a mailing address here but no title to the location: 4822 S.P. Way, Seattle, Washington . . . nothing else, eh?"

"I'm afraid not. Everything we have is there before you."

"Well, that confirms it."

"What?"

"Brock and Rosse, they are so obvious. My bet is Stevens doesn't live at this address, either. But, I have to start somewhere. Thanks for your help, Mr. Randall."

"You are welcome, but exactly how do you know I'm not a bad guy and involved with Rosse or Brock?"

Burns smiled, as he put on his fedora, "Because, my dear fellow, I am a detective."

They shook hands, Jake turned to walk out, then he stopped and said, "One more thing, I checked your complete history up to our meeting. You are clean . . . oh, and I know the guy who wrote the words etched on your wall."

Jake tipped his hat and left.

"That's two more things," Randall chuckled.

Chapter 24

Time Travel, Inc.

JAKE'S CARRIER, MIRIAM, burrowed the short trip and docked at the Post Platform under Seattle's subway station, just off 15th Avenue. "We have arrived at destination, Jake Burns. Thank you for the most stimulating ride."

"Great. You're welcome."

"I have integrated into your Knofer, and will maintain security protocols."

"I have it covered, thanks."

"I will remain here for your return trip."

"I shouldn't be too long."

Jake exited the beast and took a bubble unit to the surface. Then, he hailed a taxi and rode to the address which Oscar Randall gave to him. When the cab stopped in front of Lucian High School, he sat in the back seat silent, perplexed.

"This is it," the cab driver said.

"Are you absolutely sure?"

"Yes, sir, I have picked up kids here, on occasion, and taken them home. Granted, it's very rare, but this is 4822 S. P. Way. It's the only one in the city."

Jake shook his head, wearing a frown; he paid the cabby, got out of the car and watched it drive away.

"Now what? I guess I'll talk to the principal."

৵৹৪০৫৶

Time Travel, Inc.'s facility housed four underground floors dedicated to research and administration. The mailing address was an old post office box to keep the would-be curious away.

"Hamil Stevens had a private experimental lab extending directly off the decoy surface building. His lab was completed within the last six months, specifically to accommodate secrecy regarding Semitri and any new particle discoveries. The lab looked more like a tomb in the Valley of the Kings.

৵৹৪০৫৶

Jake Burns entered the school and walked down the hallway past several classrooms. He stopped at one, briefly, to watch through the half glass door. A teacher was demonstrating a new tool, holding up a small Knofer-like object that projected holograms in front of each student. Each student began touching the holograms and giggling. One or two noticed Burns at the door. The teacher looked at him and stopped the lecture. Burns looked embarrassed and walked on. A sign and arrow guided him into the principal's office.

"Good morning, sir. May I help you?" one woman asked. She got up from her desk and walked to the chest-high counter where Burns stood. Burns removed his hat.

"Yes, please, I'd like to see your principal. It's a police matter."

"All right, I'll try and reach him. Frankly, I am not sure if he is still here. We only have three classes going on right now. Very different hours, since the new policies went into effect."

"I noticed one class as I was walking; why only three?"

The woman smiled kindly, and replied, "We are a special needs facility and cater to single parents with strange work hours." She leaned a bit over the counter toward Burns and whispered, "You understand."

As she did so, Jake noticed out the window, next to them, that a limo had just pulled up to a shed across the parking lot behind the school. He watched as the driver got out and opened the back door. Jake nodded and smiled to the woman. She went back to her desk and paged the principal. Burns couldn't believe his eyes. The figure of the man getting out of the limo was unmistakable. It was Marion Brock. Jake had no way of knowing it was really Clone-Brock. The billionaire nodded thanks to his driver and then quickly walked around the car into the common looking brick shed. It resembled a small, old garage. The limo sped off, and Burns thought, *A high school . . . brilliant! Why can't I think of things like this?*

He turned to the woman again. "Excuse me, ma'am, is that a garage or storage facility across the parking lot, over there?"

"Oh, we don't own that. It's not part of the school. I believe it's a storage unit for one of the houses down the block, I think; but don't quote me. Would you like some coffee, Mr.? I am sorry, I didn't catch your name."

"Jake Burns, ma'am. And yours?"

"Dolly," she giggled, "Dolly, Miss Dolly Waddel. I will try paging Mr. Tate again. He hasn't answered, yet."

Jake smiled and said, "That's all right, Dolly, tell him I was here and I will be back. I see I am running a little late. Thank you so much."

Burns tipped his hat, turned and quickly walked back to the school's front door and around to the back of the building. He carefully approached the shed. As he gripped the doorknob, he turned his Knofer on, initiating its Defense Mode's weapon system. Then, he entered, and just 10 feet inside a hallway veered to the right. It was a stairwell leading downward some 100 feet or more. He stepped cautiously, took out his Ever-Life standard air gun and pointed it straight ahead into the dimly lit concrete tunnel.

At the stairs' end, a ramp continued even further down. The light changed from purple to a red tint, and as he continued to walk, the lights went out behind him. Blackness seemed to force him forward.

The sound of his footsteps was the only thing he heard. After another 200 feet or so, Burns came to a door. To the right and left above him there were small tunnels extending into the walls. The normal eye would think the entire area was a sewage run off. He tried opening the door, but it wouldn't budge. There wasn't even a sound of a lock clicking as he pushed and pulled.

Fine, now what?

Jake turned around. There was no other possible way to go.

Well, I am not going back, so?

He put his Knofer on the floor. "Examine and display the door lock."

The Knofer ticked, and within seconds, it displayed a 3-foot holographic image of the lock mechanism.

"Can you disengage?"

Jake watched a red dot in the hologram move quickly all around the image. He heard several more ticking sounds, and then the hologram disappeared. He picked up the Knofer and turned the knob. The door opened.

Voila! I love this technology.

Jake walked into a large room, which was lighted in a bluish tint. He noticed on the wall next to the door an oval with three letters in it, T.T.I. *Time Travel, Inc., this is it.*

He looked to the right, and about 50 feet away was another room that stepped downward, yet again. *This place looks like a smaller version of Time Trust.*

Jake walked across the room and opened another door without difficulty. What he saw shocked him. It looked like a morgue, filled with bodies laying on gurneys. "There have to be 200 in here."

Burns lifted the sheet covering one. "Marion Brock?"

Then, he walked a few yards and lifted another, then another and another. "They're all the same. Christ!"

He got a sick feeling in the pit of his stomach. *They are not dead, but they're not breathing.*

He looked around at the dark room and ceiling lights. *This is where they are doing it.*

He noticed movement from the far side of the room and walked toward a wall of square glass cages. Each was sealed and housed a pristine environment inside, almost surgical. What he saw made Burns very uneasy.

"Bodies . . . writhing bodies."

Within each cage, a clone of Marion Brock lay on its back, writhing, stretching, groaning and growing fatter. Jake walked from cage to cage and finally stopped at the last one in disbelief. A duplicate body had grown up out of the other, a clone from a clone rising above itself, floating until identical twins faced each other.

Jake whispered to himself, "They didn't learn this from us."

"You are quite right," a voice said behind Burns. "We developed the technique ourselves. It's weightless in there, mimicking amniotic fluid."

Jake turned around, startled, and reached for his gun.

"No need for violence here. I am Dr. Hamil Stevens. I won't harm you."

He extended his hand, and after some hesitation, Burns shook it. They stood next to each other and watched the bodies detaching as Stevens spoke, "Quite something, isn't it?"

Burns took his hand off the gun and replied, "I have never seen anything like it. I had no idea technology like this existed."

"I don't mean to be impolite here, but, who are you, and how did you get in?"

"I am Jake Burns, Chief Inspector of the Arden City Police."

He showed Stevens his badge and continued questioning, "How long does the process take, anyway? How long does the one body suspend above the other like that?"

"The growing process is two days. Separation takes about an hour. When it is complete, the top one falls onto the bottom one. The collapse is what starts them breathing; much like a baby is stimulated to breathe in the final stages of labor."

Just as Stevens said it, the top one fell. Both clones jerked involuntarily and took breaths. Then, the bottom clone pushed the top one off.

"There, see? Perfect . . . "

"What if the fall doesn't start the breathing?"

"Well, then we don't have life, now do we?"

"So you discard them if there is no reaction from the fall?"

"Not really. A buzzer sounds in another room and technicians come in to try to revive each one. But frankly, that's rare. Anyway, we have plenty more, as you can see."

"So, how do you dispose of the bodies, if they don't come around?"

"Follow me, Mr. Burns. While I'd love to share all our secrets, you are not supposed to be here."

"Actually, I got this address from your old company. Oscar Randall gave it to me. He said some very complimentary things about you and your time discoveries."

"Oh, are you interested in time travel?"

"Yes, very."

"Are you here because of clones or time?"

"Both, really, I am a detective investigating Mr. Marion Brock."

"Marion, he is eccentric, I'll give you that; but hardly worth a detective's investigation. In fact, he's due here any time. I have to run some medical tests on him. We think he was affected by a time test we ran yesterday."

"Exactly how long have you been cooped in here?"

"This place is self sufficient. I really don't leave unless I have to. Recent experiments require my complete attention. Here we are." They had walked out of the one room, down the hall and into another. "Policy dictates I keep this door locked. Please, come in."

"But policy says you can let a stranger in, just because he shows a badge?"

Stevens chuckled, "Not quite; you see, the sensors during our walk here rendered all of your communications and any weapons ineffective. You are quite harmless, unless you wish a physical confrontation."

They walked into a very high tech room, reminding Burns again of one of the Time Trust labs.

"Impressive, what is all this?'

"Without giving away every secret, I can tell you it's a time travel laboratory. The chamber is to the left, around there."

Burns gave a cursory look and asked, "So how does it work, really—time travel I mean?"

"There is no way I can explain it so you will understand, completely."

"I think I can safely say I'm qualified to hear your spiel."

"I would be of no use if I told it all, now would I? But, the short version goes something like this. You stand in the chamber, and sensors calculate the number of sub particles that make up your body."

"So, they don't count cells or molecules; they count particles?"

"Right, actually sub particles."

"That's a lot of stuff; there are trillions of cells alone in the human body."

"Yes, unimaginable numbers . . . hence the need for accuracy; so the equipment is highly sensitive, very difficult to build, and expensive."

"Hence the need for you, Dr. Stevens . . . "

"I like to think so."

" . . . and I take it, one is naked in the chamber?"

"Yes, and everything is sterile. Anyway, I designed the equipment. There is nothing like it anywhere, really. Once we have an accurate calculation, it all takes place automatically. All I do is push this, here. I've set the chamber's next user destination. It's ready to go."

"Where is he going and who is the user?"

"First, there has to be compatibility genetically, in order to displace the sub particle mix and be able to travel on the time road to whenever. As to who is going, why, Mr. Brock, I presume."

"Interesting word, compatibility; what if the genetic mix isn't there?"

"I wouldn't activate the chamber; otherwise whatever particles displaced wouldn't reverse and replace themselves in the same order."

Jake scratched his head and said, "What, come again?"

Stevens was on a roll. "Just look at this. It is a communication device that Marion gave to me. It has a record of our first test patient's information in it."

Stevens showed Jake a Knofer. Jake took it and asked, "What is it? A phone?"

"Not at all; Marion calls it his new V.A.D.—a Video Audio Device. I was able to input our test case's data from it, and I programmed the chamber, but something else triggered. The chamber started on its own. Something else must have occurred. The chamber just shut down. All activity ceased. We can't get that chamber to operate now."

"What was your power source?"

"Interesting you ask. Marion controls one himself, and I have discovered something brand new, a combination of electrical power from a latitudinal network, brand new to us. Believe it or not, I followed magnetic particle charges to the great pyramids around the world. I have a focused recovery monitor and discharge control, right over here . . . The combination of Marion's inputs and my new pyramid charges have made the difference in capacity. However, even though we have no proof, all the monitors there recorded an event take place—several, as a matter of fact. Look here. I have never seen anything like it . . . and here, I can only call this an anomaly, some sort of time distortion.

"Wait a minute. How can you say someone travelled in time, if he didn't show up in that booth? Doesn't the traveler have to be where this equipment is?"

"Yes, I always thought so, too, but, as it turns out, now I'm not sure. It's very interesting, although unexplainable at the moment. You see, just before I came here, at O.P.A.S. we made a discovery. We always knew sub particles could be in two places at the same time. We needed to figure out how to read the construct record of the subject and determine how to transmit. Once at a destination—a different time, a reverse reconstruction should take place, especially using our knowledge of cloning."

"How?'

"At one end is the construct— the subject to travel. We send the construct's information, by electromagnetic forces, through a sort of wire, and then we re-grow the sub particles just like the clones you saw out there. You've seen science fiction movies, right?"

Jake smiled. "Yes, it sounds simple enough, but what wire does the signal go through?"

"Long ago, scientists discovered the wire, so to speak. They called it the Sidron. All sub particles of everything travel on it. We just had to find out how to connect to it, plug into it."

"And, how did you do that?"

"Well, I discovered a few things at O.P.A.S., and they led us to an almost there scenario. Then, the bottom dropped out. The company needed money and new direction. They hired Oscar Randall, and I got a better offer. Here I am."

"So, you finished the experiments?"

"Not quite. Marion contracted with a very smart doctor, who found several new aspects to duplicating the construct. He discovered that man's memory or personality coagulates in one place, after death. He called it C.P.T.—Chemical Personality Transfer. That was quite a bump in the road for us, a slow down, at any rate."

"Why?"

"If we could pin down its location and measure it properly, we could reconstruct a person's memory and guarantee the same person is reconstructed at the destination. If we do that, all travel would be revolutionized, along with medical science and healthcare."

Jake found a lab chair and sat down, listening in disbelief.

"So, what happened?"

"Well, we needed the formula for C.P.T. Marion guaranteed me he could get it. After all, he was a partner with the doctor, and he was part owner of the Medical Complex where they kept the formula. He said he would get it personally. Unfortunately, the man who we picked as our first subject was arrested for murder, and the formula disappeared. We input all the information we could regarding the subject's construct to see if we could run the first test; but it failed. We didn't even have a reading in the equipment. That is when Marion brought me this."

Stevens opened a drawer and handed Jake a spinal bound book. Jake read the first page, "Particle Displacement, use of the Sidron by Dr. Jack Avuar Sheldon . . . holy crap."

"It's very thorough, but incomplete."

"The last pages are missing? I don't understand. Mr. Stevens, you know there was a Sidron event, right?"

"Actually, I needed the rest of the pages to answer that question. After all, I am a scientist."

"So Marion Brock stole the papers, but didn't get the last pages?"

"Stole? Hardly. As I said, he partnered with a research specialist to bring life back from death. Over here I have the contract." Stevens walked across the room and picked up what looked like a stack of legal documents stapled together. "Here, look at this."

Jake took the papers and read the first page.

"Look at the last page, Mr. Burns."

Jake flipped to the end and read, "Do not use electricity, use the . . . . there is nothing after that."

"Go back and look at page 2."

Jake flipped back to the second page, which read in bold type:

Property in Partnership as developed by Dr. Jack Avuar Sheldon
And financed by
Mr. Marion Brock, Brock Companies Worldwide

Jake's jaw dropped. "There are two signatures here, Dr. Jack Sheldon and Marion Brock."

"I know, and they are originals, not copies. However, as you can see, the last pages are missing in both the treatise and the contract. Dr. Sheldon owes us those pages."

"My God!"

Jake got weak in the knees and sat down. "I don't believe it. It can't be true. You're good Mr. Stevens, you are very good."

Stevens approached Burns and looked Jake straight in the eyes. "I don't particularly care if you believe me, or not; but, it is true. What do you think? I knew you were coming, or in case some stranger broke in here, I'd keep a copy of that to convince you it was true? Come on, detective, I am not that clever when it comes to this. All I want is to finish my job. I was sure the last pages would solve the puzzle, that's all."

"You must know that your testing has caused havoc within both the Sidron and in time."

"I think Mr. Brock may be linked to it somehow; I don't know how, though. Thank God I have another chamber. I talked to Mr. Brock. He said he was bringing a much more reliable source of energy. He is due anytime. Actually, I thought you were him."

ᔦ᠂ᏰᎧᏀᏯᏋ᠂ᔧ

Meanwhile, miles below Earth, as Allenfar swam toward the northwestern United States, from Time Trust in Giza, GGM Mathew Bellos studied his Knofer, along with the recordings sent to him by Abby Johnson and Jake Burns.

"Allenfar, I need to speak with Tyree Master."

CHAPTER 25

JACK IN RIO

JACK SHELDON AND ABBY JOHNSON SAT in the Ever-Life jet on a private airfield, just north of the great Christ statue in Rio de Janeiro. Only the front of the statue remained since the terrorist wars ended. It became a reminder to the world of what happened there. The Portuguese were instrumental in changing the tide of the bombings. As a result, the Brock companies invested heartily in the people of Rio.

Jack's phone rang, and as he reached for it, Abby grabbed his arm. "Before you answer, remember, keep your head."

"Are we set?"

"Yes, we are."

Jack lifted the phone to his ear and started walking down the outside stairs of the plane.

"Hello."

"Hello, Dr. Sheldon."

"Yes?"

"Do you have what we asked for?"

"Where is my wife?"

"Do you see a car coming toward you?"

"Yes, I see it."

The phone went dead. A brown four-door sedan drove up and stopped at the bottom of the plane's staircase. A large ugly man, with what looked like one eyebrow across his forehead, got out of the front door passenger side and opened the rear door for Jack. The doctor stared at the man as if he'd never seen anyone like him, and then, Jack got in the back seat. Sitting next to him was a small figure of a man.

"Hello, Doctor; my name is Rash InVoy."

He extended his hand, but Jack wasn't playing politely.

"I have heard of you. You are Marion Brock's henchman."

InVoy smiled. "Actually I am his Chief of Staff. I see you want to get right to it. Fine. Did you bring the last pages?"

"Chief of Staff, ha! You people think he's president of some country."

"Perhaps even many countries . . . did you bring the papers, or not?"

Jack was obviously angry and had to keep from striking out. "Here's how this is going to work. The pages you want are on a chip, which is directly linked to my brain through this phone. If you don't give me my wife or if you harm either one of us in anyway, the information will self-destruct. My phone is tied to my retinal print, my finger print and a password."

"Hmm, interesting threat, all I want are the pages, the right pages. We have methods of checking their accuracy. It's simple. I will take you to your wife; you give me the pages. If they verify, you both may leave. If the information is in any way false, you both die."

InVoy smiled, turned his head and looked out the window, as the car sped off.

Back in the plane, Abby Johnson tracked Jack on her Knofer. It recorded and replayed the conversation between Jack and InVoy. She sent the recording to Jake Burns and to the GGM. Then, she deployed two Carriers to follow the GPS signals and to be available at a moment's notice. After setting her Knofer to defense protocol, she deplaned and drove far enough behind InVoy's car to assure no detection.

InVoy was a shrewd character and naturally provocative. "Did you know, Doctor, this was once a great seaport, as well as quite a playground for the rich and famous?"

"Talk to me when you give me my wife."

"I see no reason to be uncivilized or impolite. We will both leave here with what we want, if you keep your end of the bargain. Perhaps you two may even decide to stay and enjoy the city life."

"I doubt it."

"Rio de Janeiro—marvelous city, home of Carnival de Brazil, festival of festivals; you must have heard of it . . . read about it . . . all the unimaginable costumes, ladies running in the streets, sex everywhere, ha! What a life . . . unfortunately, also great cover for the terrorists."

"Yeah, I heard about all of it. So, terrorists bombed and killed millions. Now you have it. I don't see any difference."

"This was the Pearl Harbor of terror . . . and yes, that made possible our acquisition of many companies down here. But, we brought their economy back from anarchy."

"Why don't you just shut up? Or tell me what flea infested hole you're taking me to."

"Ah, far be it from me to put your wife up in a flea infestation. We are going to the Copacabana Palace of Palaces, my friend, the best of the best. We rebuilt it after the wars."

Abby Johnson's Knofer recorded and sent the coordinates of the Palace to Jake Burns and the armed Ever-Life Security Team, inside one of Carriers. They reached the Corcodova station within 10 minutes and were on their way to the Palace before Jack arrived.

In the car, InVoy was dripping with arrogance and ego. "Look at that crowd, Jack, everywhere, people. Everyone is so cramped down here now, all we have to do is smile at them and they beg for whatever will lift their spirits."

"You mean you sell them drugs. I thought Brock was out of that."

"He is, as far as I know."

InVoy took a wad of rolled $1000bills out of his pocket, waved it at Jack and said, "You have to know what people really want, my friend. Watch this . . . Keith, pull over and stop."

InVoy rolled the back seat window down and called to a group of young people, in Portuguese, "Hey, you there . . . yes, you! All of you . . . come here." He stuck his head out, just enough, so they could see his face with sunglasses on. "You want to make a lot of money?"

Of the six who came over, there were two men and four women. They each nodded yes.

"Are you all related?"

They said no.

"This is $100,000 cash. That's $16,500 for each of you."

One of the girls asked, "What do you want us to do, have sex?"

"Yes," InVoy replied, "but with each other . . . right here, right now. What do you say?"

One girl turned and examined the others. "Sure, why not? What do you all say?"

"Give us the money!"

InVoy giggled at them and turned to Jack. "You see, my friend, down here money buys anything."

Jack didn't flinch. "Either let me out or take me to my wife, you pig."

InVoy shouted at Keith, "*Vamos*—we go!"

Fifteen minutes later, after driving through various streets and along a beach road, the car pulled up to the Copacabana Palace of Palaces.

"Here we are, my friend. Feast your eyes . . . you, come with me."

Little did InVoy know that Johnson and her team were in place to follow the little snake to his lair. There were 10 in the team, all inconspicuously dressed. Four at the front door entrance, two at the main elevators, two patrolling the outside back and two on the roof. Jack had no idea he had support, until, as they lead him across the lobby, he noticed Abby, herself, sitting facing the check-in desk. He tried not to react, but he looked surprised for just one fleeting second.

That was all the reaction InVoy's fat man guard had to see. Jack barely flinched, nothing the normal eye would catch, but to the trained mercenary, it was more than enough. In an instant, the guard focused on Abby. He reached for his pistol and pointed it at Jack's head. "Allright, you there! You, girl! Stand up! Stand up or so help me, he's dead, and so is the wife!"

InVoy turned, as Abby stood, and one of her team reacted from the elevators. He yelled, "Fire!"

InVoy's guard turned and saw Abby's man. At that second, a different Ever-Life man at the front door pulled his gun as well and fired at InVoy, the guard and Jack. The airburst hit them all, and the three went down fast; but the fat man pulled the trigger of his automatic weapon, as he fell. Bullets spit out everywhere. The desk clerk was hit, and as InVoy's guard hit the floor, his gun shot toward Abby. It was over in three seconds. Then, the screaming started. People ran in all directions away from the lobby. Two more Ever-Life men ran in from outside. They grabbed the shooter, tied his hands behind him and helped Jack to his feet.

"Wait, wait!" Jack yanked free and turned to see InVoy was face down. Jack bent down and turned him over only to see his belly gutted from the shots.

InVoy flopped into Jack's lap as his innards splashed all over. But, he was conscious enough to say, "Too late my friend . . . " InVoy opened Jack's hand, and placed a two-inch round wad of money in his palm. A key slipped out from the center of the roll. Then, the Chief of Staff, henchman of Marion Brock, stared into nothing. He was dead. Jack gently laid his head back onto the floor and stood up, looking at the money and key, with a twisting sick feeling in his stomach.

"Sir! Here, over here, it's Ms. Johnson."

Jack rushed across the room to her. She lay on the lap of the Team Commander. She was clearly hit in the heart. Jack took the man's hand and put it on the wound. "Press hard, here! Abby, Abby, can you hear me?"

She opened her eyes. "It's okay, do you know where Rachel is?"

"Hang on, stay with me."

"Ask for Rosse, Charlie Rosse. Don't forget the . . . " She looked at Jack with a dead stare. She was gone, too. The Commander looked up and spoke quickly.

"Sir, we will clean up here. You go with those three and find your wife. I'll meet you back at the rendezvous point, the station under the statue. I'll have a car for you in the back of the hotel . . . Sergeant Strom, stick with the doctors. You get them back to the Carriers."

"Yes, sir."

Jack kissed Abby's forehead and then got up. They all heard sirens, as Jack took one last look at Abby.

"Come on, sir, we have to go."

Jack studied the key in his hand and read the tiny red-etched word on it, "*Base* . . . what is this? What do you make of this, Strom?"

The Sergeant looked and shook his head. "I don't know . . . Base . . . maybe basement?'

"Christ, we have no time."

As pandemonium reigned in the lobby, the three ran to an elevator, entered, and Jack pushed B on the panel. When the door opened, Jack was ready to jump out, but the guards held him back. Strom shushed him and looked carefully. "Nothing but the laundry staff wearing those silly head-nets.

"Even if there was anyone here," Jack said, "we couldn't hear them over the sound of those washers and dryers."

"Come on, let's go. Easy, Doctor, you stay between us."

They walked down the hallway about 50 feet to another door. Strom tried the knob; it was locked. He looked at Jack and said, "You don't think?"

Jack took the key out, stuck it in the door and twisted the knob; it opened

The sergeant looked through and saw a man halfway down the hall closing another door. As their eyes met, the man froze, and then ran the other way leaving the door opened.

"After him!" Strom said.

One guard ran after the man, while Strom, Jack and the other guard walked into a dimly lighted room.

"Holy shit! What the hell is this?" Strom said.

Jack walked in behind him. "It's a lab; a fully loaded lab, at that."

They studied the room. There were instruments rivaling those at the Complex. In the far corner, they saw a gurney with a light over it shining on what looked like a woman's body.

"Christ!" Jack ran to her. "It's Rachel! Help me!"

She was barely breathing, and clothed in nothing but a hospital gown. Three needles stuck in her, one in each arm and one in her neck. Jack quickly checked her vitals.

"What the hell are they doing to her? She is alive, thank God. Hold her while I get these out."

At that point, the third guard came back. "He's gone, sir, disappeared."

Strom gestured, "Quickly, help us here!"

Jack rushed around the room looking for anything medical that could help. "Damn, where do they keep the good stuff? What a shithole."

He noticed several pieces of glass on the floor, blue glass. He bent down to pick one up and there it was; a corked, small two-inch blue vial that he couldn't mistake. He picked it up and studied it, but he didn't notice the figure standing at the door with a gun.

"Yes, Jack, it's a vial, like your magic potion, but enhanced. Stop! All of you! I am a pretty good shot. Stay calm, and you all might live through this."

"Rosse, you bastard! Let me tend to my wife."

"First things first, my friend. Get over there with them."

"What have you done to her?"

"Did you bring the papers, Jack? A deal is a deal. Give them to me and she's yours."

"Fine, I have to reach in my pocket; they're in my phone."

Rosse pointed, "Over there, yes there, it's a printer. Get going or I kill her."

Jack moved to the equipment, took his phone out, verified the retina scan and pointed it toward the port. "This thing is ancient. It probably doesn't even work."

"You let me worry about that. Do it Jack. Transfer the pages...I need them in black and white." Jack pushed a phone key and a page printed, then another, and finally a third.

"Hand them to me, Jack."

Rosse grabbed them out of his hand and slowly backed up to the desk in the middle of the room. On it was a cylinder, sitting vertically, roughly 12 inches high, with characters on the side. He pressed several, and a display on the top read, *Insert.*

Rosse fed the papers into a slit on the side and then turned to Jack. "Now we wait."

It seemed like hours to the Doctor. Finally, the cylinder beeped, and the display read, Confirmed, proceed.

The cylinder did not spit out the papers; rather it displayed the message: *Self destruct in five minutes.*

Rosse looked at Jack and smiled, "Thanks, Jack, you can keep the vial. She's all yours."

Then, he backed out the door, pointing the gun at Rachel, and slammed it shut behind him.

Jack ran to Rachel. Two guards ran to the door. "It's locked!"

"Sir, she's alive, but in a coma. Look at her neck."

"They were experimenting. Christ! We have to get her back to the Complex, fast."

Strom took his Knofer out, requested escape directions and the team's car. The Knofer displayed a model of the palace and notified one of the team guards of the exit location. Then, Strom turned to the doctor. "Jack, the door . . . the bastard locked it."

They both thought the same thing. Jack took the key out again and ran to the door, "Bring her!"

They all took a breath as Jack stuck the key in and turned the knob. The door opened. He held it for the guards carrying Rachel. Strom went next. "My guess is we follow Rosse's exit. We can't go back the way we came, the lobby will be filled with police. Let's go!"

They ran as quietly and quickly as they could, up the narrow staircase and exiting to the alley behind the palace. An Ever-Life crewmember waited in a car to take them all to the Carrier rendezvous station.

CHAPTER 26

MARSHALL'S REVENGE

IN THE BASEMENT of the Arden City Courthouse, Angie Bellos and Brian Sheldon were about to be escorted back up the stairs by the jailer. Halfway up, they all heard the scream.

"YOU FUCKING BASTARDS . . . LET ME OUT! BROCK! I AM GOING TO KILL YOU!"

Then they heard a crowd of cellmates yelling and banging on the doors. The guard turned and rolled his eyes. "It's that shit, Marshall, again. He provokes everybody. I hope he gets the chair."

Angie was quick to reply, "Excuse me, I am his niece. I've come to see him for the last time. Maybe I can quiet him before he drives you all crazy."

As her eyes filled with tears, the guard looked at her and said, "I have never seen you here before. He knows you?"

"I have been overseas. This is my friend. He is a lawyer. I wanted to see Davy before the verdict. I have to leave for the airport. I won't be able to see him, otherwise. Please, I just want to say hello and goodbye, give him a hug. I can quiet him. Really."

Marshall let out another wail and the three of them looked at each other.

"That bastard. Sorry, miss, he has been a thorn in my side ever since he came here. How can you stand to be related?"

"Please, it's just to say hello and goodbye, really."

The guard thought and sighed, and finally, during another yell, he agreed. They walked into the jailhouse to Marshall's 6 by 9 foot cell. "I have a surprise for you, Mr. Marshall."

He opened the cell door, and Marshall made eye contact with Angie. "Christ, it's you! What the hell are you doing here?"

The guard seemed protective and spoke for her, "Be decent, or I'll beat you to a pulp. She came to visit . . . you've got 15 minutes, young lady. Call me if you want out earlier."

Angie and Brian walked in and the guard closed the door. Marshall sat on the cot and quizzed Angie. "I never expected to see you. Your boss, Swanson, said he would see me again. Are you here for him?"

"No, I am here for me. I don't even know where to start or if anything I say will mean anything to you."

"Well, I have time. They don't take me upstairs for the verdict for a while."

Angie sat down next to him, while Brian stood uneasily at the cell door.

"I'm not sure where to begin . . . "

"Oh, just tell him, babe . . . she thinks she was transported back in time and is stuck in some time warp here. She thinks it happened here in the courthouse. So, we are here to find out where. There. Was that so hard?"

Marshall stood up, listening intently. He paced and then looked at Angie. "Christ, it does work . . . but, why are we here?"

Angie interrupted him, "What are you saying? You know about it? Tell me, tell me what's going on!"

Marshall was quick to reply, "You two shouldn't even be allowed in here. The fact that the guard let you in with me should tell you things are not what they should be here." He went to the wall and stood inches away from it, staring at it. Angie could hear him say, "D.M.006004."

As he did so, Brian whispered to Angie, "Jesus, this guy is really something; he has a voice print safe in his cell."

Marshall pressed his fingers to the wall and turned them in a circular motion. A small door, 9 x 12 inches, appeared and clicked open. He reached inside and took out two Knofers. He held one in each hand and turned to face the two young people.

Angie said, "How did you get those?"

"They are my insurance policy, girl. Sit down and be quiet."

"But, I thought you were a prisoner here, brought by Mr. Burns. How did you get those?"

"Now, be very careful how you answer me, young lady. If you play games, I'll see to it you stay with me here forever. You wouldn't want that, now would you?"

Brian stood against the cell bars and had to face outside to hide his rage. Angie simply replied, "No, I wouldn't. Tell me what you know, and I'll do everything I can with the GGM."

"Ha! *GGM* . . . you don't get it. These little gadgets are my ticket out of here. Fuck your GGM! I had these programmed long before the morgue murders. I gave samples to Brock so he would get me out, so I would be free of that hellhole. These things have a defense protocol, you know, which will bring us home from wherever we are; and that includes whatever time we may be in. Don't you see, all we have to do is take them apart, duplicate the science and voila! A time travel gizmo."

"But they're programmed to Ever-Life citizens. You're not one. Those won't function."

"Well, none of us can function without money, luv. At least that is what I told Brock. If he doesn't get me out soon, I have a special present for him. He is tied to me, no matter where I am. His little toys won't function the way he thinks. These are my insurance to get me out."

Brian couldn't control himself. "You're insane, you bastard!" He lunged at Marshall, pushed him hard and they fell against the wall. Angie moved quickly to the cell door, away from them. Brian grabbed Marshall's throat with both hands and screamed, "You fucking bastard, you killed my dad."

Angie screamed in a whisper, "Brian, stop it! Stop it!"

But, he only heard his own shouting. Marshall thrust his two hands upward between Brian's and broke his grip. Then, he struck out. Brian fell on the mattress and Marshall jumped on him. Angie leapt toward Marshall, expecting to land on him, but that didn't happen. She landed in her own bed, back in her apartment, with the covers over her. She flung the covers off and, this time, Brian wasn't there. She looked around in a panic and focused on the clock. It was 7 a.m. again. The anomaly lasted only two hours. It was shorter this time. It took her several minutes to collect her thoughts.

"Holy crap, I've got to get to the courthouse and find that sweet-spot."

CHAPTER 27

THE FATHERS' RETURN

THE THREE FATHERS LAY IN A TIME TRAVEL CARRIER, riding on a wave in the Sidron highway. But they were not in the arms of tentacles, as they were when they left Dr. Bellos' office. Now they were lying on padded lounges, next to each other. Each man slowly opened his eyes. A stranger of average height and weight stood before them.

He smiled and gestured, saying, "Hello, my friends. Welcome back. You have been resting for some time by my calculations. Do you remember what you saw?"

James was the first to speak. He sat up slowly and surveyed the empty room. "We saw the prophet, our teacher, Moses!"

Ahmir sighed, reacting, "Allah be praised, we saw the one true prophet, Mohammed; blessed be him who believes."

Kristos stood up and said calmly, "Same old, same old; we saw them both. We saw our Lord and Savior, as he willed us to. Who are you, and where are we?"

"I am a man as you see me; however, I am in truth, but a representation of this vessel you ride within."

James politely asked, "And why are we all here? Dr. Bellos said we would return to his office."

"What happened back in that cave?" Kristos asked.

"So much for the unity you conspired to achieve. You each saw something different I take it? I wonder what you heard. Let me explain a few things, which perhaps you can agree on. I represent this vehicle—a species, which is quite different from yours, in many respects. On the other hand, we are also quite similar in some."

Ahmir interrupted, "What do you mean . . . you are a representation of this vehicle? This was a statue. Then it became a transport, right? A Carrier, Dr. Bellos said."

"That is correct. I am a solid projection, given by the Carrier. We, unlike you, are a hive mindset—a collective consciousness, if that helps you understand. My name, in your language, is Tyree Master. A variation of this image is what we use when appearing to your kind. I contain and express the will and thoughts of our entire species."

The fathers studied the stranger. "And, what exactly is going on?" Kristos insisted.

"Before you leave our hospitality and end your trip, we have several questions and observations to share. Please, may I proceed?"

The fathers nodded.

"We are most curious why you negotiated with Mr. Marion Brock in the first place?"

Kristos offered, "*We* did not. I did. I was foolish to believe his parlor tricks, or to think any scientific explanation could prove God's power on Earth. I accept the responsibility."

"You miss my point . . . let's say you succeeded with Mr. Brock. Would the rest of your kind unite, as you planned, and accept one major religion?"

Kristos turned aside to think, while James replied, "I would have, knowing what I knew then, but now, no . . . And I believe none of us can speak for any other. What we believe is a matter of individual choice. Our kind has laws, which we must follow; short of that, we have free will to act and believe what we choose."

Then, Kristos added, "And it is our 'free will', our different choices that bind us when dire threats or fear overcome us."

Ahmir stepped directly in front of the stranger and said, "For God is One; and we are too, as mankind, when we need to be."

The stranger grinned. "And so it is. That is what makes you so different from us. We are of one mind." The Tyree Master walked a few feet away and the three fathers watched as a table appeared out of nowhere. He opened a drawer, took out several papers and handed them to Kristos. "Are these yours?"

Kristos read the first few lines and replied, "How did you get these? I wrote these before I met with Brock."

"We have monitored and helped many surface people over the centuries. Your kind has killed most of them. The point is, you have been contemplating for a long time how to stop the killing, haven't you?"

The man reached in the drawer again and handed duplicate copies of Kristos' notes to the other two clergy.

Kristos said, "Yes, at that time, my thinking was if we could discuss the root causes of our differences, we could compromise and stop terrorist acts. But, the more I thought, the more I became convinced that my compromising would never be accepted as doctrine. Only proof would be accepted. So, when Brock approached me, I negotiated with him."

The stranger gestured to them all, "Read the pages."

The three examined Kristos' handwritten notes.

Goal: Unity-One Faith

Basic Challenges:

1] Argument regarding the name of God:
Examples: Jesus [Christian name for the Lord God in man]; YHWH [Jewish name for God]; Allah [Islamic word for God]

Christianity *defines Jesus as a man and as Divine, God in three persons, 1] God, the Father, 2] God, the Son, 3] God, the Holy Spirit; The Holy Trinity . . . according to other faiths, Christianity pluralizes the word, God . . .*

Suggested pamphlet for dispersing, using Brock Network:

God made Himself a man to reconcile Himself with men who choose to be apart from God. In human form, as his Son, He could a] directly communicate with men; b] would show people who He is, what He is capable of, and take responsibility for giving man free will to be apart; c] God, Himself, would pay for man's iniquities - repeated sins. God would no longer punish humankind; rather, He would allow them back with Him by grace - his gift of unmerited favor; d] All men would have to do is choose to believe in Him - Worship. The sins of men are the result of free will, given by God in the first place. So, by example, because men have been incapable of understanding their plight, God would pay a ransom to Himself, and allow men to witness it; e] Men, witnessing the horror and willingness of sacrificing a father's son, in favor of all other humanity would surely make man return to Him. Moreover, Men would witness the Resurrection of His Son-Himself, showing that God has the Love and power to do anything; f] It had become evident that because of man's free will and selfish nature, only impressing mankind would persuade him back to God; and g] Finally, God would show humanity what life is like with, and without Him . . . Choose wisely.

• *Judaism* and *Islam* *reject a pluralistic definition-word for God. Contrary to Christianity, whether in Arabic, Hebrew, or any other language, they define their 'word for God' to mean ONE.*

• *In* *Islam*, *it was sinful, reprehensible, shameful and discreditable to identify the Creator in any sense other than the ONE, Almighty-Allah . . . all men are equal to each other, none to God. Men are born, live and die. It is written that Jesus was a great prophet, given power to do what he did, by Allah; but he was a man, and died as a man. Allah cannot die. To say Jesus is God means the Christian God died and is to say he was not God in the first place.*

2] Argument of Idolatry: To many **Muslims** *and* **Jews**, *Christianity has idols, representing man and woman, which are to be worshiped, such as figures, or statues of Jesus, Mary, the Saints, the Cross . . . etc. Judaism and Islam have no idols of any kind. To them, no person should be worshipped or bowed before. Pray only to the unnamed almighty ONE.*

Ahmir was the first to remark, "This is not new. For centuries now, we have respected each other's differences, and we all translate or interpret words between languages differently. The Terrorist War stopped long ago."

Kristos was quick to remind him, "Yes, the war stopped, but not the killing. Each of us is bound by our doctrine to bring peace to our brothers. These are just my notes. I tried again to explain the truth as I knew it. When Brock approached me, I was convinced proving the resurrection would unite us all. I knew it!"

Ahmir replied, "You didn't want to unite us. You wanted to convince us!"

The stranger listened, as their arguing intensified, and then, he interrupted, "You call this peace? You can't even convince each other."

The three fathers stopped.

"You three were given a great gift today in what you witnessed and who you met. My kind has no choices about such things. I speak for all of us, in all matters. Do you really think having a hive mindset about God is the answer?"

The three men looked at each other, and James quoted a platitude, "My God, our God, one God; all things are possible through Him."

Ahmir sat down on a lounge. "So, if Allah can put himself in the Quran, in a sunset, in nature, in life, surely he can put himself in a man. Allah can do what he wishes."

"Yes," Kristos said, "if we look carefully, we can see a little of Him in all of us. He can put his Divine in anything he chooses . . . even in a hive mindset."

The three fathers stood together and stared at the stranger.

The room began to flicker, and suddenly, light exploded. The three blinked and covered their eyes. When they gathered their senses, they were standing firmly next to each other around the coffee table in Bellos' office suite. There on the table lay the white book given to Kristos by *S*. Sticking out of one end, between its pages, was a folded piece of paper. Ahmir pulled it out and gave it to Kristos, who opened it and read the short note out loud:

> *My Brothers,*
>
> *To say you love someone and then demand, 'if you don't do as I say, I will have nothing to do with you,' negates choice and contradicts love. God reconciled Himself to man .*
>
> *. . help your brothers reconcile themselves to one another, and interact in like, respecting and accepting your differences.*
>
> *S*

James reached down, picked up the book and looked at it. Tears filled his eyes and he gave it to Ahmir. Ahmir held it with both hands and looked at the other two priests. Then, after a moment, without a word, he placed it back down on the table.

Kristos sighed and said, "Shall we go?"

Together, the three walked up the foyer steps. Kristos opened the door, smiled, and the three fathers walked out.

CHAPTER 28

BROCK REVEALED

INSIDE THE LAB of Time Travel, Inc., Hamil Stevens continued to enlighten Jake Burns by answering every question posed. Jake had pushed his Knofer and it should have recorded and transmitted the complete conversation to GGM. Stevens held back nothing; it was almost as if Jake were a new hire listening to an educational seminar.

"Mr. Burns, you probably noticed, I don't talk to many people in this job."

"I must admit, you are quite free with details. I didn't expect that."

"I want you to know something else."

Stevens walked across the room and picked up a metal cylinder. He brought it back to Burns and set it on its end. "Actually, these came in not long before you got here. Now, watch. I push this; read the display."

" . . . Sheldon papers . . . "

The slit on the side pushed out three pages, which Stevens handed to Burns.

"Here, look. I made minor corrections to Chamber 2 based on these; however, we haven't tested it yet. We needed an increase in the energy pattern—the power, so Marion is bringing a booster."

"Booster?"

"Yes, his other power source."

"Christ, these are Jack's last pages. Brock went back in time to get another compatible party—Nicolas, it has to be Nicolas from 1965. When is your boss due back?"

That was when another voice spoke behind Jake, "Actually, I can tell you that. You do go on, Stevens, sometimes too much, I'm afraid; and who is this?"

Jake got up and turned to see the impressive figure of Marion Brock [it was really the mad clone]. Jake instinctively began to reach for his gun, but he stopped short.

Clone-Brock just grinned and said, "I am afraid your little gadgets won't work in here. Didn't Stevens tell you?"

He extended his hand and waited for Burns. Jake took a deep breath, smiled and said, "I am Jake Burns."

Then, he shook his hand, feeling a vice for a grip.

"Welcome, Mr. Burns. You are just in time for my little surprise."

Without a word, as smooth as a quick draw artist in the Old West, Jake pulled his air gun, pointed it at Brock and fired, but nothing happened. "Hmm, well you can't blame me for trying, eh?"

"I don't blame you at all. Now that you have seen this much, and I don't doubt Stevens here has brought you up to date. Would you care to see something that may enlighten you even more?"

"You know, I can't let you continue all this."

"Please . . . Jake, is it? I know you will appreciate, and probably react a little differently, when you see what I have to show you. This way . . . Stevens, lead on. Mr. Burns, you are from down under, are you not?"

"Yes, I've come to see if we can negotiate something."

"I do love a challenge; if you know anything about me, it's that I do negotiate. Were you raised in the caverns?"

"I was a cop in New York City."

"Interesting; you're not indigenous to the colonies, then? I always thought it was a private club."

As Stevens opened another door, he asked Burns, "So how did you find us, anyway?"

"It's the detective in me, I guess. It wasn't that difficult; and, I have friends of a different kind."

Brock chuckled, "So, we have something in common; interesting."

As the three walked into another large clean room, Burns studied the layout and saw another chamber. Brock couldn't resist the urge to brag. "How do you like it all? It's my pride and joy. The lab was built by the greatest minds of our time, no disrespect intended . . . " Clone-Brock opened the chamber door and walked in. "And this; this is the next generation; right Stevens?"

"Yes, sir."

"You simply shower, it air dries you, and you are ready to go."

Brock walked out again and over to a door just to the right of the chamber. "You see Jake, may I call you Jake? You see, Jake, I needed the highest potency and most intense combination of compatible sustenance possible. Quite a mouthfull, don't you think?"

"What's your point?"

Brock stood in front of the door and turned to face the two men. "While Stevens here discovered the Pyramid Power, it just didn't push in the right direction. Actually, it didn't allow us to shove the construct off the on ramp, if you will, onto the highway. The constructs were bouncing off the ramp before they reached the Sidron. We needed the combination of powers, more compatibilities . . . hence this place. Now we need a booster. So, I have brought the last turbo charge, guaranteed to zap us all to success.

"What are you talking about?"

"Let's stop the games, my friend. The Carrier was educational, but not the final objective. I learned the how of many things while I was in there. But, you see, it was never really me in there. Oh, it is now, really Brock, I mean. Too confusing for you? He is food for the beast, in return for my freedom. I have made Semitri as many clones as he wants. It seems that Mr. Brock—to you, Real-Brock—had the first clue, right on his person, one of those charming little toys you call Knofers. Your Dave Marshall gave it to him, months ago. Brock already started the effort to duplicate them, one of his promises to his worldwide companies. It is a fun toy, but not the answer. The answer is the power of compatibility."

Jake's jaw dropped for a second time. "I should have known."

"Hah, of course, you silly man, I even know you are one, and that you are a relative of the old boy in there. Semitri left nothing to chance to get the clones. After I got out and checked the progress of our communication experts, I realized the power of these little gadgets isn't nearly enough. I needed Stevens and his pyramids, you and a little help from history. You see, my friend, you were led here."

"Jesus, you are insane."

"Well, closer to God than you think.Anyway, as it turns out, you are not just a witness to all this, you will be a participant. I needed to get more power to make the second chamber work. It's a little insurance policy, in case my Carrier friend changes his mind. It's very important to cover the bases."

Stevens blurted out, "I don't know what he means, honestly."

Clone-Brock was on a roll. "Your Dave Marshall was my first clue. He thought he could control Brock by resetting the Knofers. Ha! Then came me back from the dead. No one expected that. I took the knowledge from Semitri and we built this place in no time, clones, power, no limits. We needed Dr. Sheldon's final calculations to make corrections from the original event. Rio . . . are you getting all this, Mr. Burns?"

"I understand more with every word."

"That brings us to here and now."

Brock gestured to the door next to him. Burns and Stevens stood silently waiting. Burns wasn't going to get physical, unless he had to. Meanwhile, he was dying of curiosity. Brock faced them both and acted like the ringmaster at a circus introducing the main act. He reached in his coat pocket and took out a pair of black gloves, put them on and pulled out a thin rope. "My friends, I offer for your consideration the greatest single discovery ever made. Do you know what this is?"

He stretched out the rope between his hands. Jake was dumbfounded at first. He just said, "It looks like you're going to strangle someone."

"Hardly. This rope represents a particle displacement conduit. It represents the Sidron. My hands represent creation, one from the other. I am beyond cloning now and I have control of the Sidron."

Brock dropped the rope, pulled a Knofer out of his breast pocket and spoke into it, "Semitri, my friend, now."

The three looked at the blank, dark gray wall and watched the door change before their eyes. The rectangular door became round. Burns was not impressed. He shrugged and sarcastically remarked, "It's a door, Brock, or whoever you are; that is your big surprise, a round glowing door?"

Clone-Brock smirked and turned the knob. "Really, just a door, eh? I don't think so."

He pulled the door open, and out fell the limp bodies of Gordon Swanson and a stranger, both unconscious and soaked in sweat. Stevens and Jake quickly bent down and checked the two men.

"I've got a pulse . . . "

"Me, too . . . thank God."

Jake lifted the secretary's head and, in the same motion, he took his Knofer out and pressed it. Nothing happened. C-Brock watched it all, as if in ecstasy. "Oh, he is quite all right, more than just alive, I wager."

Burns pushed the Knofer again and spoke into it, "Alpha one! Activate alpha one!"

"I told you, your little toys won't work here. On the other hand, mine does just fine. Semitri, bring Mr. Brock to the doorway."

From out of the light inside, a chair, holding Real-Brock slid toward the door. Stevens was mesmerized.

"Mr. Brock, that's you? Which one is which?"

The voice from the chair spoke loud and clear, "Stevens, get me out of here, do something!"

C-Brock stood laughing, watching Stevens and Burns. Burns tried to revive Swanson, but he was barely breathing. "Help me, Stevens!"

Stevens had revived the other man, who now sat up and tried to digest all that was happening. Jake kept insisting, "Stevens, come here, come here!"

He and Jake moved Swanson to the wall. "Hamil, look at me, try to help him."

Then, Jake moved quickly to the stranger. As C-Brock argued with real Brock, taunting him, Burns talked to the man, "Who are you?"

"My name is Nicolas Brock."

"Christ, it's New Year's with the Brocks . . . "

"What?" the stranger said. "What the hell is this?"

"All you need to know is that you, me and them are all going to die if we don't stop the man laughing. I'm Jake Burns, a cop from New York. You have to trust me."

"Who are those two?"

"Those two? They are the crazy twins. They want to murder you, kill us and steal your company."

Burns helped Nick to his feet. Stevens watched the two Brocks and saw his opportunity. He leapt through the door, into the Carrier. C-Brock watched him but then concentrated on Nicolas and spoke into his Knofer, "Semitri, you can have them both. I don't need them or you anymore." Then, he lunged at Nicolas.

In a last ditch effort, Burns reached in his pocket and took out the small pocket watch device which Swanson gave him at his briefing. He studied it for a second and then he threw it into the Carrier. A silent red glare exploded inside Semitri. Burns could see Stevens yanking Real Brock out of the chair, and finally, after the glare stopped, Stevens was able to pull Brock out the door.

Clone Brock held onto Nicolas, but he didn't expect his ancestor to be well trained in hand-to-hand combat. Nick elbowed C-Brock and twisted him around, holding his arm behind his back.

Real Brock and Stevens made it out of the Carrier just before a second blinding blue flare ignited. Real Brock yelled to Nick, "Get him into the chamber; that will hold him!"

Stevens helped Nick, and together, they forced C-Brock into the particle chamber. Real Brock grabbed Stevens, yanking him out and slammed the door shut. C-Brock and Nick were trapped inside.

"Stevens!" Real-Brock yelled. "Turn the equipment on and get out of here."

Stevens was on automatic pilot. He reacted as directed and ran to the control panel. He pushed a series of buttons and turned around to watch. C-Brock pounded on the chamber door and screamed, while Nick held him by his waist.

Jake's eyes darted back and forth between the chamber and the Carrier. He could see that something was happening to Semitri. He yelled at Stevens, "We have to get out of here! Come on!"

Real-Brock had already looked at it all and ran, before anyone else. He made it out the door on the other side of the room, just as the first explosion hit. It came from within the Carrier. The room shook wildly. Burns and Stevens were knocked over, but were able to get back up. As they did, they saw the two men in the chamber begin to disintegrate.

"My God," Stevens said. "We have to get them out! They have their clothes on."

"Come on!" Jake yanked and pulled at Stevens. "We have to go!"

They ran back through the other door and up the hallway as fast as they could. When they reached the tunnel passage to the surface, they heard a loud explosion. Jake and Stevens made it out of the shed to the school parking lot when the shaking knocked them off their feet. The ground vibrated and they watched an area of at least four square blocks cave down a good eight feet.

"Holy mother of God," Stevens said.

Jake whispered to himself, "Gordon?" He yanked at Stevens again. "Come on, we have to go!"

But as he turned around, Jake stopped dead in his tracks. "Christ, the limo. It's gone . . . shit! Come on, my car is around front."

❧ ❧ ❧ ❧

At the same moment, within the time anomaly that had trapped Angie Bellos, Angie had made her way back to the courtroom alone. She was scared, and worse, she left her Knofer somewhere in the jail cell with Dave Marshall and Brian. She had been looking arduously for the sweet spot in Room 210. Exhausted and fatigued, she sat helplessly in the witness stand, sobbing, when the first rumble came. It sounded like thunder, far away. Then, the room began to vibrate, as if an earthquake hit. She grabbed the wooden arms of the chair and hung on. As she stood up, terrified, looking left and right, she saw it. Focused and clear, out of the corner of her eye, while everything was shaking out of control, a two-foot round rotating space, right in front of her, was the sweet spot. It wasn't a blur at all. It was the only thing in the room in focus. She only had seconds to decide. She lunged and leapt into it and fell into the arms of Brian Sheldon, knocking him over onto the courtroom floor.

"Okay, okay, Jesus! Angie?"

She looked at him, grabbed his face and kissed him hard. He tried to push her away, but she clung to him, smothering him. "Oh, my God, is it you? Is it really you?"

Her kisses became tender, and he returned them. "Yes . . . it's me. Where have you been? I've been looking all over for you. I decided to come back here, hoping to find something. Your father is crazy worried about you."

"Wait, am I here? I mean, really here?"

Brian chuckled, "Well, we were out on the steps, and then you were gone, vanished, and now you're here."

Angie started kissing him again. "Well, I don't plan on vanishing again, anytime soon. Come here you!"

CHAPTER 29

BLOOD RESULTS

TOM WHEELER FINISHED THE BLOOD analysis of their visitor, Andrew, and sent it to the GGM. While riding in Allenfar, Bellos examined it and called Wheeler back.

"Tom, I see it, but I'm not sure I believe it?"

"The analysis is solid."

"We can't send him back."

"We couldn't if we wanted to. The question is, what do we do with him?"

"Well, we are all taught that genetics make the difference around here, any suggestions?"

"We sound like two idiots, sir."

"Maybe I should take him up to the surface and give him a new life there."

"I doubt that would work, but it's your decision."

"Did you double check this?"

"I ran the normal blood tests and our genetic screening, and then the comparative analysis. Based on recent events and those analyses, there's no doubt at all."

"Well, someone has to explain it all to him; we owe him that."

"Sir, it should come from you . . . "

"Yes, I suppose."

" . . . Oh, and about your daughter, she's on her way home."

"You made my day. I'll have to tell Jake you beat him on this one. His message is coming in now . . . What's the status of Rachel?"

"I have the reports here. She is still in a deep coma; our doctors discovered she has the same crippling gene as Swanson."

"Crap! That reminds me, any news on Gordon? Oh wait, hold on; Jake's message is coming in now . . . Swanson is . . . Gordon is gone, lost in the explosions."

"What? I'm sorry, Mathew. Is there anything I can do?"

Bellos sat down in silence; and, after a moment, he answered, "No; I don't think so. I will get the details from Jake. Keep all this quiet for now. I am on my way to the Bering Straits to contract the tunnel negotiations. Then, I'm going to Arden to undergo the C. P. T. for the Post Controllers. I'll come back to Giza after that to host the funeral. Talk to Patty; ask if she would like to make any arrangements."

"I will."

"Go see our visitor, Andrew, and take him to Argone Villa, in the Masters' Cave. That should make him feel at home, if that's possible. I'll see him later."

"Fine, but I don't think anything is going to satisfy him but the truth."

CHAPTER 30

BELLOS AND MR. ANDREW

THE HUGE MASTER'S CAVE was roughly eight miles below Giza. Most colonists thought it to be the first one found within the entire Time Trust Post 2. It was over 1000 feet high and approximately a mile in diameter. There were meadows of strange and beautiful flowers and rolling hills bounding a freshwater lake. On one side of the lake's beachfront lay the stunning Argone Villa. The Villa was the most plush vacation resort in the Master's Cave; and it was a getaway spot for the GGM. His living quarters were 3500 square feet, the best of the best real estate.

Tom Wheeler had just finished giving time traveler, Mr. Andrew, a tour of the grounds, and they sat down to sip iced tea, in the log cabin living room area. Wheeler began educating the new guest, reviewing the cave's traditions and history.

"Thank you, Tom," said Mr., Andrew. " I appreciate everything, I have a lot to learn. It's all so new and different."

"A little over 980 years worth of learning, I'd say, ha!"

"Thanks for taking the time. It is overwhelming, hard to believe. What are the odds of getting me back to where I belong?"

They heard the door latch, and in walked Mathew Bellos. "Hi, you two. Boy, coming here does take away the stress of the day."

Bellos slowly walked toward Andrew, and answered his question to Wheeler, "Unfortunately, if we could send you back, I'm pretty sure you would be dead."

Andrew squinted. "I didn't think of that. I was just talking about going home . . . so, now what happens to me?"

Bellos nodded to Wheeler, "Tom, fix me something a little stronger than tea, will you?"

"Sure."

Bellos sat down in one of the three high back chairs and continued. "I'm not sure. We are in unknown territory with you, I'm afraid."

Wheeler handed Bellos a drink, as Andrew said, "That's not too comforting."

"Have you had a chance to see much here, get a feel for how we do things?"

"No, not that much, I watched a lot of video before, but it would take time. It's quite a different political system, but free enterprise seems alive and well down here, as far as I can tell."

"Yes it is, quite similar to many places you were familiar with, I'm sure."

Bellos sipped, put his Knofer on the coffee table and talked to it, "Get me Malcolm Aldridge."

Within seconds, Malcolm's image began to grow from the Knofer.

"Hello, Mathew, good to see you."

"Good to see you, too."

"I'm sorry about Gordon. Of course, I will be at the funeral."

"Thank you. I called because I need a favor."

"Just ask."

"I have a friend here. Say hi to Andrew. He's an author, among other things. He's looking for a permanent residence."

"Ah, how do you do?"

"Well at times, thanks; nice to meet you."

"You have good friends in high places."

"Apparently . . . this is all pretty new to me. Forgive me, I'm a bit overwhelmed."

"Relax; it's fine. Now, would you like to meet perhaps tomorrow and we can discuss looking at some housing?"

"Fine with me, all right."

"Malcolm, he's staying at the Argone in HS-3783. By the way, we are broadcasting Gordon's funeral tomorrow."

"That's fine . . . Andrew, how about I pick you up around 9:30 in the morning?"

Andrew suddenly seemed uneasy. "Funeral, what funeral?"

"Malcolm, perhaps you could bring Andrew to the ceremony. I have a lot to do. I'd be in your debt."

"I'll be glad to. It will give us time to chat."

"I appreciate that, thank you."

"Well, then, see you in the morning. Be well . . . nice to hear from you, Mathew."

The Knofer cut the call. Bellos took a breath and turned to Wheeler. "Give us a moment, will you, Tom?"

"Sure . . . " Wheeler extended his hand and Andrew shook it.

"Thanks for everything."

"See you later, Andrew."

Bellos was rarely tongue-tied, however, in this case, he fumbled, obviously, "There is something else you and I have to discuss."

Andrew sat back down. Bellos took several folded pieces of paper out of his back pocket and handed them to Andrew.

"What's this?"

"You should read those."

Bellos rose, walked to the bar and asked, "Would you like a drink?"

"Okay, any potato vodka."

"You and Jake . . . straight or with ice?"

"Ice, please." Andrew began reading, "Let's see; it says, Blood Test Evaluation and Analysis; born 1/07/1946; Death-Unknown . . . that's interesting. Ever-Life Citizen, 6/04/2999; Sponsor, Relative: GGM Mathew J. Bellos . . . relative?"

Bellos walked back and handed him a drink. The GGM offered a toast. "It seems we have more in common than we realized . . . bottoms up."

They both gulped the drinks, and then Bellos walked back over to the bar. "You may need another, before we are through. Originally, when you appeared here, there were three of you, all the same you, in each of those different rooms; but, each of you was a different age."

"I remember."

"Well, you got here as a result of an event, the original Sidron event, which, I am sure you will learn, was triggered by a combination of factors. But, after all has been analyzed, primarily, you are here because of our genetic ties, yours and mine. We are related. I'll try to explain."

"I have time."

"A very narcissistic man named Marion Brock is power hungry. He devised a plan to go back in time, to gather as much power as he could. However, he forgot one thing . . . "

"What's that?"

" . . . my ties as GGM with the Carriers. Even though his personal Carrier friend blocked communications with its own kind, I did go through their ceremony. That meant that all Carriers became tied to me, my DNA and mine to theirs. Since you and I are both entwined genetically, when Mr. Brock's Carrier triggered the original Sidron event, it linked to my DNA, and that linked you to the event. Do you understand?"

"Whoa . . . even if I understood what you are saying, my first reaction would be, obviously I have had relatives, too, who existed all the way up to you. What about their DNA?"

"There are specific genetic markers that fluctuate and can be either lost or intensified across generations, bridge, so to speak. We confirmed this 'bridging' just recently, through new discoveries on the surface, in fact. Anyway, they can reappear again. It's much like the evolution of spontaneous genetic jumping. Certain genes can lay dormant and after a time, spark massive genome rearrangements."

"Sounds above my pay grade."

"Believe me, our shared genetic sequences are very powerful when put together in particular ways. And that is what happened."

"I'll take your word for it."

"You don't understand."

"Exactly!"

Bellos put his glass on the bar and began gesturing to make his point. "They are specific only to you and me as the result of my becoming GGM. They are very powerful, especially when you include Carrier inputs. There is something involved in all this called a compatibility. When I became GGM, I became compatible with all Carriers, not just one."

"You realize, I have no idea what you are talking about."

"I'll tell you a little secret. I come from the surface. I really prefer slowing things down and actually talking, rather than *poof!*, all of a sudden you know it all."

"*Poof!* huh? Okay, whatever that means; or perhaps, this is just pretty good vodka?"

"That it is . . . I can see we will have to get into much more detail about this for you to really understand. For now, let me say there are certain genetic markers of yours and mine that, together, across the barrier of time, were stressed. Brock's sustenance, together with his Carrier's wherewithal, combined with his ancestor's, a man named Nicolas, and yours and mine, created a power surge within the Sidron."

"Sidron; I'll have to look it up . . . so you are saying, without our combined markers, I would be dead right now."

"Interesting way of putting it, yes."

"Can it happen again to someone else?"

"Well, it has never happened before. Who's to say? Here, within Ever-Life, genetics are everything. It seems I can't send you back, even if I could."

"So, I start over again . . . "

Andrew stood thinking, across from Bellos at the bar.

" . . . And we are related?"

"You are empty again . . . another drink?"

"Definitely! What do I call you, distant brother, or am I your grandfather's grandfather's, grandfather's ancestor?"

"We will have to ask Tom. He's keeper of the records."

Bellos poured again and quipped, "Well, if you are anything like I was when Gordon hired me, you are going to be saying 'what' quite a lot."

"So, you're hiring me?"

"Hell, no! Maybe nominate you for something."

"Perhaps I should take some notes?"

Bellos chuckled, "Don't bother, I'll have to repeat this one several times before I understand it myself."

"You know, standing here like this, with you, it reminds me of conversations I had a very long time ago . . . "Andrew got a tear in his eye. "Subject for another conversation."

Bellos sighed and raised an eyebrow. "I'm not quite sure how to begin or where to start. Have you ever been to Washington, D.C., or Mexico City?"

"Yes, D.C. several times, with family; but only to Mexico City once, alone, for about 10 days. I was on the job. I was impressed with the catacombs."

Bellos' eyes opened wide. "Ah, yes, one of our first Posts, in the Americas. Then, are you familiar with underground structures?"

"Not really. What do you mean, Posts?"

"Hmm, did you know Washington, D.C., was built on a catacomb foundation, too, quite similar to this cave structure really?"

"What ?"

Bellos chuckled, "There's that word again . . . I'll tell you what, on second thought, I think it would be more prudent if we talked after you put one of these on again."

He pulled a headset out from behind the bar and held it up to Andrew. "Remember this?"

"Yes, as a matter of fact."

"Right, good."

Bellos placed the set over Andrew's ear. "Wear it like that . . . there. Now just relax. This will only take a minute. You will probably understand more this way. We have to do something about losing the art of conversation. After you're done, we will talk more."

Andrew sipped on his drink as the inputs began.

CHAPTER 31

THE FUNERAL

A CROWD OF SEVERAL THOUSAND lined around Ever-Life's Grand Arcade in Giza's Time Trust chasm. People and dignitaries from every Post came to pay respects to the most progressive and successful GGM in the history of the colonies, Gordon Swanson. Generally, each colony held funeral ceremonies celebrating lives once a month by broadcasting a 15-minute video honoring all those who passed away. However, today was the first funeral that included a GGM in over 200 years.

Funerals and customs were quite different within Ever-Life from those on the surface. The dearly departed were neither buried nor cremated and put in an urn; rather, the most common custom was to compress the cremated remains and make diamonds or gemstones out of the ashes. It was a relatively simple process and left the families with a valuable keepsake. The great GGM Hall of History had walls covered with photographs and descriptions regarding each GGM, as well as the gemstone representing the particular Master, cut in a shape requested by the family.

On this day, adult Carriers lined up and down the grand chasm, as if they were stacked sardines. There was nothing like it recorded in the history logs. In amphitheaters throughout Ever-Life's eight Posts various families and friends of other dearly departed sat respectfully waiting. At Giza, there were the close friends and family of Gordon

Swanson. In Arden, New Mexico, there were the family and friends of Abby Johnson. Mathew Bellos would speak in honor of Swanson, and that short service would be broadcast throughout the colonies. The service was scheduled for late afternoon. Jack and Brian Sheldon had arrived by special Carrier bubble. They met with Bellos, privately, before the ceremony.

"Jack, glad you made it. How's Rachel?"

"Not good. She is still in a deep coma. Thanks for the use of Dr. LuAnne and the labs, though. I'm not sure what to do. LuAnne says neither Nanites nor the new C.P.T. has worked on her this time. She's in a place I can't go. Your team did confirm she has the same crippling gene."

"I wish there was something we could do. We know so much, but there is so much more to learn. Don't give up, my friend. We'll keep at it."

The two hugged. Jack went to sit down with his son, and Bellos stepped to the podium. "Good afternoon, my Ever-Life friends . . . welcome to this month's Life Celebration. We gather to honor all those dearly departed and pay respect for their contribution to all of us, to their families, friends, careers, and to the many of us whom they never knew but whose lives will be forever changed and better because they lived. They will be remembered and ever live through us all . . .

"Also, today is a very special day, because we lost one of our most beloved and accomplished GGMs, Mr. Gordon Swanson. He was my predecessor, mentor, and for all of us, the longest most progressive and successful GGM in our history. His life and his efforts have affected us all for the better. Let us pray:

"We thank thee, oh Lord, for giving us this man . . . thank you for your service, Gordon. You will live in our hearts and our minds, and our daily lives, every day.

" . . . And now, may each one of our stations play the short video celebrating our great GGM's service record for all of us to reflect upon. This ends today's broadcast ceremony. May God bless us."

Bellos took two steps back from the podium, and everyone stood while the Ever-Life anthem played. At the end of it, each person turned and faced the grand chasm. To everyone's surprise, all the light that everyone took for granted went out, it became pitch black. After the nervous awes of the crowd subsided, the Carriers displayed what could only be described as breathtaking—another first. They began shooting fireworks, but there were no sounds, just silent explosions of magnificent and varied colors. The beauty was indescribable. People began to clap and cheer, and wonderful music played from the monitors. The show continued for about 20 minutes. The finale was like nothing anyone had seen. When it finished, light shined again, and Bellos addressed the crowd, "Thank you all for remembering our loved ones . . . Ever-Life, everywhere!"

He stepped down from the stage and began greeting Swanson's family, close friends and loved ones who sat in the front rows. They all chatted briefly, with tears and smiles, and then they disbanded to meet in the GGM Hall of History for refreshments.

CHAPTER 32
HOPE SPRINGS

RACHEL HAD BEEN ILL FOR WEEKS since the episode in Rio. Jack had the home lab rearranged into a high-tech hospice; he continued to run tests on her every day. Unfortunately, they yielded no conclusive results. Ever-Life's labs indicated nothing new either. There was no suggested direction or prognosis. Jack had been researching the orphan diseases for the last month, trying to correlate the gene pools. He was frustrated and at his wit's end. He spent all his time back and forth to Ever-Life, but to no avail. As had become his routine, early one evening, he sat in a rocker beside his wife's bed, dozing. Rachel lay still, barely breathing. Brian was there, too, kneeling on the other side of the bed, holding one of her hands. Suddenly, for no apparent reason, she opened her eyes and saw Jack, and she squeezed Brian's fingers. "Brian . . . ?"

"Mom . . . Dad, Mom is awake."

Jack jerked up, leaned over to her and kissed her cheek. "Hello, darling."

"I must be in and out quite a bit. Come closer, both of you."

They moved quickly, and she began to talk. "I am so happy. I know you think I am going to die, but it's not true, not at all. I've been having dreams. They are so real. I am just going to change. Jack, you taught me, remember in the lab, C.P.T.? My thoughts and memories, my soul; they will live on and multiply, just as life gives new babies. Brian, promise me you will have babies?"

"Of course I will."

"Rach, save your strength, I'll get you something, just be still," said Jack softly patting her shoulder.

"No, Jack, I have to get this out. You have to listen." She looked at them both and continued, "Death is just the labor of a new birth . . . Brian, you are going to know me better than you ever did, better than you ever imagined. We will be closer than I ever hoped, and yet, you and your children will be even closer. And sometimes . . . sometimes, when you need it most, we will talk. All you have to do is love."

Then she turned to Jack. "Oh, my love, I know, I'm such a romantic. I love you so. So many said it before, better than I could; but it's true, to give and receive love is to see the face of God. I see him in you, babe. Now give me a good kiss."

They smiled, and Jack kissed her with tears rolling down his face. In that kiss, she stopped breathing.

Brian squeezed her arm and sunk his head into the bed. Jack caressed her face and cried. He got up slowly, walked to the other side of the bed and helped Brian out of the room and upstairs to Angie's waiting arms. Angie walked him to the couch, and Jack went back down into the lab and closed the door behind him. He sat on the edge of the bed staring at Rachel. With the deepest sadness, he held her hand and cried like a baby, "You can't leave me." He looked up and prayed aloud, "God, if you can hear me, now is the time."

Up in the living room, Angie comforted Brian, "Come on, Brian, let your father be with her. Let's take a breath for a few minutes, get some air. Walk with me." They both went outside.

In the lab, Jack sat whimpering. His eyes were blood red from crying. He couldn't say words any longer, but his thoughts were crystal clear, *Take me, bring her back. I saw you, I know you. I know you can take me.* He cried himself out and placed her clenched fists over the covers, trying to adjust her comfortably.

Who knows how much time passed, but then, from the far corner, Jack heard a whistling, whirling sound, like the wind through trees. He looked, and to his amazement, a small glowing statue of a Carrier appeared on the floor. It was no more than 15 inches high. He walked over, examined it and read the inscription on the base, *Allenfar.*"Christ, what is this!" Then, he startled at hearing a voice from the bed. There, sitting beside Rachel's corpse, was the Tyree Master.

"Hello, Doctor. Do you remember me?"

Jack was emotionally spent and had no patience. "I'm in no mood for games. No, I don't. Who are you and how did you get in here?"

"We met on your trip, back to the surface, in a Carrier bubble. I spoke to you and your wife."

"Yes, it is you. Well, you picked the wrong time for a visit."

"It seems your wife finally pushed the communicator, which I gave her . . . all this time, and nothing to report."

"You are too late, she's gone."

"I promised her I would help her, if you remember." He smiled at Jack and stood up. "You see, she did push it. Look, there in her hand."

Jack leaned over and opened her left fist, sure enough, there it was, the little peanut device the Tyree Master gave her in the Carrier.

"Doctor Sheldon, you of all people believe in hope, do you not?"

Jack felt his knees buckle. Catching himself, he almost missed sitting on the edge of the bed.

"Who are you?" He began to tear up again.

"I am here to remind you that nothing said has any meaning without hope. Your wife touched us in a special way. Your discoveries have touched us all in many special ways."

"But, I thought sunlight killed your kind."

"The fact is, many things can kill us, just like many things can kill you. But, I am alive, and you two proved that your love for each other reaches beyond death . . . not that others don't. It just seems like the proper thing to say at this moment."

"What?"

The master smiled. "You know, you people say that word quite a lot. It's only a word anyway, death I mean. Here, I have this for you."

Jack held out his hand and the man gave him a small two-inch blue vial.

"I trust you know what to do with this? We have made sure it will work. It's a gift. Oh, and I brought the little statue over there to remember us by."

Jack turned to glimpse it. When he turned back again, the man was gone. He looked at the vial in his hand, and then he took a deep breath, sat on the bed and buried his head on his wife's lifeless body. Tears flowed, and because he was so overcome with emotion, he didn't notice her body move at first or the slight touch of Rachel's hand caressing his head. Startled, he looked up in disbelief as her eyes opened. They both smiled, and Jack reached for her, cupping her face. "Oh, my God, Rach."

"Hi, you're a sight Come here."

They kissed as Jack's tears flooded her cheeks. "But this is impossible. Look at you . . . your color, your tone; you look so healthy . . . how? Look here, I have a vial, but I didn't give you C.P.T. Oh, thank God! Rach!"

As they hugged and cried, Rachel whispered to him, "Oh, my love, there is a power so much greater than any of this. I don't know how or why. I just know I'm thankful to see you."

CHAPTER 33

AIRLIFT, MID-JULY

A PRIVATE AIRLIFT ZOOMED far above Earth, traveling with only two passengers, Marion Brock and Charlie Rosse. An optically clear window lined one wall of the cabin. The entire vehicle was fueled by the Brock Companies' Moon mining businesses. This was the first completely automated, unmanned space vehicle not controlled or financed by a government contract. It had all the accoutrements of a high-class hotel on Earth. The two men sat comfortably looking down at the majesty of the Nile River.

Brock snickered, "It's hard to believe that 10 miles under there, men have built a way of life based on healthcare. If I hadn't discovered Swanson was holding out on me, well, I should be thankful."

"What do you think people will do, once they know about the colonies?"

"Nothing, the media frenzy will last a week, two at most. We will be fine; people are stupid. When all is said and done, my V.A.D. will make the difference up here."

Brock and Rosse had just left Brock's personal port station orbiting Earth and were now on their way to the Moon.

"Marion, for the last nine months now, your whole effort was to discover time travel. Why?"

Brock was in a good mood and knew the trip was going to take a while, so he put up with Rosse. "Given my history and the events of this year, I trust you'll understand; insurance was always the consideration."

"Sorry, I don't understand."

"I guess I shouldn't expect you to. I have a dream that my companies will revolutionize life. Can you imagine if on that silly little planet we all could travel in time, not just through it? Until me, our only choice has been to decide how to spend the time we have. What if we could make the time we have left whatever we want? That's what I wanted . . . and more than that, I wanted to break away—to break out from the prison of time. Of course, how do we do that, without the right fuel-power, in this case? Do you realize how much fuel is burned up, just trying to get out of the gravitational pull of that little planet? Hence, my multitasking to mine the Moon. Who else is doing it, the governments? I know that's all bullshit."

"So this has all been about selfishly leading the people of planet Earth into space?"

"Both. Time travel is much more than you can imagine. Think of this. As we get less dependent on the base elements of that little blue ball, we can jump from one planet to others and mine fuel as we go. But, whatever the fuel is, it has to generate power enough for time travel. Time travel is the key. It will allow us to travel far beyond our little blue ball, throughout the Galaxy and beyond. I think someone said that, sometime ago."

Rosse stared at Brock in amazement, and Brock laughed. "Ha! I really had you there for a minute. Here, read this."

Brock handed Rosse a booklet that was stamped, TOP SECRET.

"You should see your face, Charlie . . . You gullible shit. See, a little sincerity, and even you will listen. I got your attention though, didn't I?"

"You have my attention with this, too. You never mentioned this in any meeting with me."

"What did you think I was doing with that Carrier, anyway?"

"I thought you were trapped inside him."

"Up to a point, I was. He wanted me, and I found out many things; because as he grew, so did I. We know now that time travel is really possible. We will take all the knowledge we got from Stevens and the Carrier, and set up shop elsewhere."

"You mean out here?"

"I have just the right spot in mind, and there will be no threat or interference this time. Look, that's where we've been, but that's where we're going."

Rosse followed Brock's finger. He looked out the starboard window and then the front portal, watching the Moon get bigger.

"My companies have built three space stations up here and an inventory port for the distribution of space fuel needed to power all travel. There's plenty more on the Moon. That's what the Brock Companies have invested in silently for the past 35 years—space fuel. It's a whole new world. With fuel, communication and time travel up here, there are no limits."

"*Communication*—you mean the V.A.D.? I must say, it was brilliant, your introduction on the 4th of July."

KNOFER-ECHO 4: V.A.D.

**Introduced July 4, 2999 by O.P.A.S.,
Seattle, Washington
After only 10 months of combined research, the Brock
Companies present the Knofer-Echo 4, Transcontinental
Communication Device and Medical Monitor**

*Contact your Brock Company dealer for more details.

"Yep, and now we have a way to communicate up here that's light years from the old cell or satellite technology. I have 300 of these little gems back there, and we are going to deliver them to the mining camps and distribution port. Charlie, my friend, I am making you the top dog up here. It's graduation, reward time for you. You are going to run the show."

Rosse did a double take, half smiled and asked, "That's great, but, I thought this was a fact-finding mission. Marion, I'm flattered and certainly I could, would . . . yes, I . . . thank you."

"Good, it's settled. You will be impressed. The mining camps are almost 100% robotic-cyber operated. We only have 10 people in management positions, very smart guys; that makes all the difference. These little devices will enable us all to interact as though we were in the next room. This trip is as much PR as anything else. You and I needed to get away, anyway."

Brock patted Rosse on the shoulder and sat down in a comfort chair, facing Earth. Rosse sat across from him, staring at the Moon and whispering to himself, "Mining camps, 10 people, the Moon . . . "

He flipped the plastic tray down next to him, and took out a map and details of the Moon camps. There was also a picture of the mining camp robots.

"Mining camp robots, they don't look like they even talk. Maybe I should find out . . . " He took out his new Echo 4, " . . . No time like the present to say hello to these guys."

He pressed his thumb against the screen, to activate the features. Then, he tapped it repeatedly, but nothing happened.

"Uh, Marion, is your Echo working? Mine looks great but it doesn't seem to do anything. Must be the altitude."

Brock took his out and pressed his thumb on the screen, likewise, nothing. He did it several times and then muttered, "It was working fine on the port station. Here, let me see yours." He shook them both, giggling at first. "I never should have negotiated with our prison friend, Marshall. This was my failsafe. It was all about the power." He continued to press his thumbprint and shake the Echos. "My researchers said they could duplicate those lovely little Knofers I gave them."

"Knofers, what's a Knofer?"

Brock gradually became more intense, "Shit, it should work! Why doesn't it work? Stupid! Stupid! I gave them the samples. I gave them the damn samples! They worked fine. It was unprecedented, a new V.A.D. in 10 months. Unprecedented, my ass. July 4th was Nick's birthday . . . lotta good that did."

"Let's just call someone from the cockpit."

The two went forward and sat in the two captains' chairs.

"These are just for show," said Brock. "This is all automatic."

As Brock studied the lighted panel before him, both men felt the airlift suddenly stop and they heard a sputter from the rear of the cabin. Then, the panel lights went out, and the Airlift began to drift to one side. Brock quickly concentrated on the Echo 4 again.

Rosse panicked in the dark. "So are we stuck here?"

"Don't be stupid, 25,000 miles per hour is hardly stuck . . . this little thing is supposed to draw power from any source. Goddamn Sheldon . . . damn that Swanson. That's what I get for trusting them all."

Brock's hissy fit was escalating into a rage.

"Marion, I think we are passing the Moon."

The airlift jerked again, and it started to slowly tumble and spin out of control. Rosse watched Brock talking to himself, obsessed with the two Echos. At first, neither man could feel the spin because of the weightless environment; but then Rosse sensed the momentum increase, when he saw the Earth pass across the window like the Sun fast forwarding across a clear Seattle skyline. It moved from the top of the window to the bottom with ever-increasing speed, faster with each spin. Rosse pushed himself out of his seat, back to the big bay window. He could see both the Earth and Moon now. The Airlift began not only spinning side to side, but it was also flipping end over end.

"Marion, you better come and see this. Something is really wrong."

Frustrated, Brock let the Echos float. He joined Rosse and they both stared out the window at something blocking their view of the Earth as the airlift spun.

It was Allenfar, floating no more than 100 meters from the Airlift.

"Christ," Brock said, "Damn fish! I hate those things."

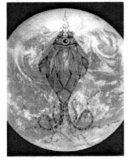

"What? What the hell are you talking about; what is that?"

Brock shook his head. Only now at the last was he to understand. "They wanted me to have the samples . . . "

Rosse's head moved side to side, trying to follow the spinning image. "What the hell are you talking about?"

Brock was enraged. His eyes bulged. He could hear the Carrier in his mind; and then, suddenly, the Tyree Master appeared in the airlift cabin behind Brock and Rosse.

"You are where you should be, Marion Brock. You will be remembered, as you wished. Oh, it seems your compatibility has released us. It has enabled us to live quite well in sunlight. Thank you. I stopped the power in your little toys. They won't work up here. We will be joining surface man, and hope to help him in many ways. It is time. Your people didn't have a clue what the power source was in the samples. They just used primitive batteries. As always, you assumed, rather than learned. Good luck and enjoy the ride."

The image before the men disappeared. Rosse grabbed Brock by his lapels and shook him. "What the hell just happened?"

Brock pushed him off and slapped his palms against the Airlift window.

"You son-of-a-bitch! You bastards! This isn't the end! This isn't over!"

Brock's view from the drifting Airlift

CHAPTER 34

AFTERSHOCK

BACK ON EARTH'S SURFACE, above Time Trust in Giza, three men walked on the ramp between the arms of the great Sphinx and talked in the sunset, GGM Mathew Bellos, his new recruit and relative, Andrew and Jake Burns. Burns spoke to Andrew in a lighthearted tone. "So, my friend, how do you like being the oldest living relative of our GGM? Come to think of it, you are the oldest living anything, hah."

"Yeah, thanks for that. When I think about it, am I really alive?"

Jake was quick to banter, "Dead or alive, I should take you to my old shrink, he would have a field day with this."

"I'll bet."

They all paused to look at the pyramids silhouetted against the sinking sun.

Andrew said, "I was just thinking, my brother loved Egyptology. He would love it here. Mind you, he'd never believe any of this, but, if he were alive, he'd love seeing this."

"Brother?"

"Yes, one of two, and a sister. She was a great lady."

"I remember you had kids."

"Oh yes, four, and grandchildren. One of my hopes is to find out what became of them. I expect to spend a lot of time with headsets."

Bellos was quick to comment, "There is a lot that isn't in the headset files. Wheeler should be able to give you vault information. You may be surprised at what you find."

"I'll remember that."

The sky was turning beautiful red and peach colors, reflecting off the clouds. Bellos studied it all, whispering, "There is truly nothing more beautiful, and not one moment the same as the last . . . I miss it."

Jake pointed to the left, "Look . . . a rainbow. Sometimes, I don't think people up here appreciate what they have . . . "

"That is because you come from up here, and you haven't seen this for a while . . . I think they do, most of them anyway, when they slow down and take a breath."

"Matt, what was that device-that watch, Gordon gave me to throw into Semitri? I thought we didn't make anything that killed."

"We didn't make that. The Carrier Council gave it to him years ago. As GGMs we have a few fail-safes."

"I don't get it?"

"The device didn't kill the Carrier. His resisting it did. The device only works from within a Carrier. Semitri fought against its effects. It tore down the wall he built up against the hive mind. The device enabled the rest of the Carriers to share the compatibility that had been denied them. He could have let it all go months ago. Anyway, by fighting the device's effects, Semitri's own power turned on him and killed him."

"I feel like I'm the one who killed Gordon."

"No, and we now know the trigger to his death was Brock's particle displacement event to kidnap him. He might as well have shot him. Also, Gordon's crippling gene has been weakening him for years. We even gave him the original C.P.T. procedure from his duplicate in Jerusalem, but it didn't kill the gene. He needed the new C.P.T. desperately. Brock's particle displacement was the last straw."

After a pause, Jake replied, "Christ, I'm the Security Chief and I never knew. Gordon was a good soul."

"Yes he was, he is. I believe he found his way. His shoes will be hard to fill. He introduced us to the surface more than any GGM in history. You two and I are the first of a new generation. We are from up here. We have to continue his work to bring the colonies and the surface together."

"How are we going to do that when sunlight kills the Carriers?"

"Yes, about that. It appears that one effect from sharing Semitri's compatibilities was that the Carriers no longer die in sunlight. Of course, it remains to be seen exactly what that means for the surface cultures."

"I wonder, too," said Andrew.

"Wonder what?" asked Jake.

"I wonder if I found my way. It has been over 900 years."

Bellos heard him but ignored him for the moment. He continued to study the sky. "I was just thinking what Gordon used to say about Ever-Life, Our job is to extend life, he'd say . . . big challenge. He made so many great advances. Under his leadership, the average lifespan within our colonies now extends three times that of those on the surface. Then, I think about Brock. In spite of all his faults, he will be remembered. He did make one hell of a contribution . . . both of them did great things. One we liked. One we didn't."

He turned to face Andrew. "You ask a great question. The answer is much more complex than my simply believing Gordon found his way. My advice, don't think about it too much. It could drive you crazy. We are going to learn much more about the Sidron. Meantime, live your life, this life. Get up and do the best you can. Fill your day; learn and be happy. There is plenty to do. At least you know the planet has lasted another 900 years."

Bellos smiled with an expression of peace.

Burns interrupted, "Yeah, some things get answered and some don't. Come on, you two; lighten up. Look over there; the way the Sun is hitting the spinning sand, it looks like a shiny dust devil."

A few hundred feet away, between the Great Pyramid of Cheops and the Sphinx, the wind blew the harmless 100-foot high tornado out of sight, and Allenfar appeared in the desert. The last of the Sun's rays reflected off his skin in a most remarkable way.

The three men fixed, startled at what happened next. A single, silent lightening charge ignited from the Pyramid's zenith to Allenfar's tongue, which extended up from his mouth like an antenna. Parts of his skin began to change, and flecks of gold appeared all over him, sparkling brightly. After only a few seconds, it was over. Bellos smiled, gestured to his companions and began walking toward the Carrier.

"Ha! They never cease to amaze me. What's next? Come on you two, our day doesn't end with the Sun going down."

✧·ᴇᴑᴄᴈ·✧

Transmission input Headset 2 complete
Andrew 10746-H2

When I opened my eyes, I saw the blinding light of an eye scope, which Sir Thomas Wheeler was shining on my pupils.

"Well, you look fine," he said.

"How long was I under this time?"

"10 minutes."

"I thought these things were instantaneous, or just a couple of minutes."

"Mostly, yes; but you seem to be different in every way."

"Thanks, now what?"

"As you were told in the headset, you have to have more sessions. I think you should take a break though and, like the GGM told you; settle a bit and get acquainted with all of this, Ever-Life, I mean. I have to run more tests before you have another session."

"I want to find out what happened to my family."

"All in good time, all in good time."

APPENDIX

Ever-Life Subterranean Posts: The following describes the Ever-Life's populated subterranean regions-Posts, worldwide. There are many transport stations within each Post. Some Carrier stations are within one mile below Earth's surface, but heavily populated colonies are a minimum of five miles below the surface.

Post 1: Includes upper East Asian Continent, Mongolia and the China Basin, stretching east and south through the Himalayas, Tibet, India and Pakistan, population: 600,000 . . . There are 250 major Transport Stations throughout the region.

Post 2: Europe, the Netherlands, England and Northern Africa . . . population: 300,000 . . . there are 320 major Transport Stations throughout the region

Post 3: North American Continent-Canada and the United States and across Alaska, including the Bering straits, population: 700,000. . . there are 230 major Transport Stations throughout the region.

Post 4: The Middle East, Turkey and the Baltic, north, including Russia and west, bounded by Afghanistan and Kazakhstan, population: 400,000 . . . there are 140 major Transport Stations throughout the region.

Post 5: Australia and the Pacific Seas, including Japanese Isles and east, including South America, population: 500,000 . . . there are 170 major Transport Stations throughout the region.

Post 6: Mid and Southern Africa and Madagascar, population: 300,000 . . . there are 100 major Transport Stations throughout the region.

Post 7: South Pole, North Pole, Atlantic Sea and all major planet fresh waterways, population: 200,000 . . . there are 150 major Transport Stations throughout the region.

Post 8: The deepest, most remote living quarters 800 miles below Earth's surface and directly below the post station at the Judah Villa in Jerusalem . . . population: 25,000 . . . there are 25 Transport Stations in the colony.

ॐ-ᏰᎯᏨᏇ-৯

A Compatibility: A particular symbiotic fusion between a genetically capable human and a Carrier. It is most rare; a potent acquisition of nourishment that motivates a Carrier to breed offspring and to share power with the hive mentality of all other Carriers. There was a time when two-way compatibilities took place, but they were rare, because the experience killed the human, thus eliminating future interaction. Two-ways were outlawed by treaty long ago.

The Void: The immeasurable, seemingly limitless, unimaginable omniscient and omnipotent everywhere, within which exists all Universes.

The Sidron: The subatomic, superconducting magnetic highway Somewhere between now and then, between this and that, deep within the smallest places of everywhere, all thoughts, feelings and power exist as independent entities; and, they seek out life, like iron filings drawn to a magnet. The Sidron exists within the void and, therefore, inhabits all universes. It is known to some sentient life forms as the bloodstream of the Cosmos; to others, it is known as the synaptic network of God; to the Carriers, it is the road for time travel.

Fluctuations/Abrasions: Creative events caused by intent or colidation, within the Sidron.

Colidation: The inter-activity and intra-activity which takes place deep within the sub-atomic world.

An Inflation: A momentous creativity within the void caused by fluctuations/abrasions within the Sidron. One has commonly been referred to as the Big Bang, or the birth of our universe.

Universal Space-Time: After an Inflation starts, Universal Space-Time is constantly expanding faster than the speed of light, and is what contains it. Past, present and future are relative terms, and they all exist within Space-Time. From one inflation—Big Bang, Space-Time explodes 360 degrees, creating a universe. Countless inflations take place within the Void, as a result of the magnetic fluctuations caused by Sidron activity. Smaller fluctuations/abrasions result in either black holes, or wormholes; and either of those can, for a time, connect two points within a universe or between universes, acting as doorways or bridges.

Soul: A singular self-awareness, a single conscious spirit, without substance It is a one of a kind organization of ideas—thoughts, feelings and power Together, in the right mix, and using choice and free will as catalysts, ideas,thoughts, emotions and power can become conscious.

Afterlife: The concept of finding peace, comfort, significance and harmony; where a sentient life's soul realizes a sense of fulfillment in the conscience of God.

Carrier Council Tyree Masters: After millions of years, the next stage in Carrier evolution is the Tyree Masters. While they operate within the boundaries of the hive mindset, each has the capacity to understand diversity and to interact with all life forms.

Standard Transport Bubble Carrier: When Carriers burrow, either they choose to swim and dredge by rotating their teeth, fins and tails resulting in tunnels, or, alternatively, they shroud themselves within a bubble-like transparent substance, which melts away rock that cools behind them, leaving no evidence they were there.

Bee Pod Program: After filling fuel cells from surface Moon camps, miners ship the cells to orbiting O.P.A.S. Space Ports for distribution to fueling stations around Earth.

Camberlane Contract: Bellos negotiated a common contract between Ever-Life's financial conglomerates on the surface, and O.P.A.S. affiliates, to destroy the Bering Strait's Quad-Bridge, in favor of repairing the The Deep Underground Tunnel System.

About the Author

Andrew Sarkady was born in Trenton, New Jersey. He studied at Washington & Jefferson College, Lake Forest College, and Northwestern University. He began making notes regarding Ever-Life in 1965, but only after fathering 4 children and a 40 year career in industrial sales did he begin to put pen to paper regarding this extraordinary manuscript. He lives in Illinois and continues to write.

Ever-Life: The C.P.T Incident

Ever-Life: Time Trust follows the first book in the Ever-Life Series—*Ever-Life: The C.P.T. Incident*—which begins this compelling tale of twists and turns, murder, love and resurrection.

Available online and at bookstores or from Christopher Matthews Publishing.

http://christophermatthewspub.com

12/15

CPSIA information can be obtained at www.ICGtesting.com
Printed in the USA
LVOW10s1546021015

456698LV00017B/649/P

9 781938 985652